Fireside Stories

by
Ginny Lee

PublishAmerica
Baltimore

First printing

ISBN: 1-59129-934-9
PUBLISHED BY PUBLISHAMERICA, LLLP
www.publishamerica.com
Baltimore

Printed in the United States of America

Acknowledgements

This book is a dream, come true. A special thanks goes to my husband Jerome, who supported my many hours of writing and computer work. A sincere thanks to my son Michael, and grandson Jadon, who have helped me by lending their computer skills to help make this book become a reality. Also, thanks to my grandchildren Rochelle and Zachery for their story illustrations. Another, thanks goes to all my family for their support in this project.

Above all, I thank God who gave me renewed health after a serious illness. It was during this affliction that God gave me the inspiration to put my thoughts into writing. All glory and honor from this achievement belongs to God. And finally, thanks to Publish America for working so diligently with me to make this dream come true. If just one person is blessed by reading this book, then it will have been worth it all.

Ginny Lee

TABLE OF CONTENTS

Andy's Angel Wings
Angels Of Charity
Caroline
Curious Cousins
Double Blessing
Hannah And Kitten Lost In Forest
Little Black Lamb
Miracle Of The Carved Nativity
More Than Camping
Other Side Of The Fence
Poor Rich Girls
Railroad To Heaven
Stranger On The Road
Throw Out The Lifeline
Triangle Of Love
Three Little Sisters
True Friend
True Christmas Spirit
Twin Trouble
Welcome Home

ANDY'S ANGEL WINGS

Andrew and Kate Bauhm had been married for fifteen years and finally found out they were soon to become parents for the first time! They had been hoping and praying for so long that some day God would grant them their wish, that they could become parents and have a child. Now that wish would be coming true.

They were thrilled and fixed up their third bedroom once more for a nursery. Several years ago they had put their name in for the adoption of a child but so far none had been granted unto them. They had fixed up this room for a child before, always in hopes that one would soon be given to them to help fill their empty arms. Andrew and Kate longed to share the love God had given them, but day by day, year by year those hopes began to fade. Now the doctor confirmed that in six months, if all goes well, hopefully Mrs. Bauhm would be giving birth to a healthy baby!

Those six months went fast for the anxious parents after waiting so long for a child that would be their very own. Finally the time was at hand. Andrew took his wife, Kate, to the hospital where she gave birth to a baby boy. They named him Andy, after his father.

When Kate first held baby Andy soon after birth, she noticed immediately that this baby was somehow different. After testing the infant the doctor confirmed with the parents the feeling they had concerning their special baby. Baby Andy was indeed moderately handicapped. Only time would tell what capabilities he would be able to develop.

Andrew and Kate wondered why their baby couldn't be normal like other babies. But after praying so long for a child, they were just thankful God filled their empty arms with this special little angel from heaven. They dearly loved him.

While still a babe in the crib, Andy always seemed fascinated by a colorful bird mobile attached to his bed. He would often try to reach for it with his tender arms.

As time went on it was evident that little Andy would not mature as fast as other children of his age. Andrew Bauhm put up a fence in the back yard; so little Andy, now a toddler, could play outside in the safety of their home. Andy, now a little past two years of age, could finally walk well enough to be able to run and play in the yard. There he loved to watch the pretty little butterflies as they fluttered about the beautiful flowers Kate had planted along the fence. He would try to catch them but of course he could not do so.

By the time Andy became four years old, he loved observing the birds just as he had so often watched them from his crib as a baby. Little Andy would try to catch the birds also, but to no avail. Kate watched her son as he ran about the back yard. She noticed how he would move his little arms, pretending to fly like the butterflies and the birds.

When Andy became five years of age, his parents enrolled him in a special school for children with learning disabilities similar to Andy's. The school, operated by a Christian couple, was highly recommended. Andy loved this school. They taught him various skills that would enable him to be accepted socially. A picture hung on the wall of the schoolroom showing an angel watching over two children as they were walking over a rugged footbridge. This picture fascinated Andy and he would often look at it.

Mrs. Allen, the instructor and owner of the training center, often referred to the children as God's special angels. She would recite verses from the Bible about angels. One of the favorite verses she quoted was Psalms 91:11. It says: "For he shall give his angels charge over you, to keep you in all your ways." Mrs. Allen would tell the children that God's angels watch over them just as the angel in the picture watched over the boy and girl as they crossed over the rugged footbridge.

Often people will stare at those who are handicapped in one way or another. Normal children will even make fun of these special children, not realizing the hurt that can be caused by their sneering remarks. Mrs. Allen had a Bible verse framed, and hanging on the wall above her desk for all to see. Those who read it were reminded to be kind to her special students. The verse, found in Matthew 18, says: "Take heed that you despise not one of these little ones; for I say unto you, That in heaven their angels do always behold the face of my Father which is in heaven."

Of course Andrew and Kate Bauhm never made fun of their little Andy and they loved him very much. Even though he was not like other children, he gave them much joy and happiness and he became their whole life. They did all they could to make Andy feel as normal as possible.

Andy, still fascinated by anything that could fly would often lay in the soft green grass and watch the clouds. It seemed to him that these fluffy white clouds could fly too. In Psalms 104 it says: "God makes the clouds his chariots: and He walks upon the wings of the wind." And in Psalms 18, verse 10, it says: "And he rode upon a cherub, and did fly; yea, he did fly upon the wings of the wind." Andy often imagined himself sitting on a cloud and sailing through the sky, as if riding on the wings of the wind. Airplanes also fascinated the young boy as they flew over his home.

One day as Mr. Bauhm was outside mowing the lawn, he noticed his son running about with his arms going up and down. Andy was saying, "Look, Daddy, I fly, I can fly, too."

Andrew decided he would make arrangements to take Andy up in an airplane so he could see what it is really like to fly. So the following week, on Andy's sixth birthday, Andrew, Kate and Andy went for a ride in a small plane at the local airport. Needless to say, the young lad was completely overwhelmed as he went on his first airplane ride. He kept saying, "I fly, I am flying."

Andy could not forget his airplane ride. That is all he talked about for the next several days. Then one day soon after that, Andrew took out his ladder to clean the spouting up on their house. He had only been on the ladder a short time when his wife, Kate, called to him. She told Andrew that he had a phone call. He climbed down from the ladder and went into the house.

Then Andy said, "I be airplane. I fly like a bird. I have wings like an angel. I fly." Up to the top of the six-foot ladder he climbed. He put his little arms out and began to flap them as if they were wings. In his heart he really thought he could fly.

Just as Andrew came out of the house to continue his job up on the ladder, he saw his young son leap from the top of the ladder, with his little arms outstretched saying once more, "I fl-y-y-y!

Andrew ran as fast as he could, but it was too late. He called for Kate, and she, too, came running. The terrified parents saw their son's lifeless body lying on the grass below the ladder. The ambulance was called, but the young boy had died of a broken neck when he fell. There was nothing anyone could do to bring Andy back to life. Andrew and Kate blamed themselves for not watching Andy more closely and they were deeply saddened by the loss of their young son.

Mrs. Allen and Andy's little classmates missed him as well. The children said that there was always something special about Andy. They said he truly was an "angel."

Meanwhile up in heaven little Andy really was flying. He had his wings now and as he flew above heaven's beautiful flowers he said, "I can fly, Mommy. I really can fly! Daddy, don't cry for me, because I am so happy now. I'm like the other angels and I can fly. I can be with Jesus all the time now! And Mommy, I told Jesus that you would be lonely without me so I asked him to please give you another little boy to take care of, because you were such a good mommy to me. If He does, perhaps I can be his guardian angel and help make sure nothing happens to him. Daddy, I don't know where my guardian angel was when I fell, but it doesn't really matter now, because I am so happy here. Someday, Daddy, you and Mommy will be here with me, won't you? I will keep watching for you and you can watch for me as I sail through the sky on the clouds and wings of the wind. I love both of you but Jesus loves me, too. He needs me here because I am now one of His special angels. Some day you will understand. I know you will!"

Meanwhile Kate and Andrew wondered about the Bible verse in Psalms that says, "For he shall give his angels charge over thee, to keep thee in all thy ways." They knew that God never makes mistakes, but why wasn't He watching over Andy when he tried to fly from the ladder? Even though their little boy was different from other normal children, he filled their lives with so much joy and happiness and they would miss him terribly.

It is said that when God closes a door, He opens a window. Two weeks after little Andy was taken from his earthly home to join the angel hosts of heaven, Andrew and Kate received a phone call. An adoption agency called to say they had a four-year-old boy and a three-year-old girl, a brother and sister, who were in desperate need of a good home. The agency wondered if the Bauhms would be interested in taking both of the children into their home. It seemed to be an answer to their prayers. Even though no one would ever be able to take the place of Andy in the hearts of Andrew and Kate, they were overjoyed at the chance to be able to be parents again, not of one but of two precious children. Their empty arms and hearts would once again be filled with the love of children.

Up in heaven Andy somehow knew that his request was being doubly granted. Now he and one of his new angel friends would both be flying down to earth to help watch over the children that were to be entrusted to the care of Andrew and Kate. He knew that now his parents would be happy again. He is very happy as well, because with his angel wings he can do what he always wanted to do, and that is, to be able to fly!

ANGELS OF CHARITY

Scott and Jenny lived with their parents in the little town of Brookville. They lived in a small, comfortable home with the Brookville brook running by the edge of their property. It was a pretty little stream with clear water running over the rocks and pebbles. Nearby a small waterfall rippled over the rocks where the children loved to play. They especially enjoyed the stream after the warm summer rains when the water was a little deeper. It was never deep enough to be very dangerous.

Mr. Carlton, their father, had lost his eyesight from being extremely diabetic. He often made his way to the brook behind their house by counting the flat stepping stones that Scott had laid in the grass from the house to the edge of the stream. Mr. Carlton loved to sit and relax there, as he listened to the water rush over the rocks. He could hear the songbirds and feel the breeze as it gently blew across his tired body, which was seemingly getting weaker as the days went by. He had been given a volume of Bible tapes and spent much time listening to the recordings of the Holy Scriptures that he could play on a small portable tape player someone from their church had given to him.

Mrs. Carlton, a kindly, gentlewoman, did sewing and altering for other people in her home so she could care for her husband. They had a very meager income. Sometimes people would give the Carltons their used clothing, which was usually made over for Scott and Jenny to wear. They sometimes felt embarrassed to go to school with other people's clothes on. They hoped no one would recognize them once their mother remodeled the hand-me-down clothes.

Scott, age thirteen, and Jenny, eleven, together had a newspaper route to help earn a little extra spending money. Scott liked to play basketball and practiced on an old wire ring he managed to put up on the old garage behind their house. Sometimes when he had basketball practice after school Jenny would deliver the papers by herself.

They always walked on their route because they had no bicycles. They were waiting for the day when they could save up enough money so each of them could at least buy a good used bicycle. Then they could ride to school and get done with their paper route faster.

The next week, when Jenny was delivering papers by herself while Scott practiced basketball after school, she came up with an extra paper for the second time that week. Scott accused his sister of skipping a customer, but Jenny assured him every customer had been given a newspaper. So Jenny gave the extra paper to an elderly lady across the street; who could not afford to buy one.

One day as Jenny was delivering the papers after school, from out of no where appeared a kindly man who asked her if she had an extra paper. It was Tuesday, the day along with Friday the week before that she had been given extra papers in her bundle. This man, whom she had never seen before, said he wanted to buy a newspaper. At first Jenny appeared to be frightened but the kindly man told her not to be afraid because he just wanted to buy a paper and then he would be on his way. Jenny gave him her extra Tuesday's paper. The man thanked her, handed her an envelope and was gone almost as quickly as he appeared.

Jenny hurriedly finished her paper route and arrived home just as Scott came home from basketball practice. Jenny told Scott and her parents about the kindly man buying her extra paper. When she took the envelope out of her delivery bag she could hardly believe her eyes, and neither could Scott and her parents, as she held out a twenty-dollar bill! At first they didn't want to believe Jenny's story, but where would Jenny get the money if it wasn't, true? And who was this stranger that gave all this money to Jenny just for a newspaper? Mrs. Carlton said the money would be put back for the bicycle Jenny wanted unless someone, somehow, reported some money missing. If that should happen, Jenny would have to return the money.

The rest of the week Scott went to basketball practice and Jenny passed the papers. On Friday, when Jenny again had an extra paper, the same kind man again appeared and asked for a newspaper, handing Jenny another envelope. Once more this man disappeared almost as quickly as he had appeared. Jenny just stood there hardly believing her eyes and wondering if her parents would believe her again.

The young, bewildered girl arrived home and eagerly opened the sealed envelope with Scott and Mrs. Carlton looking on and Mr. Carlton listening to every word. How amazed they were to find another twenty-dollar bill in the envelope. Jenny said Scott should have this money for his bicycle because after all they were both responsible for the paper route.

Mr. Carlton said perhaps this man was an angel of God, because he had been praying that somehow his children could each have a bicycle like their friends had. And because he didn't have any extra money to buy the bicycles Scott and Jenny wanted he knew someone would have to help provide the money. Sharing the funds for two bicycles would take longer. It would not take them as long to deliver their papers if they had bicycles to ride instead of having to walk their route. Then perhaps they could each have a paper route and earn twice as much money to buy some real store-bought clothes or a better sewing machine for their dear mother.

The following Tuesday Jenny again had an extra paper, and the kindly man once more appeared for his paper and gave Jenny another envelope with twenty dollars. By this time Scott was really beginning to question his sister and her new friendly customer. The young boy told his basketball coach that he was sorry but he just couldn't go to practice after school on Friday. The coach told Scott he would have to suffer the consequences if he didn't show up. But Scott just couldn't tell his coach about a mystery that he was going to try to solve.

So Friday after school Scott and Jenny together set out to deliver their daily papers. Scott had counted the papers this time and once more there was an extra paper. When the two children turned onto the street where this mystery man had appeared before, sure enough there he was, as if he knew that Jenny and Scott would soon be coming. Once more the kindly man asked for a newspaper and he handed Jenny another envelope while Scott looked on in amazement. Then as the mystery man turned to leave, Scott asked him what his name was. The kindly man just smiled and said, "Just call me Charity." Then he disappeared as if walking into a cloud.

The bewildered children hurried home and once more opened the sealed envelope as their parents watched. Again they found a twenty-dollar bill in the envelope, making a total of eighty dollars given to them by this man called Charity. Mr. and Mrs. Carlton were overwhelmed as the children once more told them about this mysterious man. Jenny asked her father if this man could be an angel of God. Mr. Carlton said it could very likely be an angel sent by God, just like the angels that visited people in Bible times, especially in the Old Testament story of Lot.

Mr. Carlton, who hadn't been feeling well lately, had been spending time by the side of the brook just talking to God and listening to his Bible tapes. It seemed he could almost hear God speaking to him in the water as it rippled over the rocks. He had often asked God to somehow provide for his children and his wife and now his prayers were being answered by unusual gifts of money from this "Angel of Charity."

Scott and Jenny had decided they would each take twenty dollars and buy a good used bicycle and the other forty dollars would be put towards a better sewing machine for their mother since she used it to supplement their income.

Next Monday when Scott went to basketball practice the coach let him play during practice, but said he couldn't play in the big benefit game coming up because he had skipped practice last Friday when he went with his sister on the paper route. Scott thought it was no use to tell the coach about this Charity Angel because he wouldn't believe him anyway.

Brookville Jr. High and grade schools always had benefit games and activities for extra school and community needs. Most all the people in town showed up for the annual festivities. Mr. Carlton had gone last year even though he couldn't see the action taking place, but he could hear it. Jenny had sung "God Bless America" in the talent contest and won five dollars. Jenny said this year Scott could be in the benefit games and she would take the paper route since all the different activities always practiced after school and either Scott or she would have to pass the papers.

Scott was disappointed when the coach said he couldn't play. He had really been practicing shooting his basketballs on his makeshift wire ring and was becoming quite good at making baskets. But then he thought of the eighty dollars they had received. Scott knew this money was worth more to his mother, father and sister and to himself than playing in some benefit game. The coach noticed how good Scott had been playing in the practice games. He was sorry he had told him he couldn't play, but rules are rules. The boys were going to play against the girls' team, and the girls really had some 'hot shots' on their team this year.

All the next week Jenny never saw the "Angel of Charity" again nor did she have any extra papers. Jenny believed, as her father did, that God truly sent the kindly mystery man to help the family in their time of need. This "Angel of Charity" never appeared again in person.

A few days later, Scott came home from basketball practice and Jenny came home from delivering papers. Together they went back to the brook to talk to their father, who often waited there for them as he sat in his chair by the creek bank. There he would listen to his children as they told him of all their day's activities at school. When they got to the back of the house they noticed his empty chair, so they went inside only to find out he was not in the house either. Quickly Mrs. Carlton and the two children ran out to the brook where they found Mr. Carlton face down by the water. Evidently the sick man had passed out as he got close to the water's edge. He must have fallen into the brook, and hit his head on a rock. This caused further injuries, which prevented him from getting up, and he drowned.

The next few days were very hard for Mrs. Carlton, Scott and Jenny. God gave them the strength they needed. After they had come home from laying their loved one to rest and committing him to God's care, Jenny took the mail in from their mailbox. She was surprised to find one more envelope, sealed and marked "Charity" with another twenty-dollar bill in it.

Mrs. Carlton thanked God for it as tears ran down from her eyes. That was just the amount needed to buy the sewing machine she had been hoping for but couldn't afford. She now could have her sewing machine and Scott and Jenny their bicycles, but these things would never replace their husband and father whom they dearly loved and missed. Mrs. Carlton was thankful her husband did not have to suffer from his illness anymore.

A week later the Brookville School benefit games were scheduled to be played. Many craft items also would be sold, some of which Mrs. Carlton had made from scraps of material. It was Saturday and it seemed like the whole town turned out for the annual festivities. In the evening the basketball game between the Junior High boys and girls was the last thing scheduled. The local school gym quickly filled with people, including Jenny and her mother. They knew Scott wasn't to play but he would be allowed to dress in his basketball outfit. He could sit on the bench with the coach and other players and just watch the game.

The game had started and the girls were really fired up. The girls were six points ahead and there were only three minutes left to play. Scott wished that he could go out on the floor and play and show the boys that the girls weren't any better than the boys were. The coach also wished he hadn't told Scott he could not play because during the practices he had been noticing how well Scott could hit the goal from just about anywhere.

Scott looked at his coach and said, "I'd like to show those boys how to beat the girls! I'd like to do it just once for my dad!"

The coach looked at Scott, and said, "Your dad isn't here and if he was, he couldn't see you play anyway, because he was blind."

Scott remembered how his dad would listen to him dribble the basketball and listen for the vibrations of the old wire ring every time Scott would make a basket. Then Mr. Carlton would say, "Good shot, Scott!"

Suddenly the coach said, "Scott, get out there and show those boys how to play. We can't let the girls beat us! Tell Tom to come to the bench."

Scott couldn't believe his ears, but said, "Yes, Sir!" And out onto the gym floor the boy ran.

Mrs. Carlton and Jenny were just as surprised to see Scott, as he grabbed the ball in the final three minutes and dribbled up and down the floor making one basket after another. The game ended and Scott somehow had made eight points. The excited boys beat the girls at last! You should have seen the excitement of the fans and especially Mrs. Carlton, Jenny and the coach, who couldn't believe what they were seeing!

The coach and the boys' team all gathered around Scott out on the gym floor and asked him how he could play like he did, making all those points so their team could win. Even the girls' team all thought Scott was some kind of a hero.

Before Scott could tell them what he wanted to say, the chairman of the benefit activities came out on the floor and called Scott over to him. Then he asked Mrs. Carlton and Jenny to come down onto the floor also. The man said the committee had decided to give half of all the benefit profit to the school to upgrade the playground equipment. The other half was to be given to Mrs. Carlton and the two children to help pay the mounting expenses they had acquired from Mr. Carlton's illness and funeral.

Jenny asked the chairman if his name was Charity, and he said no, but that all the people here could be called Charity. Then he looked at Scott and asked him how he could play ball like he did at the end of the game and make eight points so fast in just three minutes. Scott asked for the microphone and told everyone that he had always wished his dad could see him play basketball. Now for the first time his dad really could see him play. He did it all for him, because now his dad was in heaven and Jesus had given him new eyes that could see again. Scott wanted to do his very best for his dad, and for Jesus, who now had given his dad sight.

You could not find a dry eye in the crowd as Mrs. Carlton, also with tears in her eyes, stood hugging her children. With Scott in one arm and Jenny in the other, she thanked everyone for their generous love and kindness and suggested that each one go home and read I Corinthians 13.

CAROLINE

A true story is based on events dating back from 1890 to 1976.

Cherry Pie

"Papa, look over towards the shed," exclaimed nine-year-old Louis. "It looks like sister Caroline is up on the roof!"

"So she is, so she is," responded Papa, as he and Louis walked over to the shed.

Solomon, a tall stately man, looked up at his all too daring daughter and told her the roof of that shed was no place for a six-year-old girl to be. He asked her how and why she went up onto the roof.

"The old cherry tree behind the shed makes an excellent ladder, Papa," answered Caroline, as she looked down from the top of the shed. "I just wanted to see what Uncle Jacob's house looked like from up here." Jacob, who lived nearby on the same hill, was her mother's brother.

"So I see. And just what did you see at Uncle Jacob's house?" asked Papa.

"I could see Cousin Peter chasing one of the goats," responded the young Swiss miss, as the mountain breeze blew her bobbed hair across her face. "Well, maybe it wasn't a goat, maybe just his dog. Anyway I could see Peter."

"Maybe if you try yodeling to Cousin Peter he will yodel back to you. You know how yodeling echoes here in the mountains," responded Louis.

Caroline had been trying to learn to yodel like her father but so far she had not been able to do so. But knowing Caroline, she would not give up so easily.

Caroline, small in stature like her mother, and the youngest of six children, was quite a tomboy. She would rather play ball with her four older brothers,

21

if they would let her, than help her mother and sister, Anna, in the house. The name Caroline means one who is strong and this little girl surely lived up to her name.

Finally Papa beckoned for his young daughter to come down. Louis started to climb up the cherry tree to help his sister.

The little girl looked down and said, "I can help myself. I'll go down the same way I came up." With one hand she held up the skirt of her long dress and proceeded down, one limb at a time, until she reached the ground.

Louis stood in amazement as he watched his little sister come down the tree with such ease, and using just one hand. In his mind he wondered if he could do that.

"It is a good thing we just picked the cherries or you would have cherry stains all over your dress. Mama wouldn't be very happy about that, you know," said Papa as he took the hands of his two young children and headed up the path towards the house.

"By the way," Papa continued as he gently squeezed his daughter's hand, "Anna is helping Mama make some cherry pie. Don't you think you had better learn how to bake a cherry pie instead of climbing a cherry tree?"

"Maybe so," answered Caroline as she skipped along beside her papa. "But," she said, "I still would rather be outside and smell the fresh cut hay and the mountain air than smell a fresh baked cherry pie."

"That's just because you don't like to clean up and help with the dishes. But you'll be the first one to ask for a piece of pie," chided Louis, as he pulled his straw hat over his eyes to shield them from the bright lowering sun.

The sun sets early where the Solomon and Verena Liechti family live on the upper side of the mountain. They, along with other Mennonite farmers, lived together in the rolling Jura Mountains of Switzerland, not too far from the French border. The beautiful snow-capped Swiss Alps, seen off in the distance, hid the setting sun.

Because of their Mennonite religious beliefs, Solomon, along with other farmers, had to farm the land on the upper part of the mountains where the land had more rocks. The choice land toward the bottom of the mountains had been offered to non-Mennonite farmers. The Liechti family often struggled going up and down the mountain. In spite of their hardships, they were happy and content, nor did they complain. Instead they were just thankful for a place to live and earn their living.

Their big farmhouse, made of wood and stone back in the sixteen hundreds, had been built with the barn connected to it. Most Swiss homes were built with the house on top of the barn or perhaps connected side by side. This gave the farmers easier access to their cattle during the long, hard winters. Since the Liechti home had been built on the side of the mountain the main living quarters could be entered from the top part of the hill, while the barn, built below it, could be accessed from the bottom slope of the hill. Looking from the front you would just see the house, but from the back you could see the barn with the house above it. Today you would call it a split-level construction. Amazingly enough there were no screens on the windows because there were no flies, even with the livestock so close to the house.

In the summer you might sometimes see young Caroline sitting on one of the wide windowsills with her legs crossed under her long dress. She could not hang her feet down because each window had a beautiful flower box outside just below the window, filled with lovely red geraniums. Caroline had often been tempted to jump over the flower box and onto the ground below, but she knew she had better not.

Before going into the house, Papa and his two children went down into the barn to check on his three older sons, Christian, Abraham and Daniel. These boys were learning the trade of making hay rakes and pitch forks, and were actually quite good at it. Papa said supper would soon be ready and the boys should go up into the house.

Louis and Caroline raced toward the kitchen and saw two fresh cherry pies cooling on the wide kitchen windowsill beside the red geraniums. The two hungry children could hardly wait to eat.

Inside, Mama and Anna had just taken the pies and some homemade bread out of the oven. Anna was setting the table as Caroline came in the door. The red tile kitchen floor seemed to sparkle, and the young girl knew she needed to wipe her shoes before entering any further.

Mama said, "Caroline, wash your hands and finish setting the table, so Anna can help me set supper on."

"Yes, Mama," said the six year old reluctantly, as she proceeded with the task of setting the table.

Verena, Caroline's mother, was a small, frail woman and often sickly. She relied on Anna to help with the household duties. She also hoped to teach her youngest daughter to do the same. Should Anna ever leave home and get married, Verena would have to depend on help from Caroline.

Papa and the boys came in and lit the kerosene lanterns because it would soon be dark. Before long everyone was seated around the big wooden kitchen table. Since Mama was not feeling well she let Anna serve the meal. A common supper consisted of boiled potatoes with the skins left on, fresh or canned green beans, a spinach salad, especially in the summer time, and a little meat.

One of the favorite meals for the children consisted of fresh hot cornbread topped with hot home made chocolate pudding. This dish would later be carried down to future generations and is still enjoyed today. Of course they always had plenty of fresh milk from their cows and homemade bread and butter. The potatoes that were left from the evening meal were peeled and sliced in the morning, then fried for breakfast along with fresh eggs.

Solomon loved to make butter. It became one on his specialties. The family loved to eat it on Mama's fresh baked bread. It was a tradition to have bread, butter and milk with every meal.

Papa, in his deep voice, always said grace in the German-Swiss dialect, their spoken language, while the family held hands together. Holding hands while they prayed kept the children's hands from teasing the one seated next to them.

The hungry family had, no sooner consumed the main course, than Caroline said, "Where's the pie? May I please have the first piece?"

"Now just a minute, young lady," replied Mama. "I think the first piece should go to your sister Anna, who pitted the cherries and made the pie."

"But I helped pick some of the cherries. That means I can have the second piece, right, Papa?" pleaded Caroline, as she pleadingly looked up to his kindly face.

"We all helped pick the cherries," the boys agreed together.

"And since you're the youngest I think you should be last and have the smallest piece," said Christian.

"Just a minute, children. There is plenty of pie for everyone. Anna, bring the pies and I'll slice some fresh cheese to eat with them," said Papa.

"This pie really is very good, Anna," said Caroline as she ate her last bite. "Perhaps you can teach me how to make a pie after all so I can have the first piece the next time."

"That I would like to see! A tomboy making a pie!" spoke up Daniel. "It better be a good pie or I won't eat it."

"That's enough!" said Papa as he, too, finished his pie. "Boys, you better go do the chores. And Caroline, if you want to learn how to make a pie, it would be good if you started right now and helped to clean up the dishes."

Caroline could feel the sternness in her father's voice and knew she had better obey. Slowly she carried the dishes over to the sink. Anna poured some hot water in the old granite dishpan. It was too hot, so she pumped some cold water into it.

Anna turned to Caroline and said, "I'll wash the dishes and you may dry them. We can put them away together while Mama rests."

The sun had long set as Mama tucked her little Caroline in bed. The young girl insisted that Mama would tell one of her funny stories before she went to sleep. Verena was good at making up these stories and often amused her children with her tales. Before long the Swiss Miss was fast asleep in her soft feather bed. So another day came and went in the Liechti house high in the Swiss Mountains.

Winter In The Mountains

During the summer Solomon and his boys would take the cows up to the top of the mountain where the grass is fresh and sweet. Solomon could always tell where his cows were by listening for their cowbells. Caroline loved to be able occasionally to go with Papa to milk the cows. She loved to be on the mountain where she could look all around. Perhaps what she liked best of all was the sound of the cowbells as they jingled from the neck of each cow. The wild flowers were beautiful on the side of the mountain. She loved to pick them, and would carefully put the delicate flowers in her apron pocket to bring them home to her mother.

With fall fast approaching it would soon be time to bring the cows back down the mountain and into the barnyard. The barn had been well supplied with hay, which had been cut during the summer. There would be enough to feed the cattle all winter.

So the day came to get the cows and close up the milk shed high on the mountain. Solomon and his four boys walked up the path to where the cattle were.

Solomon commented to his sons that he could hardly hear the cowbells and wondered if the cattle had wandered off in the distance. The second oldest son, Abraham, assured Papa that the cattle were all together where they should be.

"Do you suppose," said Papa, as he shook his head, "that I am losing my hearing?"

The cows were gathered together with the help of the family dog, and down the hill they came. Verena, Anna and Caroline watched eagerly as the cattle neared the barnyard. It seemed even the cattle could almost sense a cold winter ahead.

All over the beautiful Swiss countryside you could see and hear the cattle coming down for the winter. As the bells gently swung from the necks of the cows, they sounded like a symphony of bells, without the distinctive melody of any one particular song. Oftentimes the cows were led through the streets of town like some big parade on the way to their winter lodging. What a sight to behold! The farmers could always tell which cow belonged to them by the special sound of their cowbells and also by the markings on each bell.

Indeed winter did arrive in all its fury. Caroline, now seven years old, walked to school down in the village as her brothers and sister had done in the past. At times the snow was so deep that they rode the sled down the hill. It wasn't nearly as much fun to pull the sled back up the hill. Solomon made some big square wooden snowshoes for his children, making it easier to walk on top of the snow. The Liechti family had a team of workhorses and father would hook them up to the old sleigh. That is how the family went to town and to church in the wintertime. More often than not, Solomon walked where he wanted to go when alone.

Solomon, a very frugal man, was actually quite well to do. One day a Mr. Geiser asked to borrow some money from Solomon. To Mr. Geiser's surprise, Solomon pulled out a sack from under his bed containing 8,000 gold francs, all in five-franc pieces. The amount of money the man wanted to borrow was so heavy that he could not carry it through the snow. The eldest son, Christian, hauled the money to Mr. Geiser's house with the horse and sleigh.

Christmas was a family time at the Liechti house. The boys would go up the mountain and cut down a small pine tree and pull it home with their sled. Homemade strings of popcorn and other ornaments decked the tree along with carefully placed candles.

The family always sang Christmas carols before opening their gifts. And of course Papa yodeled for his children. The gifts were usually homemade. Mama always knitted mittens and scarves for her family. Papa made useful items out of wood. There would be a festive Christmas dinner, sometimes shared with Uncle Jacob's family.

The most important thing about Christmas was hearing Papa read the Christmas story from the Bible. He always read the second chapter of Luke. And of course it was all in German, for that was what they spoke along with Swiss dialect. Mama would always make up a story to tell that would bring laughter to the whole family.

During the winter the family ate vegetables and meat, which Mama and Anna had canned the past summer, along with their fresh eggs and milk. The animals were well fed, too, with the hay that had been stored in the barn under the house. The men were thankful they did not have to go out into the blustery winter weather to care for their livestock.

Finally the winter was over and the snow began to melt on the beautiful mountainsides of Switzerland. The little spring flowers could be seen as they poked their delicate heads through the ground. Soon the cattle, with their cowbells, would once more parade up the path to their fresh green pastures. And soon again Mama would plant pretty red geraniums in the flower boxes below each window.

Tragedy Strikes

Warm weather had arrived. Solomon and his sons planted the garden that Verena and Anna would take care of. Before long it would be haymaking time and the men would be busy out on the fields. During the winter the boys made several hay rakes and pitchforks. They were anxious to try them. Uncle Jacob and other farmers came to buy some as well. The boys had quite a nice income because of their craftsmanship.

One day Solomon decided to take some of his rich, yellow, homemade butter and some eggs to town to sell them. He often walked along the railroad tracks when he went to town. This day was no exception. After selling his goods and purchasing some items for his wife, Solomon started for home, again walking down the railroad tracks. The clouds were lowering and the sound of thunder could be heard. He hoped he could make it home before it rained.

Then tragedy struck! Solomon had indeed become hard of hearing. With the wind blowing and whistling through the trees, Solomon did not hear the train coming up behind him. The train hit him, dragging him several yards before going on its way. It was some time before anyone found the man who had now lost his life in such a terrible way.

While all this was taking place with Solomon, his children, Christian, Abraham and Anna were at the wedding of one of their friends. When the news finally came to the three young adults attending the wedding, Abraham was so stunned by the news that he jumped over a table and raced out the door to go to his mother.

The shock of losing a husband and father was very stressful for the remaining Liechti family. The boys would have to work harder than ever to keep the farm going and to provide for their mother. Mr. Geiser, who had borrowed the money the past winter, made provisions to pay it all back to Verena and the children. Uncle Jacob, Verena's brother, would now be guardian of the younger children and in charge of their money.

Caroline, at only seven years of age, missed her papa very much. *Why, oh, why did he have to leave them the way he did?* she often wondered. Thoughts went back to the time when she was on the roof of the shed. She remembered looking down on her father as he stood under the cherry tree. She remembered how kind and gentle he had looked. How she wished she could hold his strong hands again.

Time went on and Caroline gradually outgrew her tomboyish attitude. Her mother taught her how to knit and she even learned to bake a cherry pie. Her brothers taught her how to make butter and she finally learned how to yodel and to speak in French. Her papa would be proud of her if he could hear her yodel now. Before long Caroline had become a lovely, young teenager and she looked forward to being with other young people.

On weekends the youth, from the Mennonite Church where the Liechti family attended, always gathered in homes and sang hymns. Caroline loved the fellowship of her church friends and cousins. She often went with her cousin, Peter, who was just a year older then she. How she looked forward to these gatherings! The church also served as a school where the Liechti and other Mennonite children received their education.

Most of all she loved her Savior, Jesus Christ, who gave her the hope of eternal life and the hope of seeing her father again in heaven one day. Yes, Caroline and her cousin, Peter, had both become Christians by giving their hearts to the Lord and it was very evident in their daily walk of life.

The stress of losing Solomon made it difficult for Verena to go on. The frail little woman, who used to tell funny stories, never smiled much anymore. She, too, finally passed away to be with her dear husband who had gone on before.

Then one day Anna married and the two oldest boys thought of doing the same thing. The farm was too much to keep. If one of the boys did not buy it, it would have to be sold. Caroline decided to go live with her sister, Anna, and her husband. She knew she could not stay at the farm anymore.

Uncle Jacob divided Solomon's money equally among his six children.

Caroline had purchased a new sewing machine with the money she received. Soon she began sewing for other people. With this she earned enough money to help pay for room and board. So months went by and there would yet be another change in the life of this small but spunky young lady, Caroline.

A New Adventure

"How would you like to go traveling around the world with me?" Cousin Peter asked Caroline one day.

"Surely, you must be kidding, Peter. Around the world! Why, do you know how long that would take even with the new ships they have these days?" replied Caroline.

"No, I am not kidding. I have been saving money for quite some time now and I would really like to go before I settle down and get married some day. I am really serious, Caroline. Will you go with me? You have nothing to hold you back here. When we return you will probably find a nice young man and perhaps get married like Anna did. In the meantime let's go on a trip, okay?" Peter sounded so convincing that Caroline had a hard time saying no.

Finally she said, "Okay, I'll go. Papa left me some money. I'll have my brother make me a big wooden trunk to pack my things in and off we'll go!" For a moment the young lady couldn't believe she really had agreed to such a thing as traveling around the world!

Caroline and Peter had always been close to one another and she was certain they would get along fine on this great adventure. So at age twenty, this daring young lady said good-bye to her brothers and sister, not knowing that she would never see them again. She and her cousin then took the train to the coast of France where they boarded a large ship with sails and headed west.

Caroline slept in one room of the ship, with the women and children, while Peter slept in another with the men and boys. There were not enough rooms for each family. Many people, especially women and children, became sick while out on the sea and some even died. But Caroline and Peter were strong-willed and stood the trip quite well.

What a thrill for all those on board as the ship "Chicago" neared the shores of the United States of America! The people cheered as they viewed the approaching Statue of Liberty, which had been given to the United States by the country of France from where they had sailed. As for Caroline and

Peter they could hardly believe they had arrived in the land they had heard so much about. Their rough journey across the Atlantic lasted nearly two weeks. Once on land they would take the train across America, sightseeing as they went. Their plans were to sail to the Orient once they reached the West Coast, then finally return home once again.

Back in Switzerland they had been informed of several families from their country who had migrated to the community of Kidron, Ohio, so that is where the two young cousins first headed for.

Once they reached Ohio, they stayed there for a short time. After learning about another Swiss settlement in Berne, Indiana, they decided to move on once again. Of course their big wooden trunks went with them. Peter helped Caroline with her homemade trunk that was three feet wide, two feet tall and three feet deep. It was way too heavy for Caroline to lift.

Upon reaching the Berne, Indiana, area, Peter and Caroline no longer found the soft, rolling hills like they had in the Kidron community. Neither were there any mountains like they had in their beloved Switzerland. This new community of people from Swiss-German descent lay situated on rich, flat farmland. The kindness and friendship, shown to them by the people in this small town overwhelmed the two cousins. Though they missed the beautiful snow capped alpine mountains, or 'Berge,' as they would say in their Swiss dialect, they hoped to see them again one day.

Peter and Caroline soon felt right at home in the new Mennonite Swiss-speaking community of Berne. Surprisingly enough, they both found jobs and lived with Swiss people in the community. This would give them more money to continue on their adventure around the world. Caroline found a job working for a Mr. Zuercher who, along with his family, had also come from Switzerland. Mr. Zuercher, a craftsman at making Swiss accordions, hired Caroline to work in his shop. Her small fingers were just what Mr. Zuercher needed to put the small, fragile, delicate parts of an accordion together.

A local farmer had hired Peter to work for him on his farm. There he helped milk and care for dairy cattle.

Caroline could not speak nor understand the English language very well, so she enrolled herself in the eighth grade of the local school. There she was taught the new American language. Imagine, if you will, this twenty-year-old young lady in class with eighth grade students, in a foreign land and unable to converse with them in English. Yes, Caroline was indeed spunky and willing to get the most out of life.

A New Life For Caroline

Caroline and Peter began attending the Mennonite Church in Berne and became acquainted with other young people of the community. Caroline met a tall, dark, handsome, young man by the name of Levi Habegger. He took a liking to this new Swiss miss and made her feel very welcome.

Levi's parents had also both come from Switzerland to Berne, Indiana where they were married. It is a known fact that Levi's mother was a cousin to the mother of the president of Switzerland. After their marriage they lived in a log cabin on a farm for a number of years with their five children. The cabin had two rooms downstairs and two rooms upstairs. Levi's father supported his family by farming, carving and weaving baskets. As a young lad, Levi learned to read from the German Bible.

Unlike Caroline, who in her younger years didn't seem interested in baking a cherry pie, this young man, Levi, loved to help his mother bake. He showed a great interest in drawing, especially animals. Levi also enjoyed singing around the pump organ with his family at home. It has been said that back in the old country, in times past, the Habegger family had been instrumental in the manufacturing and repair of great church pipe organs. Perhaps the music interest continued in the life of this young man as one of his many talents.

In his later teens, Levi went to Bluffton, Ohio, to attend a Mennonite college there. His intentions were to study the Bible. After a year he decided to come home and help his father. That is when he met Caroline.

Of course, like most children in the Berne area, Levi spoke German before learning to speak English. The church sermons were still preached in German. Gradually the young people were beginning to learn the English language. By now Levi had become quite handy in woodworking and carpentry.

Levi began courting Caroline with his horse and buggy. His parents fell in love with this young lady from their homeland. Needless to say Levi and Caroline also fell in love with each other. Someday Levi hoped to buy one of the new invented vehicles, the automobile, to take his young lady a ride in. But for now, the horse and buggy would do.

In the year of 1911, Caroline and Levi were married. How she wished her brothers and sister, Anna, could see how happy she was. Of course she always had Cousin Peter.

They purchased a plot of land a little southeast of Berne and there Levi would build a house and barn for his new bride. In the meantime they rented a small one-bedroom house, east of Berne, until their own home would be ready. It was in this tiny house with dark green shingles that their first child was born. Yes, little Elfrieda Verena made her entrance into the world, one warm August day, about a year after Caroline and Levi had been married.

Finally the new house had been completed and Levi moved his new family into the home he had built with the help of his father. A barn also had been constructed not too far from the house. No, it was not connected together like the houses and barns were in Switzerland. This was America and things were done differently here. A wooden fence surrounded the house so their children could play outside and not wander off. The fence would separate them from the cattle and workhorses. All farm work was done with horses. Just like the new cars, Levi hoped some day to purchase one of the new inventions of a tractor. But that might be a while yet.

Caroline seemed happy and content with her new life in America, although she often thought about her homeland and the family she left behind. Almost every week she would write a letter to one of her brothers or to her sister to keep in touch with them. She wished they would come to America also where there were so many new opportunities. Needless to say, for Caroline and Peter, the trip of going around the world ended in Indiana.

Caroline loved her little daughter and Levi provided well for his new family. In the next few years three little boys, Melvin Levi, Herman Ernest, and Daniel Gerhart were added to this Habegger household. Now Levi would have plenty of help on the farm once the boys became older. Surely Anna would be happy for her sister if she could only see all that she now had. Caroline sent some black and white photos of her family and farm to Switzerland.

Sundays were special days for the Habegger family. It was a day set apart to attend church and worship their Lord and Savior. Levi, Caroline and children would climb into their buggy and off they would go about three miles to church. It almost seemed like the horse knew the way to go to church by itself. Could it have been because the horse could hear the beautiful singing of the congregation, especially in the summer when the church windows were open? A shed had been constructed for all the horses, with their buggies, to be tied until church was over. There the animals heard the singing coming from inside the church.

Caroline kept in touch with her cousin, Peter, and saw him in church every Sunday. Thankfully he, too, had now become married and settled down in this new community. The two cousins would exchange news from their homeland. Yes, for now Caroline seemed quite content, but that would soon change.

Tragedy Strikes Again

One day, about eight years after their marriage, Levi walked two miles to Berne to purchase a young heifer. This heifer seemed quite stubborn. You might almost think it was a mule. Levi struggled with the animal for two miles, as he walked the heifer back home after purchasing it. This activity wore the man completely out. By the time he arrived home he had become exhausted. Then he became sick with pneumonia and within a week he was gone, to be with his Father in heaven. What a terrible shock for Caroline!

There, with a new farm, a stubborn heifer and four small children, Caroline became a young widow alone in a foreign land. Oddly enough, Caroline's daughter, Elfrieda, then seven years of age, was the same age Caroline was when her own father, Solomon, had died so tragically years ago.

Elfrieda, the oldest of the children, missed her daddy very much. Shortly before his death Levi purchased a child's wooden rocker from the furniture store in Berne. He carried it all the way home and gave it to his young daughter. After he had passed away, Elfrieda often sat and rocked on this little rocker. There, with tears in her eyes she longed to talk to her daddy again. The big white bow in her soft brown hair would bob back and forth as she wept and thought of her daddy. That rocker is still in the family today.

Elfrieda often thought about a particular time she had walked to school. After going about a mile, she saw several pigs on the road in front of her. Afraid to walk by them, she turned around and went back home. Levi took time out from his work and walked the two miles back to school with his young daughter, assuring her she would be okay.

But life must go on. Caroline knew she could not afford to stay on the farm. So this saddened widow, along with her four young children left their home and went to live with her husband's sister's family out on another farm. The children became very close to the family of Dan and Katie Lehman, where they lived after their father passed away. They considered their cousins as 'brothers and sisters'. That closeness would remain through out their lives. The Dan Lehman family was very good to Caroline and her children.

While Caroline lived with relatives, the Mennonite church and others helped them financially.

Levi did not believe in insurance, as many in those days did not. Levi's father felt sorry for the young widow and his four grandchildren. He decided to purchase a house in Berne for Caroline and her family. The farm had been sold to pay expenses for the fatherless family. So once again the family moved but this time to the small town of Berne. There, Caroline would spend the rest of her life.

Levi had purchased a sewing machine for his new bride soon after they had been married. Caroline made most of her children's clothing as well as her own. After moving to town she began to sew for others to earn extra money. For extra-added income, she also sold Avon products for a while.

The house they moved into had electricity. One light hung from a cord in each room. However there was no plumbing, running water or bathroom facilities, just an outside water pump and privy. Cooking had to be done on an old wood cook stove. It helped to warm the house as well.

The laundry was done by hand with a scrub board on the closed-in back porch. A clothesline was stretched inside the house in the winter to dry the clothing. In the corner of the living room stood a Victrola record player. The floors had no wall to wall carpeting. An eight by ten rug covered the center of the living and dining room floors. A covering of linoleum, of about the same size, covered the other floors with the bare wood showing about a foot around each covering. All but the back porch and kitchen walls were covered with flowered wallpaper. This writer can well remember the house and its facilities.

Caroline's youngest son was a sleepwalker. The story goes that one night the boy stepped out of bed, went down the stairs, out the door and to the neighbor's house. There, not knowing what he was doing, he picked up a throw rug from their porch brought it home and put it in his mother's washroom. When Caroline heard the door downstairs she knew her Danny Boy was on the prowl again.

A small barn, out back, housed a neighbor's cow and some chickens. The owner of these animals gave Caroline all the eggs and milk she needed so he could keep his livestock there. How she appreciated this. In the back yard a garden had been planted, so the family had fresh vegetables to eat.

Later she worked for a hatchery and an egg company. She was allowed to take the cracked eggs home for her family to use. Because she had access to so many fresh eggs, Caroline often made egg pancakes or 'datch' as she called them. These tasty pancakes, made with eggs and milk, were very thin and could almost be rolled up as crepes. She would serve these to her children using home-canned grape juice as syrup. Fresh cornbread and hot chocolate pudding soon became a favorite evening meal for Caroline's family as it had been for her in Switzerland.

Though Caroline had a small barn, a horse and buggy would be too much for her to care for, and to purchase one of those new modern cars was out of the question. Therefore the family walked wherever they needed to go unless someone offered to take them. They walked almost three fourths of a mile to church and the children walked about five blocks to school. The uptown area was about four or five blocks from their house. Cousin Peter's new family and the Dan Lehman family often took Caroline and children into their homes for Sunday dinner. Caroline appreciated this so very much. But no one could ever take the place of her beloved Levi. How she missed him!

Peter also had become a hard working man. With the experience he had gathered from working with cattle, he opened a dairy in the nearby town of Decatur. Herman, Caroline's son, still remembers going with Pete to deliver milk to his customers in a horse-drawn wagon. Pete was very good to Caroline and her children, always keeping in touch with them and helping them when help was needed.

Caroline knew she had to remain strong to raise her growing family. She put her trust and faith in her Lord and Savior, Jesus Christ. Without Him it would have been very difficult to go on. How thankful Caroline was that she had been brought up to trust in Jesus. She hoped and prayed that her four children would also gain this same trust. Somehow God gave her the endurance for each new day.

All too soon, Caroline's children became teenagers and were soon involved with other young people from the community. When her three sons were old enough to work away from home they had to get jobs to help support the struggling family. The oldest boy, Melvin, found a job in neighboring Allen County working for the Co-op. He was allowed to keep only enough money out of his salary for room and board and living expenses. The rest his salary had to go to his mother to help support her and the siblings not yet working.

Elfrieda had become quite an artist and even received a scholarship to attend an art school in Chicago. For various reasons she chose not to go and decided to stay in Berne. It has been said that when this young lady began courting the one she would later marry, Caroline had a special way of letting the young man know when it was time to go home. All the bedrooms were upstairs and a granite commode was kept in the upstairs hallway, to be used at night by the family. When Caroline thought it was time for her daughter's beau to say good night and go home, she would rattle the lid on the commode. The noise could be heard downstairs and the young man soon got the message.

So as the years went by one by one, Caroline's children became married and left home. She continued to work and support herself, still walking where she needed to go, unless someone took her in their car. In later years her three sons decided to go visit their mother's homeland of Switzerland. They encouraged their mother to go along, but she would not go perhaps because she was afraid to fly or perhaps because she knew things had changed back home and it would no longer be the same. She had her home and family in Indiana now and that is where she wanted to be.

Yes, this strong little lady, Caroline Liechti Habegger, lived until two months before her 87th birthday. She never had her husband long enough to help raise their children when she needed him the most. She never owned or drove a car, never returned to her beloved homeland, never saw her brothers or sister again, nor did she ever complete her journey around the world. But Caroline had something precious that was her whole life. She had a tremendous faith in her Lord above to help carry her through difficult times. She had four wonderful children, seventeen grandchildren and a number of great-grandchildren, who loved her dearly. She even lived to see and hold her first great-great granddaughter, Rochelle Geisel.

Yes, we believe this mighty little woman, who never complained and always had a smile, is now in Heaven with Jesus and all her loved ones who have gone on before her. I'm sure they welcomed her with open arms. You see, she also outlived her only daughter by sixteen years. Elfrieda died at the early age of forty-seven from heart disease. It was another great loss in the life of Caroline, losing her only daughter. What a reunion she must have had when she stepped inside the pearly gates! As this story is written, Caroline has one son, Herman, age 81, still living, besides all her descendants

Memories

Those of us who remember our dear grandmother will always hold a special place in our hearts for her. Grandma Habegger, as we called her, was kind, affectionate, very loving and gentle. Even though destined for much heartache, we never saw her become upset. She certainly lived up to the meaning of her name, Caroline-one who is strong.

Some of the things we remember her by are the small, two-room log cabin she moved into after her children left home. It consisted of a kitchen and living area in one room. The other room, her bedroom, had a bathroom stool and lavatory in one corner separated only by a curtain from her bed and dresser. Later she moved into a modern three-room apartment with all the conveniences, except for the old wringer washer down in the basement. There she took pride in growing beautiful rose bushes laden with many buds and flowers. She lived alone in this apartment until she went into the nursing home. She had to go there because she was accidentally struck by a bicyclist; while crossing the street. She received some abdominal injuries and after that she developed one problem after another.

We can recall the big chunks of Swiss chocolate she always kept in a big glass jar that she shared with her loved ones. How we looked forward to this treat. When we would eat at her house she still loved to fix fried or mashed potatoes, hamburger gravy, and fresh spinach or dandelion salad with boiled eggs and homemade dressing. Sometimes we had another one of her childhood favorite dishes consisting of cornbread topped with hot chocolate pudding. She also loved to make graham cracker pudding with dates for dessert, as well as ground-cherry pie. Her homemade raised yeast donuts were a favorite of everyone. Some of her grandchildren also remember eating the corn she had parched in her old iron skillet. Perhaps the most favorite food Grandma Habegger became known for was her potato salad, or as she would say, in her Swiss accent, 'Botato' salad. If you would ask her how she made it, she would say just add a little of this and that, but the secret was in her dressing and the sweet pickle relish she always added. "To make it good," she would say.

The heavy big, red, wooden trunk that Caroline brought with her to America still is in existence today. This trunk with its strong metal reinforced corners, as seen in 1998 by the author, now belongs to the descendants of Caroline's youngest son, Daniel.

Yes, we have many fond memories of this special lady, who left a great example for us to follow. She never became wealthy, yet her needs were always supplied. Loved by all that knew her, she had an abundance of love to give in return. The descendants of Caroline who remember her know that if they, as she did, truly live a Christian life, they can one day be reunited with this wonderful little mother and grandmother. Most of all we can be united with the One, Jesus Christ, who made it possible for us to be together once more as a family of God with those who have gone on before. What a glorious hope! May we all strive to live our lives pleasing to the One who made us so we can share in this great reunion is my prayer for everyone.

Written by Ginny Lee, eldest granddaughter of Caroline, in her memory. The author was privileged to go to Switzerland in 1978 and 1983. There she was able to walk on the grounds and see the area and home where her grandmother Caroline once had lived.

CURIOUS COUSINS
Based on a true story

Jadon, a young adventurous lad at the age of three, always appeared anxious to see the world around him. When he shopped or traveled with his parents, he often wandered away from them. Unaware that his parents would be concerned that he could become lost or that someone might take him, he wanted to see the world around him.

Jadon, named after a Biblical man from the Old Testament in Nehemiah, was a beautiful child with brown wavy hair and blue eyes. His loving parents always kept their eyes on him and would not let him get far out of their sight.

Isn't that how it is with God's children? Do we sometimes wander out into the world a little too far? When we do, our Heavenly Father keeps His loving eyes on us and before He allows us to get into too much trouble, He usually turns us around and brings us back to Him if we willingly let Him guide us.

Jadon loved the out of doors and he especially liked to go on camping trips with his parents, brother and sister.

One time when he was about four years of age, his family went camping with a group of families from their church. The young lad was having the time of his life. This particular camp-ground had so much to offer in the way of entertainment for the children and Jadon seemed to be taking it all in.

When it was time to go home, Jadon was not ready to leave. He innocently told his parents that he never wanted to go to heaven, he just wanted to stay at this campground. To Jadon, who had often heard his parents talk about heaven as a wonderful, great place for all who enter there, this campground was heaven on earth and he wished for nothing better!

Sometimes we become so satisfied with all this world has to offer that we tend to forget about the heavenly home our Father is preparing for all who accept Him as their Lord and Savior, and we become too content with our life here on earth. Our ultimate goal is to strive for heaven.

Zachary, a cousin to Jadon, and a charming young lad lived in the country with his parents and two older sisters. As a young child of age two or three, he seemed very inquisitive and always asked 'why' to everything that was spoken to him. There is nothing wrong with wanting to know 'why' because that is how little children, learn, by seeing and doing and finding out 'why'.

One day little Zachary, age three, was visiting his grandparents. They had games and a toy box in their basement family room. The young child began playing with a fairly good-sized chalkboard on the carpeted floor of the basement family room. He was having a good time scribbling on it with sticks of chalk, but at the same time, making a dusty mess on the carpet.

His grandmother said to him, "Zachary, why don't you take the chalk board outside on the patio and 'write' on it out there?" The youngster, with the chalk in his hand, agreed and followed his grandmother, and chalkboard, up the stairs and out onto the patio.

Grandmother went inside and several minutes later went out to check on her grandson. To her amazement the little boy was sitting on his tricycle on top of the chalkboard! Grandmother asked Zachary what he was doing with his tricycle on top of the board.

The young lad replied, "But Grandma, you said to take the chalkboard outside and 'ride' on it."

Grandmother had meant for her grandson to 'write' on it, not 'ride' on the chalkboard, but Zachary had misunderstood. He thought Grandma said to 'ride' on it. So with his tricycle he was doing just that, 'riding' on it.

Grandmother, so amused at the child's understanding of what he thought he could do, just chuckled and picked up the chalkboard and suggested to the young lad that he 'ride' with his tricycle on the patio and 'write' on the sidewalk with the chalk.

Sometime the Lord tries to talk to us and instruct us in something He wants us to do but we want to do things our way and in our own understanding. Let us always listen carefully as the Holy Spirit tries to guide us to do the will of our Heavenly Father.

Now, let's put these two little curious cousins, Jadon and Zachary, both age three, together and find out about their adventure for a day. Since Zachary had no brothers to play with, his mother at times would let one of his little cousins come to spend the day with him.

On this one particular summer day, Jadon came to play with his cousin, Zachary, who lived in the country. Behind Zachary's house grew a large field of corn. The corn stalks were at least five feet tall. Zachary's mother looked out of her kitchen window and saw the two lads swinging on the two big chain link swings that hung from a high metal frame. The boys seemed to be having a good time.

The next time Zachary's mother looked out of the window, the boys were not swinging. She thought perhaps that they went down to the playhouse or to the barn. When they failed to appear after a short length of time, Mother went looking for them but they were no where around. She noticed a couple of the very tall corn stalks bending over slightly about fifty feet from their house and wondered if the two curious cousins could have possibly wandered into the large ten acre corn field.

Zachary's mother checked in the barn and playhouse but did not find them there. She wondered if she should look for them in the cornfield. If they did go into the cornfield, which direction would they have gone? Mother called loudly for the boys but they did not answer. She became concerned and thought it was useless for her to go into the field since it covers such a large area. She notified her husband at work and Jadon's parents when the two failed to respond to her call. If the two youngsters didn't go into the cornfield, where were they?

On one side of the cornfield was a farm pond. If the boys came out near to the pond would they stay away from the water and find their way home? On the opposite side of the cornfield was a State Highway. If they came out along this road would the three-year-old boys know which way to turn to go home? Would someone see them who would recognize the boys and bring them home? Or what if someone would pick them up and take them away never to return again? There are always reports of missing children and the thought of this happening entered the minds of the boys' parents!

The grandparents were notified of their missing grandsons and were asked to pray for their safety. "Please, dear Lord," the parents and grandparents prayed, "please protect the boys and bring them safely home."

The police were called and they were prepared to look for the boys with search dogs. A family neighbor who flew a small airplane was also on standby, if needed. Perhaps someone in the plane could spot the wandering lads.

Meanwhile, unknown to the parents and loved ones, the boys had followed Zachary's cats into the field. In the cornfield the two boys wandered on through one row after another until each row began to look the same to them. When they realized they were lost, they wondered which way to turn so they would come out of the field by Zachary's house. The corn stalks were so high they could not see over them.

The two little boys had an idea or so they thought. Zachary stooped down and Jadon stood on his shoulders. Holding onto the corn stalks beside him, Zachary carefully stood up, with his cousin standing on his shoulders. Jadon tried to look over the top of the cornfield to see where they were and to see if they could locate the house. But the boys were too short, the corn too tall, and all they could see were golden corn tassels.

If they hadn't followed Zachary's farm cats into the field they wouldn't be lost now. The cats, chasing some field mice, had soon disappeared but the boys continued to walk deeper into the towering cornfield. They figured if they kept walking straight down one row, sooner or later they would come out of the field. The boys were becoming a little frightened and right now all they wanted was to find their way home. What if they couldn't find their way out and it became dark? Would they have to spend the night in the cornfield? What if a raccoon would come near to them? The boys hoped their parents would find them before dark, if they didn't find their way home first.

Somehow they knew that the same Jesus they heard about from their parents and in church, would watch over them. They were not sure just how or when they would get home. They knew they just wanted to go there.

Finally the two frightened lads came out of the field, their tender arms and legs itching from the rough leaves of the corn stalks and their hair frosted with corn tassel pollen. They came out by the highway and wondered which way to start walking towards home. Young Zachary, holding Jadon's hand, thought he knew the right way.

As they stood by the edge of the road, a man in a pick-up truck stopped when he saw the two little boys all alone wandering down the road. He asked the boys where they were going and they said 'home.' He opened his truck door and told the boys to get in. He said he would take them home but would he?

Jadon and Zachary looked at each other hesitantly because they did not know the man. They were always instructed never to get into any car with strangers. The curious cousins did get in the truck after the man persuaded them to. Then the man took off with two tired little boys sitting beside him. This man seemed friendly enough and the boys hoped they would soon be at Zachary's house.

The man, living not too far from where the lad lived, thought he recognized Zachary as a little neighbor boy. He was concerned when he saw the two lads walking quite a distance from their home along the highway. The kind, concerned neighbor man did indeed take the boys to Zachary's house where their parents were overjoyed to see them.

The police had not yet arrived and were immediately called and informed that the boys were safely home, thanks to their neighbor who had found them walking along the road. The boy's parents told them that they still shouldn't go with strangers but in this particular instance they were glad they did. The boys were glad to be home and promised never to go in a cornfield again!

Just like this true story of the boys going into the cornfield, sometimes we walk away from the call of the Lord, to look for a more exciting adventure. Then we get ourselves into trouble and become afraid and search for a way out. When we realize we are lost and don't know which way to turn, often times there are snares or hindrances, coming in the form of strangers, who could lead us further astray. If you are spiritually lost, we just pray that the One who rescues you, dear friend, is Jesus, and that you will let Him lead you home to heaven, to one day be forever with Him. It is much worse for us to be eternally lost than for a child to be lost in a cornfield and not being able to find his way out!

DOUBLE CHRISTMAS BLESSING

Life would soon be full of unexpected surprises for Jerry and Kathy Richards who lived in the suburbs of Chicago. The Richards owned and operated a prosperous health food store not too far from their home.

This couple had a good life together, but in the five years since their marriage, they remained childless. How they longed for children to fill their empty arms. It was particularly difficult for Kathy. When she saw other young mothers holding their little ones, her heart yearned to cuddle a baby of her own. Why, they often wondered, have they not been blessed with one of these precious bundles from heaven.

While they continued to pray daily for this tiny gift of life, they decided to put their name in for the adoption of a baby. The agency told them it could be months before they might be given a baby through adoption. They would continue to wait for an adopted baby, or one of their own, which ever God chose to give to them.

Kathy wondered how any mother could ever give up her baby for adoption. Or worse yet, how could any woman ever abort her baby! There are those who say an unborn baby is not a baby until it is born. The Bible clearly says in Psalms 139:13-16, "You have covered me in my mother's womb. I will praise thee; for I am fearfully and wonderfully made: marvelous are thy works; and that my soul knows right well. My substance was not hid from thee, when I was made in secret, and curiously wrought in the lowest parts of the earth. Your eyes did see my substance yet being imperfect: and in thy book all my members were written, which in continuance were fashioned, when as yet there was none of them." According to the scriptures, a baby is a baby even before it is born.

The Richards were fine Christian people who loved the Lord with all their hearts. It was very evident by the life they lived. All who came into their health food store could sense the love these two had for the Lord and for each other.

It was Saturday evening and a week before Christmas. Jerry and Kathy had closed their store for the day and decided to drive around uptown in Chicago to view the Christmas lights. Everyone had been commenting on how pretty they were. The houses and stores indeed sparkled with their decorations and colored lights. Jerry parked the car uptown and the two of them decided to walk just a short distance, to view an exciting window display a merchant had set up in a large department store. They were saddened by the fact that so many displays in the city showed only Santa Claus. Very few stores displayed anything suggesting the true meaning of Christmas.

Were people really putting the true meaning of Christmas out of their lives? Jerry thought about the Virgin Mary and the baby she gave birth to. It was this baby, Jesus, that would one day save mankind from their sins. How special this baby must have been to Mary. People are still rejecting Jesus, just as they did when He lived on earth. Jerry was thankful that Jesus came to earth, died on the cross and shed his blood there to save mankind from their sins. He then arose from the grave and ascended to heaven were He is waiting for all that have served Him on earth.

Suddenly Kathy had an awful thought! What if, Mary had aborted her baby or what if she had given him away for adoption! What then, would have happened to the people of the world? There was no one else who could have saved us from our sins. It had to be through the shed blood of Jesus Christ. Even though the Virgin Mary was ridiculed for being with child before her marriage to Joseph, she knew it was God's will and desire for her to have this special baby through the Holy Spirit.

After walking a short distance in the soft falling snow, Jerry and Kathy started back to their car. Suddenly Jerry stopped and said, "Kathy, listen! It sounds like someone is crying."

They looked around in the darkness about them but saw no one. Then they heard it again, as they walked past an alley between two big department stores. It was quite dark in the alley and Jerry didn't know if he should proceed into it or not. What if someone is just trying to trick them? On the other hand, if someone really did need help, it might be too late to notify the police first. As they stood looking down the alley, they could hear what they thought might be the cry of a young person. With a prayer on their hearts, Jerry and Kathy slowly walked arm in arm into the dark alley. To their amazement they noticed someone crouched between two garbage cans. It was a young lady about seventeen years of age. As she sat huddled to the ground, she pulled her coat tightly around her frail body.

She had been crying. Looking up, the girl saw the two figures standing in front of her. She cried out in fear and trembling, "Please, don't hurt me," she pleaded. "I can't go on anymore. It is so cold here and I'm so hungry. Please, won't you help me?"

In pity Jerry reached down, took the girl by the hand and helped her to her feet.

Kathy with a surprised look on her face said, "Jerry, I think this girl is going to have a baby!"

Jerry said to the girl, "It is a week before Christmas. You can't stay here; it is not safe. Do you have somewhere you can go?"

The sobbing girl said, "There is no where I can go."

After inviting the young lady to come sit with them in their car, Jerry and Kathy listened intently as the unhappy girl told her story about how she came to live in the alley.

This girl who called herself Mary, said she had been out with a boy one night last spring before her graduation from High School and made a bad mistake. After finding out she was going to have a baby, she became afraid and would not tell her boy friend or her parents. Her parents had always been very strict and possessive of her. They never went to church so Mary didn't go either. Mary knew, after reading some literature on the dangers of abortion that someone had given her, that she did not want to go through that procedure to get rid of the baby.

Finally, one night, Mary said she told her boy friend and her parents that she was going to have a baby. Her friend and parents became very upset and told her to get an abortion. Mary said she couldn't do that to herself and to her unborn child. Her parents said an unborn fetus is not a baby. If she did not get rid of it now, she would have to leave home. Her boy friend said he wanted no part of her or a baby and left her. She never saw him again. Mary went on to say that her parents pushed her out the door and told her never to come back again unless she gets rid of the baby. They locked the door behind her and she has not seen them for four months. Mary said she had an aunt living in Southern Illinois but she was too ashamed to ask her for help. Besides she had no money to seek help elsewhere.

Jerry asked Mary how she had been surviving these last four months and if she had seen a doctor. With tears in her eyes Mary said she has not seen a doctor and has been eating out of garbage cans and sleeping anywhere she could find a warm spot. Sometimes she spent the night in the bus station, sometimes in an outside entrance way to a place of business, but most generally she lived in the alleyways. Occasionally she could get into a soup kitchen and get something to eat. A passing bell ringer, from the Salvation Army, had given her the coat, scarf and gloves she has been wearing. Mary seemed very thankful for them.

The distressed young woman went on to say her problems all began after her Senior Prom last May. She planned to get a job to help support herself. Then she found out she was going to have a baby. After her parents threw her out she never found a job because she often felt so tired and ill. Besides, she did not have any decent clothes to hold down a job with.

The girl, with tears in her eyes said she was afraid to seek help because she did not want an abortion, but she really didn't want the baby either. Mary said she had no way to take care of it. She somehow hoped her baby would be born dead. That would solve all her problems, she thought. She would put it in a garbage can and go back to her parents, once the baby was disposed of.

Jerry and Kathy's hearts continued to go out to the girl who trembled with fear, as she poured out her heart to them. Mary begged them to please not turn her over to the police because she was afraid of what they might do to her or her baby.

Kathy looked lovingly at her husband and he looked at her. Both seemed to know what the other one was thinking. Suddenly Kathy said, "Mary, would you like to come home with us? We have an extra bedroom so there would be plenty of room. Monday I'll take you to see a doctor and we'll try to help you through this difficult time if you want us to."

"Yes," said Jerry. "Even though we just met, we do love you. It is almost Christmas, you know. More than that, Jesus loves you and wants to be your friend as well. What do you say, Mary. Will you come home with us? We will not make you have an abortion!"

Mary couldn't believe someone really cared for and loved her like this couple seemed to do. Since she had no where else to go she decided to go home with them. She had nothing to loose. Mary couldn't explain it but she felt that there was something special about these two that made her want to be with them.

On the way to Mr. and Mrs. Richards' house they stopped for something to eat. Mary had almost forgotten how good a plain hamburger and French fries tasted. The hot chocolate helped to warm and comfort her shivering body.

After arriving at the Richards' house, Mary had her first warm bath in weeks. Kathy's clothes were too small for Mary so she was fitted into one of Jerry's sweat suits. By the time she had bathed, washed and combed her hair, she looked and felt like a different girl.

Jerry and Kathy's hearts continued to reach out to this unfortunate girl. They told Mary about the Christmas story, how Jesus was born of a young virgin, also named Mary. The troubled girl listened intently as her new friends told her that Jesus is no longer a babe in the manger. Now in heaven, He is the Savior of mankind for all that give their hearts to Him. Jerry again told her how much Jesus loves her and He will forgive her sins, regardless of her past. He said if she would repent of her sins, turn her life around and ask Jesus to live in her heart, she too, could have this hope of eternal life. Then she would feel better about herself and the life she had ahead of her. Jesus would be her true friend, one who would never shut the door on her or let her down. He would help her and love her no matter what she had done.

As Mary lay in bed that night, she kept thinking about this man Jesus. Perhaps if He really loved her like the Richards couple said He did, then it must have been Jesus who brought them to her rescue. Mary, laden with child snuggled in the first warm bed she had been in for weeks. She began to pray for the first time in her life. Mary, with her hands folded over her abdomen, thanked this Jesus for bringing Jerry and Kathy into her life, when she so desperately needed help. She asked Jesus to help her make the right decisions for her baby whom she thought would be born sometime in January. Surely if there was a Jesus, He would help her.

Quite exhausted, Mary finally drifted off to sleep. When she awoke the next morning, for a moment she thought she was in a dream. Suddenly she remembered she was in the Richards' home. She sat up in bed, rubbed her eyes and glanced at a Bible lying on the dresser. She reached over and picked it up. Upon opening it her eyes fell on John 3:3 where Jesus said, "Verily, verily, I say unto you, except a man be born again, he cannot see the kingdom of God."

Mary thought of her baby, yet unborn. If she had aborted the infant within her, the baby never would have been able to see the kingdom of this earth. Likewise if she herself would not become born into the family of God she would never be able to see the heavenly kingdom of God.

Mary heard a gentle knock on the door. Wrapped in Mr. Richards' bathrobe, she opened the door and was greeted by the friendly smile of Mrs. Richards.

"How would you like to attend church with us, Mary?" Kathy asked her new houseguest. "Today is Sunday, you know."

"Oh, yes, I would like that very much. I want to hear more about this Jesus. But I haven't any decent clothes to wear. I can't go in a man's sweat suit."

Then Kathy handed her a loose fitting maternity dress. She told Mary that the lady next door recently had her fourth child and agreed to lend this dress, along with other clothing to Mary, if she wanted them. Mary tried the dress on and it fit just fine.

After breakfast, Jerry, Kathy and Mary went to church. This was the first time Mary had been to church that she could remember of. The very old story of Jesus and the plan of Salvation were very new to this troubled young lady. She took it all in like someone very thirsty wanting a glass of water. Tears ran down from Mary's eyes as she realized for the first time, what she had been missing for the past eighteen years. She wondered why her parents never took her to church. Perhaps if they had gone and had known this man, Jesus, they would not have thrown her out of the house. If she, herself, had known Jesus, she probably would never have gotten into trouble either.

After church, Mary asked to talk with the minister. She poured her heart out to him as she did to the Richards the night before. She wanted to give her heart over to the Lord, and start a new life. She invited Jesus into her heart and asked Him to forgive all of her sins. Suddenly she felt like all her burdens had been lifted. For the first time in her life she felt free from guilt. How she wished her parents could feel the same way. Mary would begin to pray for them.

Jerry, Kathy and Mary spent the rest of the day just relaxing at the Richards' home. Mary said she decided to give her baby up for adoption. Then she would go live with her Aunt Becky in southern Illinois. Her aunt was a Christian but because she had 'religion' Mary's parents would have nothing to do with her. Through the years, Aunt Becky kept in touch with Mary and daily prayed for her. Mary knew her Aunt Becky would take her in, but with a baby it might be asking too much. The baby would be better off in a good home with both a father and a mother to love and care for it. Mary said she couldn't give the baby the life it needed because she had nothing to offer the little one. Someday, hopefully, she would find a man who could truly love her and marry her for who she is. Then she could start a family again.

Mary looked at Jerry, then at Kathy. Finally she said, "You do not have any children and I can think of no one better to have my child than the ones who gave me a second chance in life. I want my baby to have that same chance." Then with tears in her eyes again, she said, "Would you be willing to take and adopt my baby? Maybe you don't want it, though. Perhaps it won't even be healthy because of the way I lived the last few months, not taking care of myself the way I should have."

Jerry stood up and pulled his wife up beside him. They looked at one another with tears now running down their cheeks. The three young adults embraced each other as if in an answer to prayer.

Mr. Richards said, "Just as the Virgin Mary gave birth to God's Son, Jesus, as the world's first Christmas gift, and loved him unconditionally, we will accept the birth of your child unconditionally. We will love it as our own, if this is what you truly want, Mary. This will be the greatest Christmas gift we could ever hope for."

"Yes, this is what I want. I know the baby will have a good Christian home if you adopt it. I will not ever have to worry about it and perhaps I can come see the child sometimes," Mary replied.

So it was agreed that the Richards would legally adopt Mary's baby. The next day, Jerry would look into the legal procedures to adopt the infant that should be born in about four weeks, according to Mary. Kathy would take Mary to the doctor for a check up the next day. In the meantime Mary could stay with them and they would prepare a room for the baby. Mary decided that after the birth of her little one, she would go live with Aunt Becky. She would do her best to find a job, start her life over and walk with the Lord, the one who saved her life from destruction.

To Kathy, it as if she was living in some kind of a dream. She was almost afraid to go to bed that night, for fear that when morning came, she would find out it was all just that, a dream. Could all this really be happening? Would her childless arms be filled shortly with this unborn infant now living in their house? Kathy had so often prayed for a baby. Little did she expect to ever receive one in this manner. If this was for real, she prayed that upon awakening in the morning it would be a reality and not just a dream.

The three adults finally went to bed. After reading the Bible and thanking God for saving her from destruction, Mary snuggled in her warm soft bed almost in unbelief of what had happened to her in the last twenty-four hours.

About four o'clock in the morning, the Richards were suddenly awakened by a knock on their bedroom door. There stood Mary in labor, about to give birth to the baby that would shortly be entrusted in their care. Kathy wondered why this baby was a month early but then with all that Mary had gone through, it didn't really surprise her.

The Richards called the local hospital and told them they were bringing in a young lady about to give birth to a baby. When they arrived, the doctors and nurses were waiting for them. Since Jerry and Kathy would soon become the legal parents of this baby, they were allowed to be in the delivery room with Mary. This would be an exciting new experience for them to actually see the birth of the baby they would be adopting for their own. They prayed with Mary that God would give her the strength needed at this time and that all would go well with her and the little one.

Thoughts began running through Kathy's mind. She didn't even have a baby bed at home. Everything happened so fast. She had nothing to even suggest the appearance of a nursery. There were no bottles, no diapers, baby clothes, nothing at all for a baby! The next few days she would be very busy indeed, preparing for their new baby's homecoming.

Suddenly Jerry and Kathy looked on with awe and amazement. They had just witnessed the birth of a precious baby boy with lots of dark hair! The infant had just began to cry when Mary gave birth to, yes, another baby, a precious little girl, also with dark hair! The second baby came as a complete surprise to everyone! They were hardly prepared for one baby let alone two of them. The twins, a boy and a girl, each weighed in at around four pounds each. This was truly an unexpected double blessing!

Mary did great and the babies appeared to be healthy. Since they were so small the doctor suggested the infants should remain in the hospital for observation for about two weeks until they are a little stronger. Kathy seemed almost relieved. That would give her time to prepare a much-needed nursery at home.

Mary told Jerry and Kathy they should name the babies since the little ones both would belong to them. They decided to name the boy, Nathan, and the girl, Natalie.

In two days, Mary had been dismissed from the hospital and went back to the Richards' home. The next two weeks were spent in purchasing baby items for the twins and a new wardrobe for Mary. It was difficult for Mary not to want to become attached to her own babies, but she knew she could not take care of them at this time in her life. So every day when Kathy went to the hospital to hold and see the babies, Mary stayed at the Richards' house, thankful for a place to be.

Mary decided to call her parents and wish them a Merry Christmas and to tell them she had given birth to twins, a boy and a girl. She told them the fine

Christian couple who had recently taken her into their home would adopt them. She soon would be going to live with her Aunt Becky, whom she had also called. Mary told her parents the same friend Aunt Becky had for so many years, had now become her friend. This friend's name was Jesus. Mary said she would be praying for them that they, too, would come to know this man, Jesus. After all, He is what Christmas is all about. If they want to get in touch with her, they could call her at Aunt Becky's house.

For Jerry and Kathy this would be the happiest Christmas since they were married. The gifts of little Nathan, the baby boy, and Natalie, the baby girl that had been entrusted so suddenly in their care was by far, way beyond their expectations. They definitely felt it was the hand of God that led them to Mary that night in the dark alley. This would be a Christmas they would never forget.

For Mary it was now the beginning of a new walk of life with her new friend Jesus. She received the greatest gift of life anyone could ever receive when she accepted Jesus into her heart. To her that was the best Christmas gift she could ever ask for. Mary, thankful she did not have an abortion, also gave the gift of life to Jerry and Kathy, when she agreed to let them adopt her babies. Mary thought about the verse the minister in church read to her in Jeremiah 1:5. It reads, "Before I formed you in the belly I knew you: and before you came forth out of the womb I sanctified you." She felt like she had done the right thing in keeping her unborn little ones so they could be sanctified and live in this fine Christian home. A home she knew she could not give to them.

Mary's Aunt Becky came to Chicago to see the twins, while still in the hospital, and to meet the people who had now become their adopted parents. She would take Mary home to live with her.

Mary, with tears in her eyes, hugged Kathy and Jerry, as she was about to depart with her Aunt Becky. For her this would be a bittersweet farewell. Soon all four were crying, including the aunt. The Richards told Mary she could come back and visit the twins anytime. After the tearful good-byes were said, Mary went home to live with her aunt. She had the promise she could come back for a visit anytime.

Mary went to live in southern Illinois. She soon found a good job and continued her walk with the Lord. As time went on she met and married, Doug, a fine Christian man. In time God did indeed bless them with three beautiful children, Aaron, Amy and Anna. Still, deep down in her heart, Mary never forgot her twins and often thought about them. But now she had a new life and a new family, thanks to the Richards for all they had done for her.

Back at the Richards' house Jerry and Kathy loved and enjoyed Nathan and Natalie dearly. Kathy thrilled that her empty arms had been doubly filled, enjoyed nurturing and caring for the precious children God had so unexpectedly blessed them with. The Richards kept their promise to bring them up in the fear and admonition of the Lord. They thanked God every day for their 'double blessings'. Often they thought of the Bible verse that says, "All things work together for good to them that love the Lord." They now knew God answered their prayers in His own time when they least expected it. Daily they sought God's guidance in raising their precious children. They continued to love and live for the Lord, and with much appreciation thanked Him for the wonderful children God had entrusted in their care.

HANNAH AND KITTEN, LOST IN FOREST

Hannah Joy, and the family dog, Miqo, lived with her parents, two brothers and big sister in an old country farmhouse. They lived near a large wooded area that had a river running through the middle of it. Hannah's parents were conservative Christians who home-schooled their children.

A friend of the family had a Siberian Husky dog that had two puppies. He could not get rid of one of the pups so he gave it to Hannah's parents, hoping the children would want it for their pet. They were delighted to have the frisky pup!

Even though they lived in the country where dogs can run freely, they kept it in a pen with a big doghouse, close to the barn, for fear it would wander into the wooded area.

Hannah (pronounced Hawn-nah), age five and several years younger than her older siblings, took a great liking to the female Husky they called Miqo (pronounced Meek-o). The young dog of silvery white with patches of gray and black and very predominant blue eyes on her white and black face took a liking to Hannah as well.

The oldest brother, of about fourteen years of age, decided to train the growing pup for a 4-H project. He worked diligently with the dog. Little Hannah became very observant in watching her brother work with Miqo.

There were times when Mother could not find her youngest daughter in the house, but she knew where to look for her. Hannah would be outside with Miqo, talking to her as if she was another child like herself. Though Miqo enjoyed the whole family she seemed very protective especially of Hannah. It was to this little girl that the dog would first run when freed from her pen. The Husky could run about with a very long rope, fastened to her collar, and tied to a big stake in the yard. Once as Hannah played with Miqo, the Husky gave a jerk as the little girl held onto the rope. Hannah received a big rope burn on her leg. It hurt for a while but that did not stop the child from playing with her new friend, Miqo.

One day Hannah was swinging outside on a big swing that hung from an old hickory tree. While gliding back and forth in the summer breeze the little girl saw a small stray yellow kitten out by the old barn. Immediately the little girl with blond hair and blue eyes, jumped off her swing, and ran towards the kitten. The kitten, not being tame, ran away from Hannah into the field and towards the woods. The child followed close behind, calling for the yellow kitty to come back.

Soon Hannah Joy and the furry kitten disappeared into the thicket. Before swinging, the young child had been in the fenced-in pen with Miqo, as she had often been before. The family kept the dog inside this fence to give her freedom from the leash except when she was taken out of the pen. The children were always to shut the gate after feeding or giving water to Miqo. Hannah had closed the gate, shutting Miqo in her pen.

Miqo saw her young companion run into the forest and barked and barked but no one seemed to notice. Since the children were home-schooled, Mother was inside with the three older siblings giving them a refresher course, as she sometimes did in the summer, making it easier to begin teaching again in September.

Meanwhile the eager, tousle-headed Hannah had followed the little butterball kitten deep into the woods. The children had been instructed never to go into the woods without adult supervision, but Hannah's desire to have the kitten made her forget that instruction, and into the thicket she went.

The kitten, being quite small, began to tire, as did Hannah who by now had no idea how to get back home. Everywhere she looked, in front of her or behind her, the trees and brush all looked the same. By now she realized she was lost. The kitten had become caught in a thorn bush and couldn't get out. A frightened Hannah Joy tried her best to free the young feline, because now it was the only friend she had near to her. With thorns in her tender fingers and tears in her blue eyes, Hannah remembered the Sunday school story of the little lost lamb caught in the briar bush. She thought about the shepherd and how he freed the lamb from the thorns and carried him back home.

Hannah knew she had to free the little fluffy butterball, who seemed to be whimpering, as she herself was, because she had no idea which way to go for home. She began to think of her parents, big sister and brothers. She wished they were here with her now. The frightened girl thought of Miqo and wished her dog was here, too. The only one she had, close to her now, was the small yellow kitten still caught in the thorn bush.

Then Hannah thought of another friend she had, that friend being Jesus. A frightened little girl then asked Jesus to help her get the kitty out of the bush and find her way home. Suddenly she noticed a big stick on the ground near her feet. She hadn't seen it before now. After picking up the stick, she pried the thorn bush apart and reached for the terrified kitten. Her tender arms were bleeding from the thorny branches that held the kitten.

The kitten, so exhausted by now, seemed willing to let the little girl take him from the prickly bush. Once free, the kitten nestled in Hannah's scratched and bleeding arms.

Suddenly it began to thunder! Hannah always ran to big sister, whom she slept with, when it was stormy, thundering and lightning, but of course big sister was no where near. Soon the rain began to fall. The thunder cracked again and again! The very frightened Hannah knew she could not get home by herself. Holding the kitten tightly in her tender aching arms, she once more asked her unseen friend Jesus, about whom her parents so often told her of, to please guide her home. Hannah thought Jesus must have put the big stick on the ground so she could get the kitty out of the thorn bush. She also trusted that Jesus would somehow get her home.

The young girl thought if only Miqo was here, the dog would lead her home and she wouldn't be so afraid. Hannah decided she better keep on walking. So with the kitty in one arm and the big stick in the other, she walked deeper into the thicket, not realizing which way she was going.

Suddenly she stepped into a hole and hurt her ankle badly. "Oh," she cried, "if only I was home with Daddy and Mommy!" Hobbling on, she never dropped the kitten. Hannah held tightly onto the kitten with the one hand, while using the big stick as a crutch with the other hand. The tired little girl continued limping on into the forest with two little paws sticking up above her bleeding arms and two furry paws hanging out below.

Finally, the girl reached the riverbank. There she saw an old shack nearby that some fishermen must have made at one time. Hungry, tired, wet and hurting from the sprained ankle, a very frightened little Hannah and her new fuzzy friend went inside the old shed and curled up on the dirt floor out of the rain.

Hannah, with tears in her blue eyes, told her little kitten that Jesus heard her prayer and put this old shack here just for them. They would wait here until Jesus brought her daddy to her. Daddy always knew what to do when things went wrong. By now he surely was looking for her, she hoped.

Suddenly she thought of a picture on the wall in her grandmother's living room of an angel watching over two small children, as they were crossing over a worn-out foot bridge. Somehow she knew Jesus would send an angel to watch over her, too. She decided to name her kitten, Angel, because the fuzzy friend now became her comfort and close companion. At least she had someone she could talk to.

Still using the big stick as a cane, the hungry little girl limped over to the door of the old, battered shed. Hannah wanted to see if she could find any bush nearby with berries on it so she and Angel could have something to eat. Then she would try to go to the river's edge, wash her bleeding arms and let the kitten drink, that is if it ever stopped raining. Hannah remembered her mother going to the edge of the woods to pick wild raspberries. Perhaps she could find some berries near this old cabin.

But as Hannah Joy propped herself near the door of the shed, a loud thunderclap roared above her. The terrified girl screamed as a large tree fell right in front of the door where she had been standing. Now she could not get out of the shed! A trembling, tired Hannah and her little Angel hobbled back to the corner of the shed and curled up once more on the damp ground floor. Huddling together, soon both child and kitten cried themselves to sleep.

Meanwhile back home, big sister wondered what had become of Hannah and thought it strange that the little blue-eyed girl hadn't come running to her for protection from the loud thunder. Big sister thought Hannah must be with Miqo in her large doghouse, where she had sometimes gone when it started to rain while she was outside playing.

But when big sister looked out of the window, she did not see Hannah with Miqo and wondered where she might be. The youngest brother quickly put on his raincoat and went to see if Hannah was in Miqo's house. As soon as the boy opened the gate, and before he could stop the dog, Miqo leaped past him and headed for the woods where she had seen the little girl run after the small stray kitten. Miqo sensed that Hannah was in trouble and the dog knew she had to find her.

Hannah's brother immediately told his mother that Hannah was not with Miqo and that the dog had run out of the pen, through the field and into the woods. When they could not find the little girl, Mother called Hannah's father at work and he came home immediately.

The storm had not subsided and it was raining very hard, with strong winds blowing the falling rain. By the time Father arrived home, he could hardy see the old farmhouse, let alone the barn.

The policemen were notified of the missing girl. Soon two men in uniform were out at the old farmhouse. They were ready to search for the youngster, who by now had fallen fast asleep near the river in the old shack, with her soft furry friend sleeping and nestled in her bleeding arms.

By now Miqo was well into the woods, hoping to find her young companion. The rain had washed Hannah's scent away so the dog could not find the girl by smell, unless Hannah was really close to the Siberian Husky. Miqo wandered throughout out the wet woods barking as she went, hoping Hannah would hear her and cry out for the dog.

The sun would soon be down. Father and the men looking for the youngster knew they had to work fast. Mother had called her family and close friends. Soon a large group of men were out in search of little Hannah while the women stayed back to pray that the little girl would soon be found, well and unharmed.

Finally the rain stopped and the lowering sun would occasionally peek through the heavy clouds. The cold, wet, hungry, little girl woke up with the kitten still at her side. Her ankle was swollen and hurting badly. She sat up, rubbed her teary eyes, and realized she still was in the old shed by the river and not at home. Hannah thought the kitty must have been afraid of the thunder, so she kept it as close to her as possible. But it was Hannah who had been frightened the most. The small, yellow kitten helped to comfort her under these terrifying conditions.

Again Hannah began to cry softly as she thought of the dream she had while sleeping. In her dream, she saw Jesus and an angel walking through the woods with her dog, Miqo, between them. These thoughts helped to comfort her a little and somehow she knew it would be Miqo who would find her.

Suddenly she saw something move across the floor! A small mouse ran in the door, stopped, and stared at Hannah. Then as quickly as the mouse came in, it disappeared. Hannah screamed and the kitten didn't even try to catch the mouse but seemed content to stay in Hannah's arms.

Then she saw a shadow moving near the door and heard a rustling noise in the fallen tree branches. Huddling closer than ever to the corner of the old shack, Hannah held fuzzy Angel very near to her. She wondered if it could possibly be Miqo. If not, who or what could it be? As she watched the shadow move, it appeared to be some kind of a dog and she cried out, "Miqo!" But it was not Miqo at all, just an old, hungry fox looking for something to eat. He could smell little Angel inside as he sniffed around the fallen tree in front of the door. A very frightened Hannah cried out once more, "Jesus, please help me and take away the fox!"

The little girl began to softly sing "Jesus Loves Me, This I Know." She thought if Jesus loved her as much as the song says he would send an angel to show Miqo the way to the shed and get rid of the old fox. Then, as Hannah sang lullaby style to her purring kitten, she saw through the fallen branches that the old fox had turned away. He went to a near-by bush and began to eat of its berries.

Hannah thought that as soon as the fox went away she would try to go pick some berries if she could get past the fallen tree and if there were any left for her and Angel. She seemed concerned for her kitten, which she now loved dearly. The kitten became a great comfort to her through all this even though it was because of the feline that Hannah had become lost, scratched, wet, hungry and sprained her ankle.

As she carefully watched the old fox through the doorway, she noticed the fox becoming rather jumpy, as if he sensed someone approaching. Then Hannah heard what she thought was a dog barking. "Miqo," she cried, "that's my Miqo. I knew she would come like Jesus said in my dream!"

Miqo had been led to the old shed by following the fox. The fox, upon seeing the dog, was ready for a fight, but Miqo was too strong for the old fox that took off running into the woods.

The Siberian Husky heard the little girl's cry and came to the door of the shed. Miqo realized she couldn't get into it because of the fallen tree. One window in the shed had long been broken out, so Miqo gave one big leap and soon found herself in the small shed with Hannah and Angel. The dog sniffed at the yellow kitten. When Miqo saw how affectionate Hannah had become towards the little animal, the dog did not appear to be jealous of it but accepted it as another little friend.

A very happy Hannah laid her touslehead on Miqo's back. The little girl wrapped her little aching arms around the dog, crying tears of joy. Hannah said, "I'm so glad to see you! An angel brought you to me didn't he, Miqo? I just know he did. My kitty's name is Angel. You'll like him, too. I know you will. If only Daddy was here!"

She knew Daddy would take care of her ankle, like he always took care of her when she was hurting. Although very happy to be with Miqo, she now longed to be in her mother's arms as well.

Miqo lay still for some time to assure Hannah she would not leave her but would stay at her side. The dog could sense that the girl was in pain. By now it was getting dark. Miqo somehow knew that she shouldn't try to lead Hannah home in the dark. Besides, how could she get out of the shed? The door to the shed was blocked and the little window was too high for Hannah to crawl out of. Miqo continued to lie on the floor, hoping to keep a trembling Hannah warm with her soft furry coat.

Soon Miqo began to stir, and jumping up on all four legs, she began to bark loudly. Hannah wondered what was wrong now as she watched the restless dog. The Husky seemed to sense someone approaching near the shed. She would not leave the shelter and stayed there with Hannah to protect her, no matter what or who might be out there.

Father and the two policemen went one way into the forest to look for Hannah while friends and relatives scattered in other directions, all carrying lanterns and flashlights as dusk had fast appeared. As Father and the policemen approached the old shack they heard the sound of a dog barking. Father immediately recognized Miqo's bark as coming from the shed. He hoped and prayed his little daughter would be in there with the dog.

Father asked the policemen to please stand back while he called to Miqo to make sure it was she. Miqo would not leave the shed but barked at Father's command. Father immediately went to the window and shined his big flashlight in. There he saw Miqo and his little girl holding a small, yellow kitten, huddled together on the floor. As soon as Hannah saw her daddy, the trembling girl began crying tears of joy once more.

The men quickly moved the tree away from the door and Hannah leaped into her daddy's arms, dropping the kitten onto the floor. Fluffy Angel stayed right by the big dog, who by now had became its friend. Father also wept tears of joy. What a happy reunion for both of them! Hannah told her daddy she was very hungry and asked him to please pick some of the berries from the bush where the fox had been eating. The policemen looked at the bush and knew that the berries were poisonous to people but not to animals. They told Hannah it was a good thing she could not get to the berries because they would have made her very sick. God surely let the tree fall in front of the door to keep her from eating the berries.

The three exhausted but happy men, along with Hannah, used their big flashlights, to head back to the old farm house where Hannah's mother, sister and brothers, relatives and friends continued to pray for Hannah Joy's safety. Hannah, now safe in her daddy's loving arms, had been wrapped in one of the policemen's jacket. The other policeman had a large handkerchief and securely wrapped it around the little girl's swollen, ailing ankle, giving it support as they headed for home. Miqo had picked up Angel by the back of his neck and carried the kitten home in this manner, walking all the way beside Father and Hannah as if continuing to protect the tired little girl.

The other men who were out looking for Hannah seemed to sense that she had been found when they heard Miqo's loud barking in the distance, and they, too, headed for home.

Soon the entire posse returned to the old farmhouse and the little girl rested safe in her mother's arms with her joyful brothers and sister around her. Mother gave her a bath, dry clothing and something to eat. Daddy wrapped her ankle again and soon she began to feel better. Before long Hannah fell fast asleep in her soft, warm bed.

The people that had been at the farmhouse were also huddled together but for a different reason now. They formed a large circle, held hands and prayed with tears in their eyes, thanking their Heavenly Father for protecting little Hannah so she could return safely home. Surely an angel of the Lord had been watching over her, protecting her from the storm, the fallen tree, and the fox, and by providing the old shack for her to stay in. The fallen tree also kept her from eating the poison berries.

How thankful her parents were for all that helped in looking for their daughter or just came and prayed with and comforted the family. Big sister thanked Jesus that Hannah was next to her in bed and went to sleep with her loving arms around the little girl. Big brother, who had been training and working with the Siberian Husky, also thanked Jesus for sending Miqo into the woods to find and comfort his little sister. He vowed to work harder than ever to train this valuable pet. Likewise the younger brother thanked Jesus for protecting his sister and promised to keep a closer watch over the young child so she wouldn't wander off again.

Before Father and Mother went to sleep they got down on their knees, as did Hannah's grandparents in their own homes, and once more thanked the Good Lord for protecting their precious little one.

The next morning when Hannah awoke, the first thing she asked for was her fluffy, yellow kitten, Angel. The oldest brother carried his five-year-old sister into the kitchen. The younger brother ran to get the kitty, who had spent the night with Miqo. He brought it to his sister, who tenderly cradled it in her arms.

As the family gathered around the table for breakfast the purring kitten was placed in a box, close to Hannah, with a bowl of milk.

After breakfast, Father read from the Bible, as he always did. The little girl said she had something to talk about, too. She said the little kitten was like the lost sheep in the Bible story and she was like the shepherd who went after the lamb. Only the shepherd in the Bible never got lost. But then Hannah said she guessed she really never was lost because Jesus knew where she was all the time. He had sent an angel to protect her from the fox, like the shepherd protected the sheep from the wolf.

Hannah went on to say that Jesus sent Miqo to find her and help protect her, like she protected the kitty and took him out of the thorn bush. It was the same as the shepherd taking the lost lamb from the briar bush. Just as the shepherd put oil on the injured lamb, the kind policemen gave their jacket and bandana for her cold, wet body and injured foot. So the policemen were like shepherds too, looking for someone who was lost. But Jesus, Miqo and her daddy were the best shepherds of all because they had found her.

The family had tears in their eyes as Hannah told all that happened to her the night before, about the storm and how frightened she was, the fallen tree, the fox, the berries and even the little mouse.

Then Father said just as Hannah risked her life to save the lost kitten and shed her blood to take it out of the thorns, so did Jesus risk His life and died on the cross, shedding His own blood to redeem our sins. Because of Jesus we, as lost sheep, can find a new life in Christ and go to heaven one day to forever be with the Lord. That is, if we give our lives completely over to Him and let Him live in our hearts and minds. Father said, as the old shed provided a refuge for Hannah Joy, so Jesus provides a refuge for us. He is someone we can turn to when we feel lost, hurt or lonely.

That afternoon the policemen came to see Hannah. They took a picture of her, Miqo and Angel to put in the local newspaper the following day, along with the story of the lost girl and how she had been found.

Needless to say, Hannah never went into the woods alone again. Neither did her brothers or sister go unless their parents went with them to see the old shack where their little sister sought refuge from the storm.

Friends, have you found your place of refuge in Jesus Christ? Why not seek Him today while He can still be found. Don't let Satan, who is like a sly, old fox, always on the run, keep you away from Jesus. Seek refuge in Him today for behold your redemption draweth nigh.

LITTLE BLACK LAMB

Midnight, born as a little black lamb, was deeply loved by his parents. To them he was very special. All his other cousins and little friends had soft, fluffy wool as white as snow, but not Midnight. You see, his wool seemed coarse and wiry, straggly and black, the kind no one would want to buy when he was old enough to sell his coat of wool. In other words, some called him a reject or a misfit, because he did not have white wool like most little lambs.

The time came for Midnight to go to school. The teacher, Mrs. Woolly, was a good teacher but she didn't know much about Jesus. Midnight loved school but he always seemed to get into trouble. He would make unnecessary noise and seemed awkward as he moved around the class room and play yard. The other lambs would often make fun of him. Mrs. Woolly would lose her patience with Midnight and decided to talk with his parents. She suggested they keep him out of school until he could learn to control himself better, because he disrupted the other lambs in class. But Midnight's parents wouldn't hear of it. They said their little lamb needed to be in school because they wanted him to be as much like the other lambs as possible. Besides God gave this little lamb to them for a reason and he needed to be taught like the rest of the lambs.

So Mrs. Woolly and Midnight's parents agreed that he could stay in school; that is, if he passed the test that all the lambs would be given. If he did not pass, he would be dismissed from school. Since it was springtime, Mrs. Woolly asked each lamb to go to the barnyard and ask Mrs. Hen for an egg. Carefully they were to break the top open and put inside each eggshell something that represents the new life of springtime.

Mrs. Woolly wondered what Midnight would put into his egg. The teacher thought the little black lamb wasn't paying much attention when the assignment was given, so he probably would bring an empty egg or perhaps no egg at all! This would be the true test if Midnight would stay in school or not.

So the time finally arrived when the little lambs were to bring their eggs to school. Fourteen little lambs came that day with their eggs, each one putting them carefully in the place Mrs. Woolly had provided for the eggs. Soon it would be time for the test!

The first egg Mrs. Woolly picked up belonged to Fluffy. Inside the egg the little lamb had put a pretty spring flower. "Very good," said Mrs. Woolly. "These little flowers are certainly a sign of new life in spring."

Next, Mrs. Woolly chose Snowflake's egg. Inside her egg sat a tiny chick that had just hatched. "Very good," said Mrs. Wooly. "A baby chick is certainly a sign of new life."

The third egg picked belonged to Curly. He had found a butterfly and put it in his egg. "Very good," said Mrs. Woolly. "This little butterfly just came out of a cocoon and this, too, is a sign of new life."

Then Mrs. Woolly picked up Midnight's egg. The teacher looked at his egg then set it down again. She was just ready to pick up another egg when Midnight said, "Mrs. Woolly, aren't you going to talk about my egg?"

"Your egg," said Mrs. Woolly, "is empty!" She knew now that he had not understood the assignment. His parents would now have to take Midnight out of school. True, he did bring an egg but that was only half of the assignment. He had brought an empty egg!

"But, Mrs. Woolly," cried Midnight, "my egg does show new life. Jesus' tomb is empty too, so that people can have a new life. My egg is like Jesus' empty tomb. Do you know about this Jesus, Mrs. Woolly?"

Mrs. Woolly did not know what to say as she turned her head with tears streaming from her eyes.

"Do you, Mrs. Woolly?" questioned Midnight. "Do you know about Jesus? My mother often tells how long, long ago sheep were at the stable when Jesus was born. When Jesus became a man, he said people were like sheep and some rejected Him, too. Then He was nailed on a cross, made from a tree and He died there to save people from their sins. But He arose from the tomb, where they laid Him, three days later so people could have a new life with Him in heaven one day. Mother says sheep may even have been on the hillside when Jesus was put to death. This story has been passed down through the ages to all the sheep and lambs and that's how we remember the story of Jesus. You do remember the story, too, Mrs. Woolly, don't you?"

With tears still in her eyes, Mrs. Woolly said, "Yes, Midnight, I remember my grandmother telling me this story when I was a young lamb like you. It sounded like a fairy tale to me so I never paid much attention to it."

The other lambs all listened quietly as Midnight told his story. After discussing the rest of the eggs the lambs had brought, Mrs. Woolly dismissed the class for the day.

Mrs. Woolly went to talk to Midnight's parents. She told them she had been wrong about Midnight and that he had understood the assignment very well. He had passed the test! From then on, no one made fun of Midnight any more but they all said how special he was.

A few weeks later Midnight became very ill and died. All the sheep and the lambs of the field gathered together as Midnight was laid to his rest. To the surprise of Midnight's parents, Mrs. Woolly and thirteen little lambs from school each laid an empty egg shell on top of Midnight's resting place in remembrance of the story he had told a few weeks earlier of Jesus and the empty tomb.

We all know that lambs and sheep of the animal kingdom do not go to heaven when they die, but if we, like little Midnight, take seriously the death and resurrection of Jesus, we, as people, can also have the hope of a new life in heaven one day!

Miracle of the Carved Nativity

Ed, better known as Gramps, Miller was an elderly gentleman who lived alone in his little house at the edge of town. His wife, Nola, had died after an extended illness about a year ago. Ed had some insurance but much of his wife's medical bills and prescriptions were to be paid by Ed himself. Nola had been diabetic and had had one complication after another, finally losing her eyesight after fifteen years of affliction. Needless to say, all these expenses left Ed almost penniless.

Their only child, Bobby, had died of pneumonia when he was ten years old during a very hard winter. Mr. Miller, or Gramps as the town's people called him, was partially disabled because of arthritis.

Gramps had an older model Chevy that needed new tires and a lot of work to make it run again, but since he didn't have the money to fix it he walked where he needed to go. The doctor said it was good for Gramps to walk, otherwise he would get stiff from his arthritis.

Gramps Miller usually sat in his little old house carving things from wood to keep his fingers nimble. In the summer time you could see Gramps outside on his old wooden porch swing reading the Bible or carving wood.

Ed walked to a little Bible believing community church every Sunday where just a handful of people attended. Most of them were elderly like him. It seemed to him like the younger generation did not have time for God and going to church anymore. Everyone thought only of himself or herself. But if there was a ball game or sports activity, plenty of people would be there, taking part. Gramps wondered what his own son, Bobby, would have been like had he still been living. Would he have gone to church or would he have taken part in the activities of the world on Sunday? He would have been forty years old by now and could very well have had children of his own. But now Gramps was all alone. He had no wife, no son, no grandchildren, and no family living near to him.

Ed Miller, was thankful that he had Jesus as his personal friend. He spent much time reading the Bible and in prayer. Ed had no TV, but he did have an old record player and a radio that someone had given to his wife, Nola, when she became so ill. The records he had were of the good old gospel songs that were slowly being replaced by modern contemporary songs. The good old-fashioned religion is what Ed liked the best.

The neighborhood children would at times make fun of Gramps. They said his house was haunted because it was becoming so run down. Children in the neighborhood said that he was a rich old miser who was too tight to spend his money. They often made fun of the patched overalls he wore with all its pockets. The children said he always kept a book in his pocket. They had seen the elderly man take it out and look at it. The children did not know that the book Gramps kept in his big overall pocket was the Bible. Gramps liked to keep this precious Book near to his heart. He kept it in the big pocket on the bib of his overalls.

He would heat his house with wood in the winter time getting wood wherever he could find some. Gramps still had Bobby's little, old red wagon. It was with this little wagon that the old man, with snow-white hair, would often walk a mile or two just for a wagonload of wood.

One fall day, Gramps, in his overalls, was walking home with his load of wood. Two boys, who lived not too far from his house, jumped out from behind some bushes. They upset his wagonload of wood; then off they ran. Poor Gramps stooped down and loaded his wood back onto the wagon. He thanked God that the boys did not knock him down and that the wagon did not get broken, old as it was.

With Halloween soon approaching, Gramps figured that the boys would be doing something to him or to his property again, as they had done in the past. Sure enough, a week before Halloween, as Gramps sat inside, carving by his dim light, he heard a thud on the side of his house. He took his flashlight and went out to see what had happened. Tomatoes had bombarded the side of his house. Ed loved stewed tomatoes, but not on the side of his house. It wasn't but a few minutes after this had happened that it started to rain very hard. The wind blew in just the right direction, washing the tomatoes off his house. Gramps took the little Bible out of his overall pocket and held it close to his chest. He looked out of the window and thanked God for washing the side of his house. He was also thankful that the flying tomatoes broke no windows.

The next morning the two boys walked to school past Mr. Miller's house, hoping to see the tomato artwork they had created on the side of his house the night before. To their amazement there was not one trace of splattered tomatoes anywhere. They couldn't believe that the rain could have washed Gramps' house so clean.

Two days later after the sun went down, the two boys, Jimmy and Ben decided to pay another visit to the old man's house. Once again, as Ed was reading his Bible, he heard a thud on his porch. The two boys decided to do their dirty work up on the porch this time, so if it rained again nothing would be washed off. Ed took his flashlight with its dim batteries and went out on the porch to see what happened. Much to his surprise, there were a dozen hard-boiled eggs broken on his porch and they were quite easy to sweep up.

It seemed that Jimmy had taken the wrong box of eggs from his mother's refrigerator. She had boiled a dozen eggs, putting them back into the egg carton to be used later, and had forgotten to mark them as being boiled. For the next week Jimmy was not allowed to have his daily egg sandwich for breakfast because his mother found out he had taken her eggs. But that didn't bother him as much as the fact that the boiled eggs he mistakenly had thrown on Mr. Miller's porch left no big mess for Gramps to clean up.

For some reason Jimmy really liked to pick on Gramps Miller. Ben, Jimmy's friend, just went along with Jimmy for the fun of it, but it was Jimmy who did most of the dirty work. What impressed Ben about Gramps was that he never seemed to get upset and he liked the way he whistled. Whittling and whistling made Gramps feel better. He often whistled as he whittled or carved something out of the wooden scraps that people would sometimes bring to him.

Some day Ed Miller hoped to sell the carvings to get enough money for a new roof, which his house badly needed. For sometime now, he had been working on a nativity scene, which included Mary, Joseph, Baby Jesus in a manger, the stable, an angel, a shepherd boy and a sheep. Gramps had hoped to get them done by Christmas. He had hoped to wholesale them to the Variety Store in town. If people liked them, he could make more nativity sets to sell.

Saturday Gramps walked to the grocery store to buy the few necessary food items his budget could afford. It had been snowing all day and there were about four inches already on the ground. Gramps was cautious as he approached the same bushes where Ben and Jimmy had jumped out when he had his wagonload of wood. He wanted to avoid any more trouble. Suddenly he heard a noise and ducked just in time to avoid being hit by a snowball. Instead, the snowball whizzed by him and onto the windshield of a passing car. Jimmy, all alone this time, took off running into the night as soon as he saw what he had done to the passing car. The boy disappeared before the owner of the car could catch him. Again Gramps looked up into the sky, put his hand over the Bible in his overall pocket, and thanked God that the snowball did not hit him. The elderly gentleman also thanked God that no damage was done to the passing car.

Gramps continued his walk to the grocery store. After arriving, he purchased some bread, milk and rolled oats, so he could eat some oatmeal and toast. He couldn't buy a lot of fancy foods because he didn't have that kind of money, and rolled oats go a long way. Gramps often wished he had enough money to buy so much food that he would have to take Bobby's wagon to carry the items home. But the way it was, he could carry everything home in one sack.

Gramps wondered why Ben wasn't with Jimmy when he threw the snowball. For some reason he always thought Jimmy was the instigator of all the mischievous acts that had happened. There was something about Ben that almost made Gramps want to like the boy. Could it be because Ben was a boy that reminded Gramps a lot of his own son, Bobby, before he had become sick and died? Ben was now twelve years old. His son, Bobby, who had been big for his age, was just ten years old when he died. Gramps had hoped that Ben really was a good boy and he wished, too, that Jimmy wouldn't be so mischievous. He wondered if the boys and their parents ever went to church or ever read the Bible. Gramps would now pray for these two boys every night.

About three weeks before Christmas, Gramps finished carving the nativity pieces and wrapped them in old newspapers. He decided he would take them to the Variety Store to see if the owner would be interested in buying them. It seemed when he held and wrapped Baby Jesus that an extra warm feeling came over him that he couldn't explain. He would be thankful for any amount of money he could get for his work of art. He put the wrapped carved pieces carefully into a paper sack and started out for the store. Gramps was not proud of his work but thanked God that his fingers were still able to do this carving. He seemed pleased with the way they had turned out.

The white-haired man was not going to take any chances this time walking to the store. He decided to walk on the other side of the street away from the bushes where the boys would usually hide out. This street was well lit, that is why he went this way instead of on one of the side streets. This was also the closest way for Gramps to walk. It was cold and snowing again, so Gramps bundled up, wearing his overalls, heavy old coat, scarf, hat and gloves. The cold weather bothered Gramps' arthritis, so he bundled up well to stay warm. The elderly man whistled as he walked down the street. He carried his work of art, the carved nativity set, carefully under his arms.

When Gramps was about halfway to the store, suddenly from out of nowhere, Jimmy appeared in front of him. Gramps could see another boy standing between two houses, but it was dark and he couldn't tell for sure who it might be. Gramps thought it might possibly have been Ben, who told Jimmy to let the old man alone. Jimmy accused Gramps of being a miser man and carrying a bag full of money. The only time Jimmy ever saw Gramps carrying a sack with something in it was when he walked home from the store after buying his groceries. Why would the old man be going to town with a full sack of money, Jimmy thought, if he was not going to buy something big with it?

Mischievous Jimmy had waited, making sure no cars were coming, then he quickly stepped out in front of Gramps. The boy grabbed his sack while giving him a little shove so anyone seeing him would think he had stumbled. Gramps' glasses flew off and he fell to his knees. When Ben saw what Jimmy had done, he decided to let Jimmy go. He stepped out on the sidewalk to help Gramps. Ben picked up he old man's hat that had fallen off, handed it to him and helped him to his feet. The boy found Gramps' glasses and gave them to him. The elderly gentleman couldn't thank Ben enough for helping him.

For the first time Ben really had a good look at the old man. The boy watched, as there on the sidewalk, looking up into the soft falling snow, Gramps thanked God that he had not broken any bones, not even his glasses. He thanked God for sending the kind boy whom had helped him. Then Gramps said something Ben did not understand. The old man, with hair as white as the snow on the ground, told his God right there and then, to please bless the one who had his nativity set, and especially Baby Jesus. Ben asked Gramps what he had in his sack. Gramps said it was the nativity scene that he had carved. He had been on his way to the store with it, hoping to sell it for a little extra money, so he could make some repairs on his house.

Then almost as quickly as Jimmy had appeared, Ben disappeared into the night. He ran to find Jimmy and this thing called the nativity and some little baby named, Jesus. He never did find Jimmy that night, but he did find the sack full of the carved nativity pieces all unwrapped and laying under the bushes. All the pieces were there except for Baby Jesus. But Ben didn't know that Baby Jesus was missing because he did not know who He was or what He even looked like.

Meanwhile Gramps, wondering why Ben had left him so quickly, turned around and walked slowly back to his little house. He was not whistling now, but instead he was praying for his safety and that somehow God would continue to supply his needs, and return the nativity set to him. He praised God for the blessings he did have and asked to be content with such.

Ed Miller would begin to carve another nativity set, but he knew he would not get it done in time for Christmas this season. He would patch up his roof with a few more old shingles in the spring to keep it from leaking for another year. He had now given up hope on ever fixing his old car.

Ben arrived home with his sack full of carvings and hid them in his room. Tomorrow he would plan to take them to the old man's house after school.

The next day in school Jimmy didn't say too much and he seemed like an altogether different boy from what he had been the day before. Just what happened to make the difference in Jimmy, neither Ben nor Jimmy seemed to be able to understand. Ben thought he liked the new Jimmy better than the old mischievous boy he had known. Ben thought perhaps Jimmy might be sick and in a day or two he would probably be the same old Jimmy again. All Jimmy said to Ben that day was that Gramps didn't have any money in his bag, just some old pieces of wood. Ben said he knew that, and that he had found the sack after Jimmy had thrown it under the bushes. Ben said he picked it up and planned to take it back to Gramps. Ben asked Jimmy to go along with him but Jimmy said he had to go straight home after school. Ben also went home after school. When no one was looking he took the sack of nativity pieces, without Baby Jesus, and headed for Gramps' old house.

As Ben walked to Gramps' house, many thoughts came to his mind. There was something about Gramps that Ben rather liked. Could it be because Gramps reminded him of the grandpa he had lost almost two years ago from a heart attack? Ben, who had been very close to his grandpa, missed him very much and resented the fact that he had died. He especially missed the times when his grandpa would take him fishing in the summer time. Grandpa had gone to church every Sunday, but Ben's family always seemed too busy to go. Suddenly it was as if someone had turned on a light bulb in Ben's mind. He finally remembered the story his grandpa had told him about the birth of Jesus. He had also told the boy about Jesus' death on the cross, and even raising from the dead. His grandpa had said if we give our hearts completely over to Jesus, we could go to this place Grandpa called, heaven. It had all seemed like some kind of a fairy tale to Ben when his grandpa would talk to him about this man named Jesus. But now, somehow these words about Jesus were all coming back to Ben. Could it perhaps be because he was holding the nativity and that Gramps' prayer, about anyone coming in contact with the nativity would be blessed, was being answered?

As Ben approached Gramps' house, he wondered if the old man's house really was haunted. Perhaps the dim lights that Gramps burned at night made it appear to be haunted. Ben also wondered how he would explain to Gramps that he happened to have his sack of carvings. Ben slowly walked onto Gramps' porch and knocked on the door. The door opened and for a moment Ben thought he could almost see his own grandpa standing there. Gramps looked at Ben and he, too, thought for a moment that his son, Bobby, was standing there, but then, he knew it couldn't be.

The elderly man invited Ben in and immediately a warm feeling for each other developed between the two of them. Ben carefully unpacked each piece of the nativity and laid them on Gramps' old table. The boy told Gramps how he had found the sack of carvings under the bushes. Jimmy had left them there after he had hoped to find money in the sack. Instead all he found were some old wood statues, as Jimmy called them. Ben glanced around Gramps' house from where he stood and saw that it was very neat and clean. But to Ben everything was old and badly in need of repair. Then he looked at Gramps, who seemed puzzled about something. Gramps asked Ben where Baby Jesus was, because you can't have Christmas without Him. Ben assured the old gentleman in overalls that he had brought all the pieces he found, the night before, by the bushes. Then Ben asked Gramps where he had been going with these carvings the past night and did he carve them all by himself?

Ben remembered what his own grandpa told him about Jesus, and wondered if this was the same Baby Jesus Gramps was now talking about. If this was the same baby, then He must really be someone special. Ben knew that somehow this baby had to be found! Gramps told Ben that he was taking the nativity to the store in hopes of selling it. He would then use the money to repair his roof next summer, if possible.

The concerned young boy and the older white-haired gentleman took a liking for each other, and suddenly it seemed as if they had been friends for a long time. And then for some reason Ben turned, ran out of the house, and yelled back to Gramps that he would be back soon. Gramps wondered what the boy was up to now. He watched Ben disappear down the street, thanking God for his new friend who had brought his nativity set back.

Gramps prayed that somehow Baby Jesus could be found and returned so he could take them to the store in time for Christmas. He had asked God, when he finished his carvings, that He would bless whoever next came in contact with the nativity. It now seemed to Gramps that God already had blessed Ben, giving the boy a change of heart towards the old man. But he still had Jimmy to contend with. Or did he? When Jimmy had taken the carvings from Gramps, he had looked at each piece and then put them back in the sack, that is, each piece except for one!

When Jimmy was five years old he had lost his little three-year-old brother, Timmy, in a drowning accident in his uncle's farm pond. It was Jimmy who had first found his brother. The little boy had been taken from the water, wrapped in a blanket and laid on a pile of clean hay near the pond. But it had been too late; his little brother had already drowned. Jimmy's family went to church every Sunday, but Jimmy still blamed God for letting his little brother drown. So now as he picked up this one piece of carving of Baby Jesus, it reminded him of his little brother. He had carefully put this carving in his pocket and took it with him, while leaving the other nativity pieces under the bushes.

As soon as Jimmy took Baby Jesus, it seemed as if something strange happened to him that he could not explain. He no longer wanted to hurt Gramps or anyone else. So this is why Ben noticed that his friend, Jimmy, appeared to be different in school that day. It was as if someone had told Jimmy that if he wanted to see his little brother, Timmy, again then he must love Jesus and not blame God for what had happened to the little fellow. Gramps had been praying that whoever next possessed the nativity would be truly blessed. Now Jimmy had the best part of it with the carving of Baby Jesus. The boy was truly being blessed.

Ben arrived at Jimmy's house and knocked on the door. He asked to see Jimmy. The boy's mother said she noticed something different about her son today but she could not explain why. Jimmy came to the door and Ben asked him if he had the Baby Jesus that was in Gramps' sack. Jimmy said he did. Ben told Jimmy that Gramps would not be able to have Christmas without Baby Jesus and would he please take it back to him?

Soon the two boys were walking down the street together to the old man's house, not to throw tomatoes or eggs but to deliver Baby Jesus. On the way to Gramps' house, Ben told Jimmy why Gramps was going to sell the nativity set. He told his friend about Gramps' need for a new roof. The old man also needed a lot of other repairs done around his house. Ben said that Gramps really was a nice old man.

When the two boys arrived at Gramps' house, the elderly man was sitting in his rocker, in his faded overalls, waiting for Ben to return. Gramps seemed surprised to see Jimmy along with Ben. Gramps had begun carving another Baby Jesus while Ben was gone. Jimmy stood beside the old, white-haired man in the rocker, and handed him the carved baby he had carried in his pocket. Jimmy told Gramps that he was sorry for all the mischievous things he had done to him. He told Gramps that he wouldn't have to be afraid of him anymore. Jimmy went on to tell the elderly man that there was something about the Baby Jesus that made him feel different inside, but he couldn't explain what it was.

Gramps told the boys that it is not the Baby Jesus who helps us. It is Jesus as a man, who died for us. He went on to say that Jesus shed His blood on the cross for our sins and arose again from the dead, so that some day we can go to heaven if we live for Him. It is Jesus, the man, who can help us, Gramps told the boys. Gramps took his little Bible out of his overall pocket and opened to the second chapter of Luke. The two boys sat on the floor and listened quietly as the old man read the Christmas story to them. To Jimmy it was a familiar story with a new meaning now. To Ben it was a new, exciting story, just like his own grandpa had once told him. But it didn't seem like a fairy tale now; it seemed so very real.

Gramps said he had to go after more wood for his wood stove. Also, now that he had his nativity pieces back, he planned to stop at the Variety Store to see if he could still sell his work in time for Christmas. Gramps told the boys they had better go home before their parents might worry about them. But the boys didn't want to go home, so off they went, all three of them. Gramps walked in the middle, with Ben on one side carrying the nativity and Jimmy on the other side pulling the old, rusty, red wagon.

They reached the Variety Store just before it closed. All three went inside and Gramps Miller showed the carved nativity pieces to the owner of the store. The man said he would be happy to try to sell the nativity set for Mr. Miller, but the man would not promise that it would sell. The elderly gentleman all bundled up in his winter coat, and the two boys then set out to buy a wagonload of wood. Gramps almost felt like a boy himself again as he and the two boys loaded his wagon with wood. The snow was softly falling as all three of them walked back to Gramps' house. Ben and Jimmy took turns pulling the old wagon with its load of wood. While one pulled the wagon, the other boy held onto Gramps' hand. This time as they walked past the bushes you could hear Gramps whistling. He no longer had to be afraid that the boys would jump out of the bushes and scare him. What a good feeling the old man, with hair as white as the soft falling snow, now had!

After they unloaded the wood for Gramps, the boys hurried home, each explaining to their parents where they had been and what they had been doing. The boys' parents would hardly believe their stories at first. But the boys told them to call the storeowner and the man they got the wood from, to verify their stories.

Then Jimmy had an idea, and he invited Ben to come to church with him the following Sunday to help with his plan. Ben's parents were willing to let him go.

There was still a week and a half before Christmas. For the next ten days Gramps never saw the boys and he wondered why. Gramps put up the few Christmas decorations he had. He planned to spend Christmas Day attending his little church in the morning, then walk back home and have his oatmeal for dinner. He thought he might have just enough money to buy a few oranges for his Christmas dinner. For Gramps there would be no presents, just the presence of his dear friend, Jesus, who had long been his daily companion.

During those ten days, word had gotten around about the unusual nativity scene on display in the Variety Store. Many people came in to see and touch it, but the manager said it wasn't for sale. He, too, had a plan. It seemed as though all that came in contact with the carved nativity scene wanted to buy it or order one like it, and each potential customer went away truly blessed.

At last Christmas Eve had arrived. Gramps Miller was sitting inside his house reading the Bible when suddenly he heard beautiful singing outside. He put on his coat and hat and stepped out onto his porch in time to see what he thought must be the whole town coming towards his house. They were carrying flashlights so they could see and sacks of groceries, while singing Christmas carols.

Suddenly from out of the crowd came the two boys, Ben and Jimmy. They walked up on the old porch and stood at Gramps' side, each holding one of his hands that were now quivering. When the singing stopped, the boys told Gramps they had surprise for him. First, Jimmy's father, a carpenter by trade, stepped out of the crowd and said he was going to fix up Gramps' house for no charge at all. Then Ben's father, a mechanic, said he would fix up Gramps' old Chevy, and even put new tires on it. Then he would not have to get wood with his little wagon anymore. Another man said he had more wood than he knew what to do with and Gramps could have all the wood he wanted for free. Then one by one the carolers brought their sacks of groceries and put them on Gramps' porch. Hardly able to believe what he was seeing, the surprised man watched and listened with tears in his eyes and his hands raised to heaven. Once again Ed thanked Jesus for His kindness and mercy and asked God to bless all these dear friends and neighbors.

Then Ben and Jimmy said they had one more surprise. So many people wanted to buy Gramps' nativity that the store manager had decided to auction it off to the highest bidder. So there on Gramps' porch in the soft, falling snow, the carved nativity, complete with Baby Jesus, was auctioned off. When the bid was up to $300.00 the preacher of Jimmy's church said that you couldn't really put a price on Baby Jesus because He paid the price already for all of us as a man, when He died on the cross for our sins. So then the preacher bid $500.00 and bought the nativity scene and placed it on display in his church where it still is to this day. And his church has never been the same since, with his congregation growing spiritually stronger all the time! Could it be because Baby Jesus was there, not only as a Baby but also as the Son of God? Ben's family also decided to start going to church there.

The $500.00 would put a new roof on Gramps' house. Gramps thanked the people over and over and told them he loved them all. He especially loved Ben and Jimmy, his newly "adopted" grandsons, who were now carrying all the groceries inside Gramps' house. Then Gramps asked the boys how they managed to get all the people to come to his house. The boys said that it was easy. They simply told everyone in church and in school and all those they met in town that a special Baby Jesus was in the Variety Store and that they could go see Him. As the people went into the store to see and touch this Baby Jesus, a sign said, "If you want a chance to buy this nativity set, bring a sack of groceries and a flashlight to Gramps, Ed Miller's, house on Christmas Eve." The boys had also asked their parents and others to help fix up Gramps' old house and car.

So many people wanted to buy the nativity set that Gramps had orders to fill for next year's Christmas. He didn't know if he would get them all done, but at least now he would have an income all year, as he sells his carved nativities one by one. He will be given fifty dollars for each nativity set he carves.

The boys said this was their best Christmas because Baby Jesus now had a new meaning to them. Besides that, they now have a new "grandpa" to help take the place of the grandpa and little brother they had lost. Gramps promised to take both boys fishing when summer comes again. The elderly gentleman, in overalls, had prayed that all that would come in contact with the nativity would be blessed. Now the blessings all came back to Gramps, who said this was his best Christmas ever, since he had lost his wife and son. He said that God had truly given him a miracle through his carved Nativity and Baby Jesus!

MORE THAN CAMPING

Ryan and Micah were cousins who both enjoyed nature. They loved to spend time in God's great outdoor cathedral, as they called it. The summer, after graduating from high school, the two teenage boys decided to go on a weekend camping expedition in the hills of southern Indiana.

When they arrived at the State Park campground where they would be staying for two nights, dusk had already settled in. They set up camp in the primitive section of the campground because they liked to rough it.

Once in their sleeping bags inside the tent, they laid awake and listened to all the night sounds of crickets, katydids, tree frogs and even an owl. To the boys it sounded like a nocturnal symphony, written just for them by their Creator, the Almighty God.

Not until morning had they realized their tent was set up next to a poison-ivy bed. Fortunately for the two boys, neither one seemed to contact the uncomfortable itchy rash so many people get from this weed. They hoped they were still immune from the stuff.

Micah reminded Ryan of the story their grandpa often told. It was about the time when he, as a young lad, once rolled in a poison-ivy patch just so he would get the rash. And why did he want to do that? Because he thought it felt so good to scratch it. Needless to say Grandpa did get an awful rash, so badly his eyes swelled shut for a time. He became so miserable that he had to stay home for several weeks. After that Grandpa stayed away from the three-leafed weed. Even though the boys seemed to be immune from poison ivy they still stayed away from the plants as much as possible. There could always be a first time for contacting poison ivy.

After they enjoyed the pancakes made on the open fire the boys read from the Bible and prayed, asking for God's protection for the day. The boys had given their hearts and lives over to Jesus about a year ago and would never think of starting out for the day without first talking to their Creator. In all their endeavors they sought to do His will.

It appeared to be a beautiful summer day and the two cousins decided to go hiking on one of the rugged trails that started and ended near the campground. The boys were in excellent condition physically and knew they could easily walk the eight-mile trail back to their campsite before dusk. They packed a lunch to be eaten along the way and took an emergency kit consisting of a hunting knife, a rope, flashlight, and a first aid kit in their backpacks and started out on the trail.

The wind whistled through the pine trees and reminded them of the verse they had read after breakfast during their devotions. The verse in Isaiah 55:12 said, "For you shall go out with joy, and be led forth with peace: the mountains and the hills shall break forth before you into singing and all the trees of the field shall clap their hands." Surely it did seem like the hills were singing and the trees clapping their hands as the wind rushed through the trails in this beautiful State Park. The boys enjoyed God's handi-work as they saw it in His marvelous creation all around them. It seemed as though everywhere they went God's presence could be felt and heard.

About three miles down the trail the boys saw a small opening under a rocky ledge. Micah, the smaller one of the two, decided to crawl into it to see if it might possibly be a small cave. Once inside he used his flashlight to look around. It was only a very small one-room cavity but what he saw and heard was very frightening and as he quickly turned around to crawl out, he yelled, "Snakes!"

You see, inside this small cave, if you want to call it one, lived a nest of rattlesnakes and Micah, after seeing them knew he had to get out and get out FAST!

As Ryan stood by, waiting for his cousin to come out, he noticed a mature rattle snake creeping towards the opening of the small cave nearby to where he stood. Perhaps the snake was going in to protect his young ones now that he sensed intruders were in his territory. Ryan froze, but knew he had to do something and act fast. There lay a six-inch rock near the mouth of the cave, close to the big rattler. If he could pick up the stone perhaps he would be able to drop it on the reptile. He knew every move and every second counted. To get the rock seemed out of the question since the rattler now curled up next to it, gazed from one boy to the other.

Meanwhile just inside the small opening, Micah began to pray for God's protection as the snakes, sensing an intruder in their den, slowly moved in the young man's direction. Micah earnestly prayed, pleading silently to the Almighty God to please shut the mouths of the snakes as He had once closed the mouths of the lions when Daniel had been thrown into their den.

Suddenly outside the cave, it was almost as if someone took control of Ryan's arm as he swiftly drew his hunting knife from its sheath, thrusting it into the head of the coiled rattler. Both boys looked at one another in amazement. Ryan said, "Let's get out of here!"

In a jiffy Micah came out of the opening in the rocks and the two boys hurriedly took off down the trail, their hearts pounding. It wasn't long before they stopped to rest on a fallen log, discussing the excitement they had just encountered.

Micah said, "Whew, that was close! You want to know something, Ryan? When I saw those creepy reptiles, they reminded me of Satan's demons, all coming towards me, and I began to pray hard! As soon as I asked God to shut their mouths all the snakes stopped where they were and just stared at me."

Ryan said, "I, too, had been praying that God would take control of the situation and the big rattler that came so close to both of us. And, wow, did He ever take control! I still don't know how I threw that knife so quickly and accurately like I did. All I can say is that God took control of my arm, and that's all there is to it!"

"You always were good at throwing darts and hitting the bulls eye, but this time you scored better than that," exclaimed Micah. "Through God's guidance you saved our lives from possibly being bitten by that crafty reptile."

Then the two young men paused, thanked the Good Lord for His protection and asked for further guidance for the rest of the day. Once more they started down the trail.

It was such a beautiful sunny day when they woke up that morning but soon they noticed dark clouds moving in and they could hear the sound of approaching thunder. Not wanting to turn back, they continued forward on the trail that now ran along side a beautiful rippling creek. It was the same creek the boys had gone canoeing on last year with some of their friends. It seemed to be a relatively safe creek to go swimming and canoeing in, except when heavy rains come. Then the water gets too high, causing a dangerous undertow near the bottom of the creek.

Suddenly the lowering clouds became very dark, the wind began to blow and the thunder cracked louder and louder. The weather forecast had not called for rain and the boys were not prepared for this kind of weather. A heavy cloud burst dropped buckets of rain and the boys knew the creek would fill up fast. It remained fairly warm, around 75 degrees, so they were not too concerned about getting wet and cold. They wondered about their tent and camping supplies they had left behind.

Suddenly the thunder cracked loudly, as a bolt of lightening must have struck near by. Still on the trail, the teens spotted an over hanging rock ledge up ahead and hurriedly ran under it for protection, hoping no snakes would be there.

The wind blew furiously causing white caps on the swelling waters and the waves slapped against the big boulders lodged here and there through out the creek bed. In Psalms 98:8 it says, "Let the floods clap their hands," and that's exactly what it sounded like as the waters rushed by with fury.

The young men decided to wait out the storm under this rocky ledge and would take time to eat their lunch. Just as they were about to partake of their food, they heard someone calling, "Help!" Micah said he hoped no one got caught canoeing in this awful storm. Again they heard the cry for help. The teens stepped out from under the protective ledge to look for some one who might be in distress.

Then Micah exclaimed, "Look, Ryan, someone is coming on a rubber tube floating helplessly toward us, calling for help. We must help this person, but how?"

Ryan said, "God took care of the snakes and provided a rocky ledge as a shelter for us in this storm and He will help us now. I just know He will"

The teens began to pray as the person in the tube drifted closer and closer. The current seemed very swift and the waters still were rising. If the tube should hit a snag and deflate, whoever was adrift in it could possibly be pulled under into the churning waters and drown. Surely whoever was riding in this tube had a life preserver on, they hoped. The blinding rain made it difficult to tell if this person was a man, woman or perhaps even a child.

The boys stood as close to the water's edge as possible in the drenching rain, listening to the pleading cries for help coming their way. Right now the boys didn't care if they were getting soaked from the rain or missed their lunch. They just knew someone needed help and they had to do whatever possible to help this person in distress.

The black rubber tube and its passenger were almost in front of the boys. Suddenly, again, it was though someone took control of Ryan's arm. He quickly grabbed his rope, tied a loop in it and tossed it out over the swelling creek waters just as the runaway tube appeared in front of him.

Ryan yelled, "Hang on!" as the circled rope fell just below the shoulders of the frightened young man floating in the run away tube.

"You did it, Ryan, you really did it!" exclaimed Micah.

Carefully the two cousins quickly pulled the tube and a stunned young teenager, who did not have a life vest on, to shore, helping him and the tube out of the water. The trio now soaked from the rain all huddled together under the rocky ledge, almost in unbelief of what Ryan had done.

The frightened teen, whose name was Jarrod, said, "I have heard how cowboys lasso a horse or a cow, but never have I seen a hiker lasso someone out in the water and pull him in! How did you ever learn to do a trick like that?"

Ryan admitted he would sometimes lasso a rope just for the fun of it using his dog as his target. But he said it surely had to be God who took control of his arm and the rope, making it possible for him to rescue someone in distress. He knew he could not have done it in his own strength and power.

Together the trio returned to the shelter of the rocky ledge. There, Micah knelt in prayer in his soggy jeans and once more thanked God for helping them rescue Jarrod. He asked for further guidance and protection during the rest of the journey back to the campground. Then he quoted Psalm 46:1, "God is our refuge and strength, a very present help in trouble." He also added a few words from verse three saying, "Though the waters thereof roar and be troubled. For surely," he said, "the waters were troubled today."

Thankful they had packed plenty to eat, the two hungry campers once more began to take their lunch from its waterproof container, and willingly shared it with their new companion.

The storm began to subside and the thunder could be heard fading into the distance. What seemed like hours to the three boys actually was about thirty minutes. Jarrod, quite exhausted, told his two new companions he intended to be in the water only for a short time in the area where his family was having a picnic along the creek and near the campground. Before he knew it, he had drifted downstream on the rippling waters, with the unexpected storm catching him unprepared. He knew his family would be concerned for his whereabouts and he couldn't thank Ryan and Micah enough for rescuing him from the turbulent waters.

The boys continued on their hike and finally approached the old suspension footbridge they needed to cross, in order to get back to the campground and picnic area. The wind and the rain had subsided somewhat but the water still remained high and swift below the bridge. The three young men couldn't believe what they saw as they came to the bridge. Lightening must have struck the huge tree across the creek causing a large part of it to fall across the old bridge. The hand rails and bridge supports were made of rope and the tree actually snapped the rope on one side of the bridge as the large limb fell on it with great force.

This bridge was just a mile from the campground and they were so near the end of their trail. If they couldn't cross the swelling creek here they would have to go back seven miles to where they started. The clouds were still lingering low and it would be dark before they would be able to get back, if they had to reverse the trail.

Should the three of them try to hold onto the rubber tube together, use their feet as paddles and try to make it across the swift waters? What if they couldn't make it across, would they drift helplessly down stream?

Once more Micah began to pray that God would direct them to make the right decisions and asked for protection and guidance in getting back to camp. Surely The One who calms the seas and the storms would help them again. The boys knew the undercurrent was swift and feared trying to cross the water in the tube.

Micah reminded Ryan and Jarrod of the picture where the angel protects two little children as they walk over a broken footbridge. He said, "The angel of the Lord will be with us. Remember it says in Psalms 91:11-12, "For he shall give his angels charge over you, to keep you in all your ways. They shall bear you up in their hands, lest you dash your foot against a stone." He continued, "The only way across is by going over on this bridge. What do you think?"

Ryan thought they should try it. Jarrod didn't like the idea of doing that but there appeared to be no other choice. He couldn't believe the faith his new friends had and how they prayed and trusted in Jesus, a man that he knew so little about. He saw they had something he didn't have, but whatever it was he thought it wasn't all that bad. If their God could help Ryan throw the rope like he did and pull him ashore then this God must be someone worth trusting. He hoped an angel would be watching over him like Micah said.

Micah said the bridge could very well be unsafe to cross but never the less he decided, that was the way to go. He suggested the other two go across first, one at a time hanging onto the one rope that still remained in tact. Ryan the biggest of the three decided to go first. If the bridge held him, it probably would be safe for the other two. Then again his weight might weaken it more, especially near where the tree had fallen, about six feet from the other shore.

Ryan slowly stepped onto the creaking boards and started across. When he came to the large tree limb that straddled the crippled bridge, he had to climb over it. The tree seemed to be balancing on the bridge and he had to be very careful not to upset it, heavy as it was. Carefully as he took his last step over the limb, the whole bridge seemed to drop down about six inches. Ryan stood still a minute, then cautiously proceeded the rest of the way across the bridge, praying as he went. He made it to the other side and told Jarrod to try crossing over but to go very slowly and steady.

Jarrod cautiously stepped onto the crippled bridge looking down at the water rushing beneath him. Micah said, "Don't look down, Jarrod, just keep your eyes on the other shore. Remember the picture I told you about with the angel watching over the children on the bridge? Well, an angel will watch over you, too. In Isaiah it says, "For I the Lord your God will hold your right hand, saying unto you, fear not: I will help you." So let Him hold your hand, Jarrod, and you will make it, I know you will. In the meantime I'll be praying for you."

Jarrod slowly began his walk across the bridge and as he approached the fallen tree, suddenly they heard someone say, "Hey you, out there, what do you think you're doing? That bridge isn't safe to be walking on!"

It was the Conservation Officer who had been sent out to look for Jarrod after his parents reported him missing. He thought that perhaps he just might find him near the bridge. He was stunned to see Jarrod or anyone treading so feebly on this old broken bridge.

Ryan turned to the officer and told him he had just crossed over the bridge himself and Jarrod will make it as well, and so will his cousin still waiting on the other side of the creek.

Jarrod slowly stepped over the fallen tree and in doing so one of the boards gave way under his foot. He caught himself just in time and hung onto the one remaining rope tighter than ever. He said, "If you are really out there, Lord, please do take my hand and help me!" Then he slowly pulled himself up, and made it to the end of the bridge where Ryan and the puzzled officer stood.

The officer asked Jarrod to show him some kind of identification and the boy reached into his wet trousers and verified his identity. The man told him that his family had been concerned about him when he never came back to the picnic area after the storm. They were all out looking for him.

Then Jarrod told the officer these other two young men were sent here from God to rescue him from the swelling creek waters. The officer didn't know what to think as Ryan and Micah both on opposite sides of the creek began to pray once more asking God to help protect Micah as he crossed the bridge. This man knew the battered bridge wasn't safe but it would soon be dark and he really didn't want to leave Micah on the other side until morning when the waters would begin to recede. He guessed the young man should carefully cross the bridge, at his own risk of however, hoping his God would protect him as well.

Ryan threw one end of his rope across the creek, over to Micah to tie around Jarrod's tube. With the help of the rope, Ryan would try to keep the tube in the water just below Micah, to be used in case of emergency if needed.

Micah began his treacherous journey across the ill-fated bridge, treading ever so carefully. Ryan began to quote the Bible verse in Psalms that says, "God is our refuge and strength, a very present help in trouble."

Jarrod, who never had taken much interest in God before now, and the officer along with Ryan, were all three praying in their own way as their friend crept slowly towards the fallen tree. Would the bridge hold out? It seemed to weaken each time the other two crossed over it. Ryan tightened the rope on the tube trying to keep it in the water close to Micah, should he happen to need it. The waters were flowing so swiftly if someone was in a tube it would be difficult to keep them from being swept downstream.

The weight of the bridge and fallen tree was too much for the one hand rail rope left. The rope began to pull apart as Micah carefully stepped over the tree. He noticed the frayed rope, as did the ones standing on the shore. Suddenly the rope snapped and the bridge dropped from under the young man's feet! At that moment Micah took one big leap over the last six feet of the bridge towards the shore. In an instant found himself standing face to face with the Conservation Officer.

The bewildered man said, "Well, I never in all my life saw anyone leap so far so quickly as you did young man. Who are you, some kind of a super man?"

"No, Sir," said Micah. "It must have been the angel of the Lord that carried me here. On my own strength, I could not have done it. It had to come from God."

The officer said they better get back to the camp and picnic grounds where Jarrod's family may be waiting. He said no one would believe what he had just witnessed so the boys better come and help explain it for him.

Ryan said, "Before we leave here we need to thank the Good Lord for protecting all of us the way He did just now."

So the two cousins knelt on the muddy ground and thanked their Creator for His goodness and mercy. Before they stood up Jarrod was on his knees between them saying he saw enough today in these two special friends that whatever they had he wanted as well. In other words, he wanted to know and trust this God and His Son, Jesus, as his Savior, as they do.

Ryan and Micah put their arms around the wet, shivering youth that sobbingly said, "If I would have drowned today, I know I wouldn't have gone to heaven. After seeing your faith and hearing your prayers today, I want the happiness and trust in God that you both have. You're different somehow and seem so content and eager to help strangers and I want to be like that, too. Will you please help me?"

The officer stood by in amazement as Ryan and Micah told Jarrod how to become a true believer in Jesus Christ. They quoted John 3:16 saying, "For God so loved the world that He gave His only begotten Son, that whosoever believes on Him should not perish, but have everlasting life." Micah went on to say that Jesus loves everyone but hates sin. We need to ask Jesus to forgive all our sins so He can dwell in our hearts if we ask Him to take control of our lives.

All this seemed so new to Jarrod who longed to know more about this faith and trust, that the other boys had in this man called, Jesus. Kneeling down between his new friends, Jarrod asked Jesus to come into his heart. He pleaded for forgiveness of all his past sins, promising to make restitution for everything wrong he had done in the past.

Ryan told Jarrod that the book of Romans and the first four Gospels in the New Testament would be good for him to read. They would help him to understand more. He told Jarrod how Jesus died for us, shedding His blood on the cross, because He loved us so much. Then He arose from the grave so we, too, can have eternal life in heaven one day. He assured the young man that we never need to fear death if we are truly born again Christians. Then when we leave this earth the angels will carry us across the river to heaven to forever be with our Creator.

Jarrod said, "So this is why you were not afraid to cross the bridge? You knew God would help you make it to the other side, giving you the strength and courage needed. And you had faith to believe His guardian angel would be watching over you."

The two cousins somehow knew Jarrod understood what they were trying to tell him and the Conservation Officer also seemed deeply touched by the story of God's plan of Salvation.

Somehow it didn't seem to bother the three teenagers that they were still in their wet clothing. Right now they had more important things to think about.

Soon the man and the three boys started back to the campground and picnic area. Suddenly Jarrod said, "I feel like a new person and it seems like even the trees around me are rejoicing. For the first time I can really sense God's presence around me and it feels so good."

Micah said, "Even the angels in heaven rejoice over one sinner that repents and in Psalms 96 it does say, the trees of the wood rejoice also, so you have reasons to feel the presence of God around you, Jarrod."

Once they arrived at the picnic area Jarrod's family rejoiced that their son had been found. The boy told them all that he had been through and his parents were amazed that he still seemed so happy in spite of it all. The Officer tried to explain to his parents what had happened to their son. He told them how two brave young men had rescued the young man. Somehow he just couldn't say it like he wanted to. With tears in his eyes the troubled man told Ryan and Micah to tell their story about how they saved Jarrod's life. The puzzled man then walked to his nearby truck and drove away.

Ryan walked to the campground and picked up a New Testament he had there. He came back to the picnic area and gave it to Jarrod, who accepted it gladly and promised his two new friends he would read it and find a good Bible believing church to go to. He also promised he would write to them letting them know how he is progressing in his new spiritual walk of life with Jesus.

Jarrod's parents offered to pay the boys for saving their son from the swiftly flowing creek waters. Ryan and Micah both said the price had already been paid and they received more than any payment they could have possibly have hoped for when Jarrod gave his heart over to the Lord. To them that was worth more than anything. With tears in his eyes, Jarrod hugged his new friends as they parted one from another.

It was dark as the two cousins returned to their tent site. They made a campfire and put on dry clothing. After roasting hot dogs and heating a can of pork and beans they made pudgy pies over the open fire, with brown bread and peach pie filling. To them supper had never tasted so good.

Using the light of their kerosene lantern, they read the Bible and each one thanked the Good Lord for His wonderful protection given them during this passing day. But most of all for not only helping them to save the life of a young man from the turbulent waters, but for saving the soul of this person God had sent their way, to give him a new lease on life.

Amazingly enough the sleeping bags inside the tent stayed dry. As they lay down to sleep, once more they could hear God's symphony of insects, katydids and tree frogs. In the distance they could hear the sound of the owl again as if telling them all is well, go to sleep. To Ryan and Micah these creatures never sounded so good and they seemed to be saying repeatedly, "God is our refuge and our strength, God is our refuge and our strength."

As for Jarrod, he was about to have the best night's sleep he ever had. Not only because someone cared enough to rescue him from the troubled waters of the creek but also because Jesus cared enough to die on the cross to save him from the troubled waters of his life.

Friend, if you seem to be floating hopelessly through life on troubled waters, why not put your trust and hopes in Jesus Christ? He is the only one who can give you complete peace, rest and contentment for your soul. Why not let Him be your refuge and strength in the time of trouble? Then some day you can go camping, forever in Canaan's Happy Land.

THE OTHER SIDE OF THE FENCE

Debi moved with her father and mother, Mr. and Mrs. Butler, away from the only home the girl had ever known. They had been living in a lovely home in a respectable neighborhood of the big city. About ten miles away from the pollution of the big city industries, they found an old farmhouse nestled among the pines, on top of a hill. Here, they had a lovely view of the surrounding farmland.

Seven-year-old Debi had asthma quite badly and the pollution seemed to be the major cause of her health problems. The doctor had advised the Butlers to move out to the country. There, away from the polluted air, they hoped the fresh air would allow their daughter, Debi, to breathe easier.

It was a difficult decision to make. Mr. Butler would be further away from his job and his daughter would have no one to play with out on the farm. But the Butlers decided they would make the move because Debi, their little sunbeam and they often called her, was their whole life. They definitely wanted what was best for her. If it meant leaving the city then that is what they would do.

Debi adjusted to the farm but she greatly missed her playmates from their former neighborhood. To have a cat or a dog seemed to be out of the question because of the girl's allergies. Debi often wished she had a brother or sister to play with. That, too, was out of the question. Mrs. Butler had a serious illness after the birth of their little daughter. The doctor said she would not be able to have more children.

Debi also had to change schools, but that seemed to be no problem for the little girl. With her freckled face accented by two big dimples and long, silky red hair, this youngster knew no strangers. You couldn't help but fall in love with this precious little girl. Her green eyes sparkled even when she did not smile. Already, after six weeks out on the farm, the youngster began feeling better.

School was out and Debi's grandparents invited her and her cousin, Chris, to spend a few days back in the city with them. Mr. and Mrs. Butler thought it would do the girl good to visit the city again. A few days wouldn't hurt her asthma if she didn't play too hard. Besides it would be good for her to be with her cousin, Chris, age eight.

Debi looked forward to going to the city to visit her grandparents. Even though there were not any little girls nearby her grandparent's house she always enjoyed being with her grandmother. She would be glad to see Chris again but he and Grandpa usually spent the time together fishing somewhere. Grandma would often let her granddaughter, Debi, make cookies while visiting at her house. This was a special treat for the little girl who loved eating, as well as baking the cookies.

So the day came when the two young cousins were to go to their grandparents house at the edge of the city. Debi, as excited as any seven-year old would be, had her little bags packed hours before her parents were to take her to the city. The little girl had her red hair neatly braided and tied with pretty bows to match her dress. Debi had tucked some pictures that she had colored for her grandparents, neatly inside her little overnight carrying case.

It was late afternoon when the two cousins arrived at their grandparent's home. Excitement showed on their faces as they unpacked their belongings in the bedrooms they each would have. Already Grandpa and Chris were making plans to go fishing the next day. Grandpa bought a new fishing pole just for his grandson. Grandma had a new doll for her granddaughter, and the girl immediately fell in love with the cuddly rag doll.

The next day the children were up early. They both agreed that they were too excited to sleep any longer. After breakfast Grandpa read from the big Bible as he did every morning. He then prayed for the protection and guidance of his family as they begin another new day.

Grandpa and Chris soon gathered their bucket of wiggly worms and left for the fishing pond, several miles away. Grandma had packed a picnic lunch for them to eat when they became hungry. Hopefully they would bring some fish back for supper.

Grandma got out her big mixing bowl and the ingredients for making cookies. Debi pulled a little step stool up to the cupboard and stood there while Grandma tied one of her big aprons around her granddaughter. Grandma then tied the little girl's pigtails together gently in a big bow behind Debi's head. This way her hair wouldn't fall into the mixing bowl as she leaned forward. Grandma noticed how the sun shone in through her kitchen window making Debi's hair glisten as though sunbeams were dancing on her head.

Grandmother chuckled as she watched her little sunbeam roll out the cookie dough and cut it with cookie cutters. The little girl had more flour on her apron, arms and face than she did on the cupboard top. After the cookies came out of the oven Debi decorated the different shaped cookies with icing and raisins. The kitchen smelled so good from the cookies as they baked in the oven and the youngster could hardly wait until she could have one to eat.

Debi and Grandma ate lunch together and sampled the cookies they had made. The little girl, as well as the grandmother, seemed pleasantly surprised at the way the cookies had turned out. Grandmother suggested to Debi that she take her new doll outside in the back yard. This would give the elderly lady a chance to clean up her kitchen.

A high chain link fence had recently been installed around the field behind the grandparent's home. A new, children's home or orphanage had been built to accommodate the homeless children of the area. The ten-acre land at the edge of the city where this home had been built had all been enclosed with this fence. It was supposed to keep the residents of this new facility from getting lost or running away. Occasionally the grandparents could see the children playing near the large brick building they called home.

Grandpa and Grandma often wondered where all these children came from. Why didn't the parents of these children raise them like they should have? Will they ever be adopted out or will they be orphans the rest of their lives? The hearts of this elderly couple went out to these children.

Debi climbed up on the big swing that Grandpa had hung from the old oak tree in his back yard. She held tightly to the new rag doll Grandma had given to her. Debi's long pigtails continued to glisten in the sun as they bobbed back and forth while the child made the swing go as high as her little legs could reach. The happy little girl sang, "Jesus wants me for a sunbeam," as she went back and forth on the old swing.

Suddenly Debi noticed a little girl about her own size standing nearby on the other side of the high fence. The little girl lived at the orphanage and had wondered away from her play area. Debi, still clinging to her doll, jumped off of the swing and walked over to the fence. She stared in awe at the girl on the other side the fence.

"Who are you and where did you come from?" Debi asked the other little girl. Then she asked, "How old are you?"

"M-my name is V-Vicki and I live over there," said the girl across the fence as she pointed to the big brick building across the field. "I-I'm six years old."

"Look!" said Debi. "You have red hair and freckles just like I do. Only your hair is pretty and curly. Mine is straight so I often have my hair in braids but I don't like them." Debi went on to say, "The boys in school often pull my hair when it is in pigtails. I like your curly hair better."

"B-but you have pretty teeth," replied Vicki as she held onto the fence. "M-y teeth stick out so far on top that others call me, B-Buck-Teeth. T-that is why I walked over here. I-I saw you swinging on that b-big swing and I wanted to see what it's l-like to be on the other side of the f-fence. Here, away from the others, no one calls me B-Buck-Teeth."

"I'll never call you Buck-Teeth, Vicki," responded Debi as she reached her hand through the fence touching Vicki's freckled arm. Then she said, "Look, Vicki, you have freckles all over just like I do."

The two girls stood facing each other, their freckled hands now clasped together on the big chain link fence.

"Your d-doll is so pretty," said Vicki shyly. "You must be very rich to live in that p-pretty house."

"I don't live here," replied Debi. "My grandparents do. I'm just visiting them for three days, and then I'm going back home in the country. Vicki, where are your mommy and daddy or grandpa and grandma?" Debi continued to ask.

"I-I don't have any family. N-nobody wants me," the girl with curly red hair said sadly. "My m-mommy was very young when I was born so she gave me to the orphanage. No one would adopt me because of my t-teeth, red hair and freckles. I-I wish I had a grandpa and grandma to visit like you do b-but I have no one." Debi saw tears in the eyes of this freckle-faced girl that no one wanted.

"Aren't there any other children you can play with in that big house over there?" quizzed Debi, pointing to the big building Vicki called home. "Surely you have someone who loves you," she said sympathetically.

"M-my mommy came just two times to see me, but that was when I was three years old. I-I can hardly remember her. Since then she n-never came back," sobbed the broken hearted girl on the other side of the fence.

Suddenly Debi cried, "Look, you're a sunbeam, too!"

"W-what's a sunbeam?" asked Vicki.

"My daddy says when the sun shines just right on my hair I look like a sunbeam. He says I'm his little sunbeam and that I'm Jesus' sunbeam, too," replied Debi as the sun glistened on her braided hair as well as on Vicki's.

"W-who is Jesus?" asked the girl from the orphanage.

"You mean you don't know who Jesus is?" asked Debi still holding the hands of her new friend across the fence. "Don't you ever go to Sunday school? Jesus lives in heaven and some day I want to see Him there. He loves everybody on earth, even the bad people. But He doesn't like what they do."

"Y-you mean this Jesus loves me, too?" the little six year old girl from the orphanage asked. "I never go to S-Sunday School to learn about Jesus. We have a chapel on Sunday morning at the orphanage that we all go to, but they don't talk about Jesus. They just say we have to be g-good, obey their rules and do what they tell us to do. I wish I could live on your s-side of the fence.

Then I would have a d-daddy and mommy, grandpa and grandma like you do. D-does this Jesus really love me, Debi?" the girl with curly red hair continued to asked, as she wiped the tears from her sad, green eyes.

"Yes, He does, He really does," was Debi's reply.

The matron from the orphanage, who had seen Vicki wonder away, suddenly walked up to the two girls. The women sternly took Vicki by the arm and pulled her away from the fence.

"P-please let me stay a little longer so I can t-talk to my new friend. P-please," pleaded the freckle-faced orphan with protruding teeth.

"No, you can not stay, you broke the rules by coming here. Now you will have to be punished!" snapped the matron as she led the girl away. "You will have to make all the beds in your dorm for the next week!" the lady snapped.

Debi stood there with tears in her own eyes as she watched her new friend being led away against her will. Vicki turned her head back to look once more at Debi. With tears running down the cheeks of the girl no one wanted she slowly put up her hand and waved good-by to the girl holding the new rag doll. It was the prettiest rag doll Vicki had ever seen. The elderly matron gave Vicki's arm a jerk and led her back to the big brick building that the little girl called home.

Unknown to Debi, her grandmother had been standing by the kitchen window, watching all that had been taking place between the two red-haired girls. Grandmother could not believe how much the two girls favored one another. You could almost think they were related somehow. The elderly lady could not understand completely all that the little girls were saying, but she could tell they had become friends. These two girls were so close to one another and yet so far apart.

As Grandmother stood pondering over the girls, she heard her husband's car pull into the driveway. She wondered what kind of a day they had together. Before she could collect all her thoughts, her grandson, Chris came running up to the door. "Grandma," he said, "I am hungry. Is supper almost ready? Grandpa's very hungry, too. He's bringing the fish we caught. Can we eat them tonight?"

Then Chris turned around and saw Debi slowly walking up to the back door of her grandparent's house. She stopped to pick up a dandelion that had gone to seed. Chris watched as his cousin blew the little white seeds into the summer's breeze while tears were flowing down her freckled cheeks.

As she reached for the back door, Chris asked, "What's the matter with you, Debi? Are your allergies making you cry? Maybe you better put that dandelion down."

Before the little girl could say anything, Grandma said, "Let's wash our hands, children. Supper is ready now. Tomorrow, Chris, we can eat the fish you and Grandpa caught."

After putting the fish in fresh water, Grandpa came in and also washed his hands and face. He glanced at Debi and noticed her unusually sad face. "What is wrong with our little sunbeam?" Grandpa quizzed. "She looks so sad."

"Oh, Grandpa," Debi said sadly, "It's a long story."

"Let's sit down and eat supper," remarked Grandmother. "Then afterwards if Debi wants to tell us her story we can all listen together. Is that okay, Debi?"

"I guess so," said Debi softly as she gently placed her pigtails behind her shoulders. She continued saying, "Something inside of me aches and I'm really not very hungry."

"Your allergies are probably making your tummy hurt, aren't they, Debi?" said her cousin Chris.

"No, I don't think so," replied Grandma. "It's a kind of an ache that Jesus will have to heal. It's an ache for a lonely little friend, right Debi?"

"How did you know, Grandma? Did you see that poor little girl from the orphanage, on the other side of the back fence?" Debi asked, as she slowly looked up at her grandmother's, loving face.

"Yes, I did. I couldn't help but notice her because she looked so much like our own little sunbeam. Her lovely red hair, though curly, and her freckles are very much like yours, Debi."

"Did you see the sunbeams in her hair, too?" asked the young girl as she tried to finish her supper.

"Yes, I certainly did," replied Grandma.

After supper, Grandpa and Chris went out to clean the fish they had caught that day. Debi again stood on the little stool by the kitchen sink beside her grandmother. With a dishtowel in her hand the little girl tried to wipe the dishes for her grandmother, but her mind was not on drying dishes. Finally Debi began to tell her grandmother all about the little girl from the other side of the fence.

"If someone could just fix her teeth, then the other children wouldn't make fun of her like they do," cried Debi. "And that lady was so mean to her when she pulled her away from the fence. I hope they didn't punish Vicki too hard," the little girl continued as she wiped the same plate over and over.

"When I say my prayers tonight, I'm going to ask Jesus to help her and to somehow fix her teeth. Grandma, they really do stick out."

"Yes, we really do need to pray for that little girl. Somehow I feel that God will hear and answer your prayers."

"Do you really think so, Grandma?" cried Debi. "I hope you are right. I feel so sorry for her."

The next day, after lunch, Chris and Debi's grandparents took the children back to their respective homes. Debi never saw the little girl, from across the fence again.

The cousins thanked their grandparents for the wonderful time they had and asked if they could come back again before the summer would be over. The grandparents assured the children that they could.

Back home at her house in the country, the little girl in pigtails, told her parents all about her new friend from the orphanage. She told her parents that the little girl never gets to go to church. For the next several days all Debi could think about was the girl across the fence from her grandparent's back yard.

Meanwhile Grandma had told Grandpa all about the little freckled girl from the orphanage. She told him how much she looked like their granddaughter, Debi. The grandparents decided they would go to the orphanage the next day and check on this lonely little girl. They wanted to see if there was any way possible that they could donate the money needed, to have Vicki's teeth fixed. If the girl needed braces, they would be willing to pay for them.

So the elderly couple went to the orphanage. They talked to the administrator there and told him how they came to find out about this unfortunate little girl. The man in charge agreed to let this elderly couple pay the necessary monies to have Vicki's teeth fixed. He could not believe that anyone would come and just offer to pay some child's dental bill. Especially for a child they have never really met.

The administrator seemed to be impressed with this elderly couple and asked them if they would like to see the child they offered to help. Grandfather had not yet seen Vicki and seemed eager to see her. The little girl was in the playroom. There was another room adjacent to the playroom that had dark windows in it. There, people could come in and view the orphaned children without them knowing they were being watched.

The sun shone through a window into the playroom. A ray of sunlight beamed on Vicki's curly red hair.

"Look," replied Grandfather, "there she is, a little sunbeam just like our own granddaughter! But she looks so sad. No one seems to be playing with her."

"Debi said children made fun of her because of her teeth and I guess she was right. Once she gets her braces and her teeth no longer protrude, perhaps it will go better for her," exclaimed Grandmother.

The administrator said he would make the necessary dental appointments for Vicki as soon as possible. He told the elderly couple that they could check on the little girl's progress anytime they wanted to. The man thanked Debi's grandparents for their concern for this little girl whom no one ever seemed to want. After watching the sad little girl for about twenty minutes, the grandparents left for home.

The elderly couple felt good about what they had done for this unfortunate, lonely child. She reminded them in so many ways of Debi. Later that night after they thought their granddaughter would be in bed, they called and talked to their son, Mr. Butler and his wife.

Mr. Butler answered the phone. His parents asked if their daughter-in-law could listen on their other phone. Then the elderly couple told their son and his wife that they had been to the orphanage that afternoon and saw this little girl who lived on the other side of the fence near their home. They said they had talked with the administrator and he agreed to let them pay to have braces put on Vicki's teeth.

Debi's father told his parents that they too, had been talking about this unfortunate child from the orphanage. Ever since their own daughter had told them about this sad little girl with freckles and red curly hair, they could not get her off their minds.

The grandparents said that is why they wanted to talk with them. Perhaps this other little sunbeam, that has no real home or parents, could be adopted.

The Butlers spoke up, saying they, too, had the same thoughts. They planned to check into that possibility the following day. In the meantime they were not to say anything about this to Debi. They did not want to build up her hopes, should they not be able to carry out their plan, for whatever reason.

The next day, Mr. and Mrs. Butler again took their little daughter to visit her grandparents. Little did Debi think she would be visiting them so quickly again, but like always she was delighted to go. Just maybe she thought she might be able to see her new friend from the orphanage. But then she thought, perhaps the little girl would be closely watched and would not be allowed to wander near the fence again.

Debi had no idea that her parents went to talk to the administrator from the orphanage. The Butlers expressed their desire to see the little girl with protruding teeth. They were taken into the room next to the playroom. There they could see this precious little child that until now no one wanted. Not having seen this girl before, they had no trouble picking her out from amongst the others because of the description Debi gave of her. Or could it be that it was because she again played all by herself, making it easier to find her?

"Just look at her!" replied Mrs. Butler. "She truly is another little sunbeam! Even with her protruding teeth there is something about that girl that makes me want to go to her and give her a big hug."

"You know, I feel the same way," Mr. Butler responded. "And to think this girl has never been wanted! No wonder she feels so sad and lonely. She has never even been taken to Sunday school. I would love to take her in my arms and tell her all about Jesus. One thing we know for sure, Jesus loves her, too."

"From the way you talk I gather that you are really seriously thinking of adopting this poor freckle faced girl with protruding teeth?" asked the administrator.

Mr. and Mrs. Butler looked at each other. They paused for a moment then together they said, "Yes, we are!"

"You see, Sir, we have a little girl of our own very much like this child. She has red hair and freckles also. Our daughter is a year older than this little one but I feel they would be very good for one another. They each need a sister and we would like to have another daughter," replied Mr. Butler as his wife agreed by nodding her head.

"Before any decision is finalized it is customary for prospective parents to spend a day with the child they wish to adopt," the administrator said.

"How about a week from Sunday?" spoke up Mr. Butler. "Since it is summer time, after church we could all go on a picnic. Then we could go to the zoo for a while. We can't spend too much time at the zoo because our own child is allergic to the animals. What do you think, Dear?" asked Mr. Butler as he looked at his wife who was all smiles.

"That would be just great!" she answered.

"Fine, then it is all set. A week from Sunday it will be. The girl will be ready to be picked up at 8:30 in the morning. Monday of next week Vicki gets her first braces put on. You will get to see her with them," stated the administrator. "It is very kind of your parents to do this for a child they hardly even know."

"Our own daughter has great faith in prayers. She has prayed many times for a brother or sister. Up until now those prayers have not been answered," said Mrs. Butler. "And now lately she has also been praying that somehow Jesus would fix Vicki's teeth. It seems like both of her prayers may now be answered. We have been praying for a child as well. Now we feel that God heard our prayers, when He brought these two girls, from opposite sides of the fence, together. They truly are God's little sunbeams."

"That is right, Sir," replied Debi's father. "Ever since our daughter met Vicki, she has been praying that someone would adopt the girl and fix her teeth. Her faith will really be strengthened next Sunday when she sees her little friend with braces on. We are not going to tell our daughter about this until that Sunday morning."

"The legal work and papers will be completed as quickly as possible," said the administrator of the orphanage. "It should be just a matter of a few days. It is possible that by the time you pick her up a week from Sunday she may be able to go home with you permanently. She will then become your daughter and responsibility.

Mr. and Mrs. Butler left the institution knowing in their hearts that they did the right thing. For years they trusted in the Lord and sought His guidance. They truly did as Proverbs 3: 5-6 says, "Trust in the Lord with all your heart; and lean not unto your own understanding. In all your ways acknowledge him, and He shall direct your paths." They both vowed to bring up the two girls in the way the Lord would have them to be taught. They promised to faithfully take them to church and instruct them in God's Holy Word. Mr. and Mrs. Butler and their parents had the hope of eternal life through the saving blood of God's son, Jesus. This is the hope they wished to instill in the two little girls God has now placed in their care.

Finally the day arrived that Mr. and Mrs. Butler had been waiting for. Mrs. Butler went upstairs in their big country home to awaken their daughter, Debi, for church. She found the little girl clutching her rag doll as she lay in bed. The sun was shining in through the window and onto her auburn red hair. Mrs. Butler bent down and kissed her little girl and said, "Good morning, Little Sunbeam."

Then Mrs. Butler looked at the empty bunk bed that Debi had been sharing with her dolls and stuffed animals. In her mind she envisioned another little girl, very similar to her own, sharing this room with Debi. She still could not believe all this was happening. "Isn't God wonderful," she thought as she looked at her daughter who by now had awakened.

"And just what are you thinking about, my little sunbeam?" Mrs. Butler asked her daughter as they both sat on the edge of the bottom bunk bed.

"It's Vicki. I just can't forget her, Mommy," was Debi's reply. "How I wish she could go to Sunday school with me, just once."

"My dear child," said Mrs. Butler as she took her precious daughter in her arms, "we have a surprise for you. Jesus has heard your prayers. Today your friend, Vicki, will be going to Sunday school with you. Breakfast is soon ready, so hurry now and prepare for church. We have a big day planned for all of us. We will go pick up Vicki and take her to church with us, that is if you want us to."

The little girl could hardly believe what she was hearing. She replied, "Do I want to? Oh, Mommy, I want that more than anything in the whole wide world! I'll even give her the doll Grandma gave to me. Grandma won't care, will she?" Debi said as she flung her freckled arms around her mother. Then she cried, "Oh, Mommy, I love you so much!"

Mrs. Butler began to brush her daughter's hair and said, "I love you, too, my little sunbeam. It won't be necessary to give Vicki your doll. You will find out why later. We better hurry now, because we will be leaving early to go pick up your little friend."

Debi was so excited she could hardly eat her breakfast. The child and her parents climbed into the family car and started out for the day's activities. Debi sat in the back seat and began singing, "Jesus Wants Me for a Sunbeam."

The Butlers arrived at the orphanage and all three went inside to pick up the girl from the other side of the fence. Vicki had been told she would be spending the day with some people but had not been told it would be the Butler family. When the little freckle faced orphan, with braces on her teeth, was brought into the reception room, her eyes opened wide as she saw Debi. Up until now, she had not seen her little friend since they had talked together behind Debi's grandparent's house with the fence between them. Vicki ran straight to Debi with her fluffy red curls bouncing about her head. She threw her little freckled arms around her new friend and with tears in her green eyes said, "I n-never thought I would see you again! D-do I really get to g-go away with you today? Is this your d-daddy and mommy? They look so n-nice!"

"Yes," spoke Mr. Butler, "you get to go with us today. And you look very nice, also."

Just then Debi stepped back and looked at her new friend. Suddenly she cried, "Look, Daddy and Mommy, God answered another prayer. Someone put braces on Vicki's teeth!"

"That is right. Your grandparents are going to have Vicki's teeth fixed with braces," replied Mr. Butler. "Come along now, girls or we will be late for Sunday school."

"D-did you say Sunday school? Y-you mean I get to go to S-Sunday school for once?" cried Vicki. "Oh, I hope this day n-never ends!"

The grandparents were waiting at church for their son's family. Vicki was introduced to them and then she threw her little arms around them and thanked them for the braces on her teeth. Everyone fell in love with this charming curly headed, freckled girl. They could not get over the fact that the two little girls looked so much alike. Some wondered if they might even be related, but of course they were not.

After church, Debi, her parents, grandparents and their little guest from the orphanage all went to the zoo. There they had their picnic lunch. The grandparents then gave Vicki her very own doll. It was just like the one that they had given their own granddaughter, the day she met her little friend from across the fence.

Suddenly Vicki jumped up into the grandfather's arms and threw her freckled arms around his neck. She said with tears in her eyes, "I-wish you were my grandpa. I never had any g-grandparents. If I ever do, I h-hope they are just like you and Debi's grandma. T-thank you for fixing my teeth. T-thank you for the doll." The youngster looked down at Debi and continued saying, "I-I'm going to name her Debi. When I go b-back to the orphanage, the doll will make me think of D-Debi and all of you. I will talk to my dolly and pretend that I-I am talking to Debi, then I won't b-be so lonesome. Oh thank you, thank you!" Then the little girl brushed the curls from her face and planted a big kiss on the grandfather's cheek.

Grandpa, with tears in his eyes, did not know what to say. Finally he looked at the little one still in his arms and said, "You are very special to us. We love you and Jesus loves you, too. You are a precious sunbeam, just like our Debi." Then Grandfather gently stroked her hair as the sun glisten on the soft curls around her freckled face.

Nearby were two park benches. Debi's father spoke up and said, "Come over here everyone. Mother and I have something to tell you."

The elderly grandparents and Debi's mother sat on one bench. Facing them on the other bench sat Mr. Butler with his daughter, Debi, on one knee and Vicki on the other. His big strong arms were around the girls. He looked at his daughter, then at the little girl from the orphanage, as he fought to hold back the tears.

Finally he said, "Girls, we have been praying for a long time that God would give us another child. Until now we did not know if it would ever happen. And now, in a most unique way, God has brought you two precious little sunbeams together. Mother and I decided not to keep you girls separated any longer." He took his big handkerchief out from his pocket and wiped his eyes. Then he continued saying, "Vicki, we want to adopt you and have you for our very own daughter. Debi, you will have a new sister and we will all be one happy family. What do you say, girls? Is this all right with the two of you?"

Almost spontaneously the two girls each threw their freckled arms around Mr. Butler and said together, "Yes! That means we will be sisters!"

Then Vicki, with tears streaming from her happy face cried, "D-Debi was right. There really is a J-Jesus! She told me that Jesus loves me and if I-I prayed to Him and asked for a r-real mommy and daddy He would give them to me. And n-now I'll have them for r-real! I-I want to love this J-Jesus I heard about in S-Sunday School today, forever! A-and I'm going to l-love you forever too, --D-Daddy!" cried Vicki as she flung her tender arms tightly around Mr. Butler's neck.

With tears in her eyes, Mrs. Butler walked over to the bench where her husband sat with the two girls. Then she took Vicki in her arms and said, "Yes, dear child, I too, love you very much and want you to be our daughter. Debi and you will be sisters forever and you will always be a part of our family from now on, if you will have us."

"I-I can't believe that someone r-really wants to adopt me. F-Finally I will have a real mommy and daddy! O-oh I love you s-so much---Mommy," said the little girl as she hung onto Mrs. Butler, giving her the biggest hug and kisses the little girl could possibly give.

Then the curly headed child climbed onto the laps of the elderly grandparents. With tears still in her sparkling green eyes, she clutched her doll and cried, "N-now I finally have a grandpa and a grandma. Oh, G-Grandpa, I love you," and she planted another big kiss on his cheek. Leaning over to Grandma she said, "Oh, G-Grandma, I love you, too. T-thank you for the b-beautiful doll. When I come to v-visit you at your house now, I'll be on the right side of the f-fence, won't I? And I will n-never have to g-go back to that, other p-place!" The little girl then planted a big kiss on the grandmother's cheek.

At last the little girl stood in front of her new sister, Debi. She took a hold of both of her hands and said, "D-Debi, you will be the best s-sister I could ever have and I-I'll try to be the best s-sister you could ever want. I-I just want us to be sisters forever!"

The two girls with hands clasped so tightly together that Vicki's doll fell to the ground, began jumping around in circles, their red hair bouncing as they jumped. Each one cried, "I have a sister, I finally have a sister!"

Suddenly Vicki stopped and looked at her doll on the sidewalk. She said, "N-now I won't have to talk to my d-doll and think it is you, Debi. I can talk to y-you forever. O-oh, I-I am so h-happy!"

Debi then went to her parents and threw her loving arms around them saying, "Thank you, Daddy and Mommy for my new sister, I love you so much and I love my new sister, too! This is the best present I could ever want!"

"Don't thank us," replied Father. "Thank Jesus. We love you too, Debi, because we wanted you and you were born to us as a special gift from God." Then looking at the curly headed girl in dental braces, he said, "We love you too, Vicki, because we wanted you also and chose you as a special added gift from God."

Then Grandfather stood up and said, "Everyone please stand up and let us form a circle, holding hands together."

As they did so, Grandfather led the family in a prayer of thanksgiving right there outside on the picnic grounds. He thanked God for making their family complete. When he had finished praying the sun seemed to shine down extra bright on top of the two happy little girls.

Debi said, "Look at Vicki. There are sunbeams all over her curly hair."

Then Vicki spoke up saying, "T-they are on your p-pigtails, too. Y-your hair is full of s-sunbeams. And I f-feel like my whole insides are f-full of sunbeams. I'm so h-happy!"

The two girls held hands once again and both crawled up on a big swing that hung from a nearby tree. Soon they were both singing, "Jesus wants me for a Sunbeam, to shine for Him each day." Their little feet were going back and forth, beneath the swing, as if to keep in rhythm with the song they were singing.

To the Butlers and the grandparents, these two charming girls in all their similarities, truly were precious sunbeams. God brought into their lives, one through natural birth and one through adoption. Thanks be to God their family was now complete. As time went on, Vicki's teeth no longer protruded and even her stuttering all but ceased, just because someone loved and cared for her.

Dear friend, God loves and cares for you and wants to adopt you into His family of believers. You can be His child if you give your heart and life over to Him and accept Him into your heart. He loves you and sent His Son, Jesus, who gave His life for you so that you could have the hope of eternal life. Then you can become a brother or sister to Jesus and be adopted into the family of God.

The Butlers chose little Vicki through adoption to be their daughter and a sister to Debi. God wants to adopt you, too, to be His child and a brother or sister to His Son Jesus. In Ephesians chapter one it says, "He has chosen us in Him before the foundation of the world, that we should be holy and without blame before Him in love, having predestined us to adoption as sons by Jesus Christ to Himself, according to the good pleasure of His will." So, you see He does want to adopt us.

Friend, why not give Jesus your heart today? You never need to be, on the other side of the fence, away from God. Stay close to Him and you will always be on the right side.

POOR RICH GIRLS

Julie, age fifteen, lived with her parents, Mr. and Mr. Noble, just a few miles from the big city of Springfield. The Nobles were owners of a large sod farm and were quite well to do. They sold their green grassy sod to customers who wanted instant grass around their homes or place of business. Mr. Noble had an irrigation system to help water his sod fields, but nothing took the place of water like the rains from heaven.

Speaking of heaven, the Nobles didn't really believe in a heaven or a hell, but thought when your life on earth ended there was nothing more to it, no life after death. In other words they did not believe in the Holy Scriptures.

Julie went to church with her grandmother occasionally for Easter or Christmas festivities. Other than that her Sundays were spent at home watching TV while her parents slept in. Anything that Julie wanted, Julie received. Mrs. Noble worked in an office as a secretary in Springfield and her job paid well, so anytime Julie wanted something, her mother bought it for her. But the thing Julie wanted most was to be loved. Julie had a beautiful white cat she called Snowball, and it was to Snowball that she would tell all of her troubles, since her parents were often too busy to listen to her and spend time with her.

You would think that a young girl who had the best clothes and all the material things she ever wanted would be happy, but she wasn't. Julie's parents made her wear the very best clothes to school. To her classmates it appeared that Julie seemed to think she was richer and better than the rest of them. Because of this, they often snubbed and rejected her, thus causing her to withdraw from the rest of the students.

It was to Julie's kitten, Snowball, that this lonely girl would often confide at night in the quietness of her bedroom. Julie could talk to and love Snowball and not feel rejected by this furry friend. Snowball would at least listen to her talk, which was more than she could say for her parents. They always appeared to be too busy to take time out for their daughter.

About four miles away from the Noble farm, Kayla Kolsen, also fifteen lived with her parents and two brothers. The Kolsens were God-fearing people. They, too, lived on a farm, consisting of a few cows and some chickens, which supplied the family with milk, eggs and meat. Along with that they raised tomatoes. At harvest time the whole family could be seen in the fields picking the plump red tomatoes. They also raised some grain and hay to help feed what little livestock they had.

About five years ago the Kolsen's barn burned down during an electrical storm and much of their farming machinery was destroyed. Mrs. Kolsen, home alone at the time the fire broke out, ran into the barn to try to save the farm truck her husband had just purchased. She got the truck out just before the barn roof collapsed. In doing so, her legs were badly burned and much medical treatment was needed in the years to come to help save her legs. The insurance paid only about half of their loss and the Kolsens had been struggling financially ever since.

Kayla, coming from a financially strapped home, often wondered what it would be like to have just a little of what Julie had. Kayla did not have the very latest style in clothing. In fact, her mother, who did not work outside of the home because of her bad burns, made many of Kayla's school outfits. Mrs. Kolsen, was a very good seamstress, and she also did some sewing for other people to help supplement their income.

The girls at school never made fun of Kayla's clothing because she always looked nice no matter what she wore. When Kayla tried to be friends with Julie, then the other girls in their class would call them the 'poor rich twosome.' For that reason Kayla often ignored Julie so she could be with the other girls.

Kayla's mother was aware of Julie's situation and asked her daughter to invite Julie to go to church with them. Kayla was afraid everyone would make fun of Julie if she brought her to church, because if she dressed so fancy just to go to school what would the girl wear to church?

The Bible says to "love one another" and Kayla knew this, but it seemed so hard for her to get close to Julie. And Julie, who wanted so to be able to reach out to Kayla and be like her, had a hard time showing love to Kayla or anyone else, perhaps because the girl's parents showed very little love to her. They just cared more or less for themselves. Julie often wished she would be poor and loved like Kayla.

One Sunday morning in Sunday school, Kayla's teacher suggested that the next Sunday everyone should bring someone who didn't attend church anywhere on a regular basis. Right away Kayla thought of Julie, but she did not really want to invite her. Perhaps someone else would ask her to go with him or her. But who would? There were only two others in her Sunday school class that were in her grade in school, and one of them was a boy.

It wasn't until Friday of the following week that Kayla finally asked Julie if she would like to go to church with her family on Sunday. Julie jumped at the opportunity and willingly accepted the invitation. It was then that she told Kayla how much she had always envied her. Julie told her she would much rather be a poor girl, who is loved, with homemade clothes, than a rich girl who has everything but love. Julie also told Kayla that she could see the love that radiated in her two older brothers and how well they got along with everyone. The two boys, ages seventeen and eighteen, had given their hearts to Jesus recently and had been baptized. Kayla was seriously thinking about doing the same thing.

That night at the supper table, Kayla told her parents that she had invited Julie to go to church on Sunday and how eager the girl appeared to go with them. She also told them that Julie said she would rather be poor like herself than rich, because she wasn't happy and didn't have many friends like Kayla had. Mr. Kolsen said the family should pray for Julie so she would be receptive to what would be said in church on Sunday.

Sunday morning came and the Kolsen family drove up the lane to the Noble farmhouse in their old station wagon. Kayla walked up onto the front porch of the big country house. For a moment she almost wished she could live in a home as pretty as this. She knocked on the door and stood gazing at the house in front of her. To Kayla it almost appeared to be some sort of a mansion. She thought of Julie and how lucky she must be to live in a place like this. But Julie was not happy here in this lovely place.

Mr. Noble came to the door with Julie. The man let Kayla know that he was not very happy to let his daughter go with the Kolsen family to church. He did not care to have anyone see his daughter riding around in the Kolsen's old car! But Mrs. Noble said Julie could go just so the TV would be off. Then she could get caught up on her sleep. Mr. Noble said Julie could go today, but he wouldn't make any promises for future Sundays. Julie wondered why her dad even cared if she went or not. He never seemed to care about anything else she ever did.

Surprisingly enough, Julie did not come in a fancy dress but somehow was able to get out of the house in more casual attire; yet it was very fitting for Sunday school. She appeared to be all smiles as she climbed into the old car beside Kayla.

The Sunday school teacher talked on the Book of Revelation and warned the teenagers that the Rapture to heaven of all true believers could be very soon. A true believer is one who has given his heart and life over to Jesus Christ and lives completely for Him. The Bible says, "You must repent of your sin and be born again," if you want to go to heaven when you die. Otherwise you will spend eternity in hell and eternity is forever and ever. This is the commitment that Kayla's brothers recently made. They, along with their parents, now also had this hope of eternal life.

Julie had never heard anything like this before, especially about life after death, and she listened very attentively. After Sunday school, the two girls went into the sanctuary to the church service. There, once again Julie heard the Word of God preached like she never knew before. She heard that someone now loves her more than her parents love her, and that someone is Jesus. She wanted to know more about this man.

As the Kolsens took Julie home from church she thanked them for taking her. She told them she would like to go again next Sunday, but someone would have to take her because her parents would never go with her. For once Kayla really felt compassionate towards the rich girl and invited her to go with them again the following Sunday.

The following week in school, the two girls were often seen together. They were again labeled as the 'poor rich girls.' Somehow Kayla did not mind, as she and Julie were becoming good friends. Kayla looked past Julie's fancy clothes and saw the heart of a girl who needed a friend. She also had been searching in her own heart for something that had been missing. She kept thinking about what her Sunday school teacher had said last Sunday. He said, "Where would you spend eternity if you died tonight?" This really made Kayla think, and Julie could not forget it either.

When Julie asked her parents why they never went to church, they said it was old fashioned. They told their daughter they had no time for such ridiculous teachings, but if she wanted to go to church they guessed it would be okay. It just wasn't for them.

In the quietness of her bedroom, Julie told her kitten, Snowball, that she finally had a new friend at school. Kayla, the girl she always wanted to be close to, had at last become her best friend. Snowball seemed to understand as she purred as Julie stroked her soft white, fluffy fur.

Mr. Noble had a big order for his grassy sod before the cold weather set in, and hoped it would rain at the right time so the grass would be extra thick and green. And a few miles away, the Kolsen family prayed for warm, sunshiny weather so their tomato crop would ripen. The rains could burst the tomatoes and cause them to rot if the fields became too wet. So each family had their special needs and wishes.

Julie and Kayla had at last become the best of friends. The rich girl with the best of clothes and the poor girl with her homemade outfits were quite a twosome. The other classmates were finally beginning to like Julie as well. They saw that behind this lonely girl was someone very much like them.

Kayla was convicted to give her heart and life over to her Creator, Jesus Christ, and told Julie she didn't want to risk one more day without Jesus in her heart. She did not want to take the chance of not going to heaven should something happen to her before taking this most important step.

Julie had now gone to Sunday school and church enough to know that she, too, should do the same thing. She had learned at Kayla's church that after the Rapture of the true believers, those left behind on earth would be facing very perilous times. If they did not worship the coming Anti-Christ, who would be the evil ruler once the true Christians are taken away, they might very well have to give up their lives in order to go to heaven. This Anti-Christ would make everyone take a mark on their hand or forehead in order to be able to buy or sell anything. Those who did not take this mark could not buy or sell anything and would undoubtedly lose their lives.

Neither Kayla nor Julie wanted any part of this life after the Rapture during the terrible tribulation. So they both decided to give their hearts and lives over to Jesus.

Mr. and Mrs. Noble began to see a change in their daughter's life. They couldn't believe how happy she now seemed to be. They were almost puzzled as to how Julie's life could change so quickly. They did not want to admit or believe that they, too, needed this so-called religion in their own lives as well. Julie read her new Bible often and began to pray for her parents that they could see the error of their way of living and would go to church with her.

The Kolsens also saw a change in their daughter. Kayla seemed to be so happy and bubbly at home and at school. Her face radiated the love she now had for her Lord and Savior. The friends at school could see the change in her life and in Julie's as well.

By now Julie's father was very concerned for his sod fields, because if it didn't rain soon he would lose the grass he had contracted to sell. He told his daughter if the God she was now praying to seemed as real as she thought He was, then she better start praying for rain and pray hard. If it didn't rain soon, then he would know for sure that this God Julie now prayed to was not for real.

A few miles away Kayla, her parents, and brothers were all praying that the weather would continue to be favorable so they could harvest a good tomato crop. They needed lots of sunshine now, but they prayed that God's will would be done and not their will.

We know that God answers prayers in the way that is best for us, and that it rains on the just and the unjust. We do not always understand the way God answers prayers. He may say yes, no or wait awhile to our petitions.

The hard, soaking rains did come, just the kind of rain Mr. Noble wanted for his sod fields. But a few miles away fields of tomatoes had begun to ripen. The rains beat the plants to the ground, causing the red fruit to burst open. Then the tomatoes could rot if they stayed wet on the ground too long. And that is what happened, the Kolsens lost most of their tomatoes and income for the season.

Kayla wondered why God allowed this to happen. They were planning to buy a different car and fix up their house a bit with the money from the tomato harvest. Their old station wagon seemed to be on its last leg. Mr. Kolsen said God makes no mistakes and that "all things work together for good to them that love the Lord." Somehow they would make the old car last another year. Kayla thought of the nice car that Julie's parents had and thought it wasn't fair that the Nobles had so much and her family had so little. But then she knew God was in control and she dared not be envious. After all she had parents who loved her and went with her to church. That meant more to her than Julie's fancy home and car.

Julie's parents promised her that if she prayed and it rained so that their grassy fields would be saved, they would go to church with her the next Sunday. They kept their word! Kayla couldn't believe her ears when Julie told her not to pick her up for church because her parents were going to take her. The Kolsen family prayed that Mr. and Mrs. Noble would be receptive to the Word of God as it would be preached the following Sunday.

The Kolsen's prayers were being answered, not for a tomato harvest but for a spiritual harvest. The Nobles were very receptive to the Word of God and realized they, too, had been living in sin. So now instead of sleeping in every Sunday morning, Julie's parents were actually taking her to church and loving every minute of it. In fact they, too, now made a commitment of repentance and gave their hearts and lives over to Jesus.

Even Snowball seemed to be more content than before. The soft, furry white kitten purred as Julie told her pet how happy she now was. Jesus had come into her parents' lives as well as her own life and their house had at last become one happy household.

Mr. Kolsen knew now why his prayer was not answered for sunshine on his tomatoes. It was because God wanted His Son to shine in the hearts of the Nobles. Because of the prayers and faith of their daughter, Julie, whom they had taken to church, they, too, came to know Christ as their personal Savior. And Julie knew if it had not been for Kayla that she would not have gone to church and heard the true Word of God spoken, so that she and her parents could now have this hope of Eternal life after death. How thankful she was for God's love, and now her parents were showing her love like she never had before.

Mr. Noble had planned to trade their nice car in on a new one this year whether his sod field prospered or not. He also saw the need of his daughter's friend, Kayla, and her family for the use of a different car. Mr. Noble seemed to be a different man now. He wanted to give his present car, which was much newer than the Kolsen's old car, to them. It was in appreciation for all they had done for their daughter and for them as well. If it hadn't been for the Kolsen family taking Julie to church, they perhaps never would have gone either and would not have found their Salvation in Jesus. Giving their car to the Kolsens was the least the Nobles could do for them.

At first Mr. Kolsen did not want to accept the gift of this car to their family, but then he thought how God works in miraculous ways. God allowed his tomato crop to be lost so that two more souls could be saved and added to the Kingdom of Heaven, so he humbly accepted the car. He knew that these dear souls were worth more than all the tomatoes in the world.

Julie and Kayla no longer envied one another but had truly become the best of friends. Their classmates no longer made fun of them, and they became loved by all. Instead of being poor, rich girls in material things, they were now both spiritually rich. It was because they had the love of God in their hearts. They had the hope of having Eternal Life after death in heaven one day to be forever with their Lord and Savior, Jesus Christ.

So, you see, you never know how God answers prayers. He works in ways we often don't understand, but we need to have faith to believe that "all things work together for good to them that love the Lord." And we, like the Noble family, can be rich and still be poor Spiritually, or like the Kolsen family we can be poor and still be very rich Spiritually. Our prayer for you, dear reader is that you will become Spiritually rich.

LIFE'S RAILROAD TO HEAVEN

It was not an easy life for Margie Birkley. She had been born in 1920 to a young couple who faced a lot of hardships financially. Two years later a little brother joined the struggling family. Margie can remember hearing her father say that he should never have gotten married. Margie and her little brother felt they were somewhat to blame for the problems their parents were having.

As a young girl she would often listen to the click, clack of the old train and steam engine that came through her town. She would wonder where it might be going and where it came from. Thoughts of running away on the train often entered her mind.

Then the Great Depression hit. In 1930 when Margie turned ten years old, her parents took her and her brother, Cory, age eight, to an orphanage and left them there. The children never saw their parents again. It was very hard for Margie and Cory, but they made the best of their situation. The separation from their parents brought the children closer to each other. God was looking over their lives and had a plan for each of them that they were not aware of. For Margie it would be far from pleasant. They were only in the orphanage about a year when they were separated and put in foster homes apart from each other. Later the two children were adopted separately; by families who had taken them into their respective homes.

Margie and Cory saw each other only once after that, when Margie was about thirteen years old. Ever since Margie was a baby she seemed sickly and frail. In time she grew up to be a lovely young lady in spite of her illness. Margie met and fell in love with a young man who seemed to be nice on the outside and could put on a good front. Inside he was a selfish, miserable person who liked to drink and occasionally would get drunk. Margie found this out only too late. After they were married about five years, her husband left her with the two small children, Mindi, age four, and Tommy, age two. Margie knew that at times history seemed to repeat itself, but why did it almost have to happen to her own children as it happened to her when she was but a child? Determined to keep her children, Margie vowed she would never give them up! Often she thought of her parents and especially her brother, Cory, and wondered whatever happened to them. But now she was resigned to the fact that she might never see them again and would devote all of her attention to her beloved children.

Margie got a job in a grocery store during the day so she would be home in the evening with Mindi and Tommy. They began attending a little Bible Believing Church near their apartment. For the first time in her life Margie found a true friend she could depend on and one that loved her as no one else ever had. That friend was Jesus. Her children loved to go to Sunday school also and to hear stories about this new friend, Jesus.

The illness that Margie had when she was younger seemed to be coming back. It was getting harder all the time for her to go to work, but she put her trust and faith in her new found friend, Jesus Christ. Somehow she felt that He would help her through the days ahead. Margie often told her children that life resembled a mountain railroad, going up and down over bumpy tracks and sometimes through dark tunnels. But there always seems to be a light, no matter how dim or bright, at the end of each tunnel.

Margie was getting so weak and tired that she had to quit her job. She spent much time reading the Bible to herself and to her children. She prayed with them that the railroad they would be traveling on in their lifetime would be smooth and not bumpy like hers has been. If they would just put their trust in Jesus, He would take them on Life's Railway to heaven some day. All they needed to do was to accept God's plan of Salvation into their hearts when God calls them to do so. Then they would be given a one-way ticket to Heaven.

Margie could feel that her time on earth was getting shorter. Soon she would pass through the dark tunnel of death in this life only to wake up to the wonderful light of her heavenly home. Margie knew she would be forever with her dearest and closest friend, Jesus. He had given His life for her so that she could have the Blessed Hope of Eternal Life now that she had committed her life to Him.

Margie made arrangements with a fine Christian couple, at the church where they attended, to take care of her children when she would no longer be able to do so. She sat down with her children, Mindi and Tommy, and explained to them the situation that soon might be at hand. Margie gave

Mindi the locket she once wore as a little girl. It had a small picture of her inside of it. To Tommy she gave a small framed picture of herself and her brother, Cory, taken just after they went to live at the orphanage. They were about the age then that her two children were now, with Mindi being nine and Tommy seven. Margie told her children that they would soon be living with their friends from church, the Walkers, because she had become too ill to care for them. She would very soon be taking her final ride on the Railroad to Heaven.

Mindi and Tommy were very sad indeed and didn't want to lose their mommy. They asked her if they could go on the train with her because they wanted to go where she was going. Their mother said that when the right time comes for Jesus to call them home to heaven then and only then could they come and be with her. They had to be good and live fully for Jesus in order to go to heaven. Margie knew her children would go to heaven in their tender years if something happened to them now. But she also had to prepare them for the years ahead, as they continued down their Railroad of Life. She hoped they would follow on the tracks of Jesus, as she had.

Then the day came when Margie left this earth with its troubles and trials and went to her Eternal Home to forever be with her Lord and Savior, Jesus Christ.

Mindi and Tommy, now orphaned like their mother had been when she was but a young girl, took their few belongings and went to live with Mr. and Mrs. Walker. The Walkers were good to the children and the children liked them as well, but they missed their mother so very much.

Two weeks after their mother died, Mindi told Tommy they were going to go to their mommy. She told her brother that if their mommy went away on the Railroad to Heaven that they could get on the train and go find her. Tommy liked the idea and agreed to go with his sister.

So one morning before school they packed as much as they could in their school bags. After school, instead of going home to Mr. and Mrs. Walker, they would walk to the train station several blocks away from where they now lived. Mindi had it all figured out. Mommy had told them that to go on Life's Railway to Heaven all you need is a one-way ticket, because when you get to heaven you never come back. Mommy had told Mindi that the ticket to heaven was free, because Jesus paid for it when He died on the cross for their sins. Just in case the people at the train station wouldn't believe her story, she took with her enough money to buy two tickets, one for her and one for Tommy.

After school Tommy waited for his sister, as planned. The two of them made it to the train station just in time. Mindi asked for two tickets to the other side of the nearest mountain, for Heaven must be on the other side. They purchased their tickets and went aboard the train. Mindi had packed a little extra lunch in each of their school bags so they could eat it if they became hungry on the train before they arrived at their destination. They had no idea how long it would take to get to Heaven. But if they would go to sleep like their mommy did, perhaps they would wake up in heaven also like their mother said she would do when she slipped into her final earthly sleep.

After about thirty minutes on the train, the conductor came by and asked each one for their ticket. Mindi gave their tickets to the conductor and he asked where they were going. With tears in her eyes Mindi told the man that she and her brother were going to take the train over the rough tracks and mountain-side that their mommy said would be on the train. It should take them to heaven to be with their mommy who went there on Heaven's Railway two weeks ago. The conductor asked where their daddy or grandparents were and the children said they didn't have any relatives anymore. By this time the people seated around them had heard their story and they, as well as the conductor, also had tears in their eyes.

Back at the home of Mr. and Mrs. Walker, every one became very concerned for the whereabouts of the children who never came home from school. A search had begun to find them, but little did they think to check the train station.

The conductor noticed the golden locket Mindi wore around her neck. Thinking that perhaps there just might be some picture or identification inside, the man asked Mindi if she would show him what was inside her locket. Mindi, who hoped that she could trust the kindly conductor, showed him the locket that had a picture of her mother inside of it. Her mother, the late Margie Birkley Thomas, was about eleven years old when the picture was taken.

Then Tommy spoke up and said he had a picture to show also, and taking out the small, framed picture from his school bag, he, too, showed his picture to the now very interested and concerned conductor.

The man could not believe his eyes when he saw Tommy's picture and asked if there was anything written on the back. Tommy didn't know but told the conductor he could look and see. Sure enough on the back of the picture, that he had already recognized, was the words, Margie and Cory. It was the same picture he had at home that was taken of him and his sister soon after they went to live in the orphanage.

In his mind the conductor was beginning to put together one more piece of the puzzle of his life. Could it really be possible that the girl in these two pictures was really his long lost sister? The children told him the girl in the picture was their mommy when she was little like they were now. The boy was her brother whom she had so missed but never knew what had become of him.

The conductor, Cory Birkley, sat down in the seat between the two children, hugged them and wept, with the other passengers around them weeping as well. Then he told Mindi and Tommy that he was Cory, the little boy in Tommy's picture, and since he was their mother's brother that would make him their uncle. Mindi told him all about their mommy and how hard she had worked and how sick she was. And Tommy said he couldn't remember ever having a daddy. But Mommy had told them that he wasn't a kind, loving man and he had left them when they were quite small.

Cory, the conductor, told the children to stay right there, that he had an errand to attend to, as the train was about to make a scheduled short stop. Then he would be right back.

Tommy asked Mindi if she thought this man, who said he was their uncle, would take them to heaven to see their mommy or perhaps take them back to

Mr. and Mrs. Walker. Mindi said not to worry because Jesus would take care of them wherever they went since they were on Heaven's Railroad.

When Cory returned to the children he told them that the three of them would be getting off at the next train stop. Right away Tommy hoped they soon would be in heaven to be with their mommy, but Mindi was beginning to think otherwise. She hoped she could trust this new friend who said he was their uncle and wondered if he really was. The way he had cried when he saw the pictures of their mother, Mindi knew he must be their mommy's brother. But what was he going to do with the children now, she wondered?

The next train stop, in forty-five minutes, would be in a town about an hour's drive from where conductor Cory lived. He had sent a message to his dear wife, Miriam, at the last train stop, asking her to meet him at the next train station as soon as she could. He told her to bring the little picture he had at home of his sister Margie and himself, when they were children. Cory told Miriam all about the two children. He was positive they belonged to his late sister, and that they were no doubt his niece and nephew.

Meanwhile Miriam notified the police and the Walkers that the children were found and were safe and unharmed. They were riding on the train, hoping to find their mommy, who had gone to heaven.

Conductor Cory took the children to the dining car and bought them something to eat. By now they were somewhat frightened as to what would become of them, and they were getting tired as well.

When the train stopped at the next town, Cory and the two children stepped off of the train. The three of them waited at the station for about a half an hour for Andy's wife, Miriam, to get there. While they were waiting, Andy placed a long distance phone call to the Walkers and assured them that the children were okay. The children also got to talk briefly with them. Andy had told the Walkers that since he was the closest relative to the children he would like to take them home to live with him and his wife.

As soon as he hung up the phone, Miriam arrived with a big smile and a picture in her hand. The children recognized it as being the same as the one Tommy had in his school bag. Now they knew for sure that conductor Andy was indeed their uncle. Miriam fell in love with Mindi and Tommy at once, and the children liked her, too.

As they drove out to the Birkley farm, Cory told the children that they, too, went to church every Sunday. He said they were are all on Life's Railroad, traveling to heaven, some just get there before others. Then Conductor Cory told the children that for years he and Miriam had been praying that God might give them children, but so far it wasn't to be. Now he felt God had heard and answered their prayers by putting the children on the train and leading them to him and his wife so they could take care of them as their own mother would want them to be cared for.

Cory still couldn't believe that after all these years as conductor on this train, he had been going through the very town where his sister, Margie, was living and didn't even know it. But now he was going to make it up to her the best he could. He planned to apply for legal adoption papers for Mindi and Tommy, the niece and nephew he never knew he had.

As for Mindi and Tommy, since they found out they couldn't go to their mommy after all, they were happy and content to become the children of their Uncle Cory and Miriam. They were thankful that Jesus had given them a real home and a new mommy and daddy who loved them. Now they wouldn't have to go live in an orphanage. They would continue to love Jesus and go to church every Sunday so they could someday, after all, go on Life's Railroad to Heaven to see their mommy once again.

STRANGER OF THE ROAD

Adversities would soon change the life of a young woman, changes that would affect the rest of her life. Keith and Susan King both raised in the same community in northern Indiana moved to Nashville, Tennessee soon after they were married. Keith had been offered a fantastic opportunity in a thriving business and decided to take his new bride there to live. They loved Nashville, as it lay nestled among the beautiful hills of Tennessee.

They attended a small church of Christian believers. Since they had no relatives close by, they felt secure with their fellowship. Keith and Susan had both become Christians, giving their hearts over to Christ, during their teenage years. They relied on God's strength and guidance in their walk of life.

Two years after their marriage, God blessed them with a little girl. They named this precious bundle from heaven, Heidi. Then three years later they were again blessed with a precious baby. This time a little boy, by the name of Erick, came to live with the King family.

Life seemed to be going well with this All-American family. Then one day Keith was diagnosed with the dreaded disease of leukemia. He fought very hard to combat this illness but his strength grew weaker and weaker.

The Bible says that, "All things work together for good to them that love the Lord." Susan wondered why this had to happen to them. They truly loved the Lord, and knew that He made no mistakes. They would continue to serve and trust Him no matter what.

Finally, Keith's weak body gave in to his illness and Jesus took him to his eternal home in heaven. Susan's loss was now heaven's gain. She knew that someday she would see him again, because of the promises in God's Holy Word. The Bible assures us that if we are truly a born again child of God, we will go to heaven when our journey on earth is over.

The Scriptures in the Bible that gave Susan that hope are found in I Thessalonians chapter four. In verses thirteen through eighteen it reads: "But I would not have you to be ignorant, brethren, concerning those who have fallen asleep, lest you sorrow as others who have no hope. For if we believe that Jesus died and rose again, even so God will bring with Him those who sleep in Jesus.

"For this we say to you by the word of the Lord, that we who are alive and remain until the coming of the Lord will by no means precede those who are asleep. For the Lord himself shall descend from heaven with a shout, with the voice of the archangel, and with the trumpet of God. And the dead in Christ shall rise first. Then we who are alive and remain shall be caught up together with them in the clouds to meet the Lord in the air. And so shall we ever be with the Lord. Therefore comfort one another with these words."

Susan, confident that Keith had given his heart to the Lord several years ago, knew she would see him again in the heavenly clouds one day. Still, she and the children missed him so very much. Susan wondered why God took him home so soon when they had so much going for them together as a family. Susan knew she should not doubt God because He was in control. He knew and did what was best for them, even though she did not always understand His ways.

Keith had left his family with a good life insurance policy. Financially, Susan and the children had nothing to worry about. But how they missed their husband and father! Money would never be able to replace their loved one.

Susan continued to stay in Nashville for the next year and relied on the mental support of her church friends. She didn't know what she would have done without them. They were a great help and comfort to her since all of her family lived out of state. Heidi and Erick tried their best to adjust to life without a father. The young boy especially missed his daddy.

One day Susan told her children they were going to drive up to northern Indiana to visit their grandparents and cousins. If she could find a job and a house, she might consider moving her little family there. The children were delighted to think of living close to their grandparents.

Indeed, they would miss beautiful Tennessee but Susan felt like she had to start a new life over again for the children's sake. Being closer to her parents would help fill some of her lonely hours. She prayed that God would direct her to make the right decisions.

Mrs. King packed enough clothing for two weeks and started out on the Interstate Highway, in their light blue car. Erick, age five, and Heidi, age eight, were delighted. Each had their own little travel kit to help keep them entertained during the seven-hour drive. Leaving early in the morning, they hoped to be at her parent's home in Indiana later that afternoon, if all went well.

When they were about three hours down the road, Susan decided to stop at a rest park for a short break and let the children move around a bit. After using the rest room facilities the children went outside to watch some little dogs that people were taking for a 'doggie walk.' Susan walked over to the outside vending machines to get some snacks for the children to eat on the way.

Suddenly a young man stood directly behind Susan and quietly demanded that she not say a word and hand over her purse. When she refused he told her he had a gun, which she felt pressed against her back. He ordered her to get into her own car, on the passenger's side. He had seen the family get out of their car a few minutes earlier and knew it belonged to her. If she cooperated and gave him her keys he said she wouldn't get hurt. She told him to take her purse, keys and the car but please let her go because she had two children here. The young man would not listen but forced Susan into her own car just as Heidi and Erick walked towards the car. The bewildered children stood in disbelief as they saw their mother take off in their light blue car with another person driving.

"Mommy, Mommy," they both cried, as they stood in a state of shock! Sadly they watched their mommy disappear down the road. Again they cried out, "Come back, Mommy!"

But it was too late. The car soon disappeared out of sight. Why did their mommy leave in their own car with another person driving? And who was this man that Mommy went away with? Will she come back, they wondered? And why did she leave without them? Erick began to cry as Heidi, wiping tears from her own eyes, put her arm around her little brother. They stood still on the sidewalk, almost in a state of shock as they both gazed in the direction their mother had disappeared. No one around appeared to be interested in what had just happened. No one that is, except three teenage boys sitting in a car nearby that were laughing as if excited that the incident had taken place. The car with the three boys then drove away.

Meanwhile the two frightened children went back inside the comfort center and told the attendant what had just happened. He could hardly believe their story. The attendant told them that their parents probably thought the children were in the car and drove off. As soon as they see otherwise, they will come back, he assured them. Heidi tried to explain to the attendant that the man in the car was not their daddy and they had no idea who he was or where he came from.

A salesman standing nearby overheard the conversation with the children. A few minutes ago, he said four tough looking teenage boys were talking in the restroom about stealing a car. To him it sounded like three of the boys were demanding that the fourth boy steal a car from someone. This salesman did not think the boys knew he was in the restroom when he heard them talking. They left before he came out and now it appeared as if they really were serious in what they were talking about. The theft and abduction really had taken place.

Right away the attendant notified the police. A description of the car and of Mrs. King was given in hopes of locating them. When the police arrived they decided to take the children to the police station in a nearby city. As the frightened children sat in the back seat crying and asking for their mommy, suddenly a man appeared on the seat beside them. Though the policeman could not see or hear the man in the back seat he could hear the children talking to someone. To Heidi and Erick this stranger was very real. This kindly man told the children not to be afraid. He said he would see to it that their mommy would be okay. He also told them they would be well taken care of at the police station. The children asked the man who he was and he just said, "God sent me here." Then he disappeared.

The policeman, driving the car, asked the children who they were talking to and little Erick said, "God was just here, but He left." The puzzled man thought the children must really be tired and frightened to imagine such a thing.

Finally they arrived at the police station and the children were made comfortable in the lounge area, after being fed some lunch. Each one was given a Teddy Bear and a blanket and told to try to sleep. Erick asked Heidi if she thought God really did send the man in the car? If not, where did he come from and why did he disappear so quickly? Heidi said she had to believe the man because he said he would take care of their mommy. If he didn't take care of her, who else would? Somehow these young children were no longer afraid and with the Teddy Bears cuddled in their arms they soon drifted off to sleep.

Heidi had told the police they were on their way to visit their grandparents in Indiana. Upon the girl's information, the grandparents were notified of the incident that had taken place. Susan's parents told the police they would immediately drive down to be with the children. They, too, prayed for the safety of their daughter. Surely God knew how much the children needed their mother, especially since they had lost their father.

Meanwhile the kidnapper and car thief, with Mrs. King sitting nervously beside him, had pulled off the Interstate Highway onto some side road. Susan had no idea where she was headed for. The young boy, whom Susan thought must only be about sixteen or seventeen, appeared big for his age. He ordered her to sit still and not try anything that might upset him. After all he had a gun in his pocket, didn't he? Susan did not realize that it was just a toy gun because it looked so very real.

Susan told the boy that regardless what he had done in the past he could be forgiven, because Jesus loved him. She told him the Bible says in Romans that, "The wages of sin is death but the gift of God is eternal life through Jesus Christ our Lord." Susan said God hates sin but loves the sinner.

She continued to question him about his family and his life, all the while praying for and thinking about her own children. Where were they by now and who has them? Would she ever see them again, she wondered? Her abductor seemed so young. In a few years her son could be doing the same thing. Somehow she almost felt sorry for this boy and began to pray for him.

As they drove down one road after another she prayed that God would deliver her from being captive of this young man. She wondered what went wrong in his home life to make him do a thing like this.

Finally he asked her, "Can't you do anything else but pray?"

Susan replied, "What else is there to do? Besides I think you need it worse than I do! By the way," she continued, "what is your name?" The boy didn't answer, so she began singing the song, "All the way my Savior leads me; cheers each winding path I tread—"

The boy finally said, "My name is Dave. Now what else do you want to know? Can't you do anything else but pray and sing? That makes me nervous!"

"Somehow," said Susan, "I feel that you are not a bad boy at all but just got involved with the wrong crowd, right? Why, I bet you even knew the song I just sang, didn't you?"

The boy now trembling, said, "One more word and I'll point the gun to your head!"

Susan noticed that the gas gage in the car was getting low. She hoped this boy, Dave, would soon stop at a gas station before they ran out on some back road. If they made it to a gas station, hopefully she could signal for help, somehow. If they didn't make it, what would become of her and her car? What would the boy do to her, she wondered? Surely by now, the police were out looking for her. Susan thought about her children. She hoped and prayed they were okay. Susan imagined how frightened they must be by now. She didn't know they were fast asleep with their new Teddy Bears somewhere in a police station.

Susan, thankful that her abductor hadn't tied her hands or her feet together, continued to pray silently. Dave told her if she didn't move or talk anymore, she would not get hurt. She wanted to believe him. He just did not seem like a criminal to her, but more like a frightened teenager.

Also driving down the same road but in the opposite direction, was Michael Lane. He had been listening to a Christian Radio Station when suddenly he noticed a man standing in the middle of the road. Michael stopped the car and asked the stranger if he needed assistance. The man said he didn't, but that someone down the road does. The stranger asked Mr. Lane to please drive him to the next town? Michael had never seen this man before, but somehow he felt like he had known him for a long time. Mr. Lane asked the stranger if his car had stalled somewhere down the road. The man told Michael, it hadn't, and that he just sort of 'flew in.' Michael appeared to be puzzled. He did not know what to think about this stranger that just appeared out of nowhere.

The man told Michael to drive to the next town and stop at the second gas station. Michael, still parked along the side of the road, looked at his gas gage. He reminded this stranger whom he had now picked up, that he had plenty of gas and didn't need to go to a gas station. The man told Michael to go there anyway. When he gets to this station there would be a light blue car there with a woman who needs help.

"You are to help this lady," said the man. Then as quickly as he had appeared on the road, he disappeared.

Michael Lane sat in his car and shook his head in bewilderment. Then he proceeded on to the next town as instructed by the stranger.

By now it was late afternoon. Susan and her abductor had made it to the next town. In an answer to prayer the boy pulled up to the gas station for refueling. It appeared to Susan that Dave seemed quite confused, almost as if he did not know what to do next.

He put the car keys in his pocket and took money out of Susan's purse. Just as Dave went inside to pay for the gas, Michael Lane pulled up in his car, stopping right behind the light blue car. It was there, just like the stranger said it would be. In his mind, he was trying to figure out what was going on. Suddenly he saw a lady get out of the car. It appeared as though she didn't want anyone to see her.

As she quickly walked past Michael's car she looked at him and said, "Please help me!"

The ladies' restroom, in the station, had an outside entrance. Susan ran to the door, quickly opened it, went inside, and locked the door behind her. She thought if she stayed in there long enough, the boy would give up and would drive off without her, taking her car with him.

Michael, still puzzled over what had happened, realized God surely must have sent one of His messengers from heaven, instructing him to somehow help this lady in distress. Not realizing she had been abducted, he wondered what kind of help she needed.

Michael Lane walked over to the ladies' restroom and stood outside as if waiting for his wife or daughter to come out. Suddenly Dave came out of the station and noticed his passenger had left her car. Determined to find her, he also went to the door of the ladies' restroom, thinking she might be in there. He began to knock on it. He then turned to Mr. Lane and stared at him for a minute or two. As the two men looked at each other, it almost seemed like they should know one another, but how could they? They had never met before. Finally Dave asked Michael if he had noticed anyone going into the ladies' restroom. Dave told Michael he was looking for his sister.

For some unknown reason, Mr. Lane did not think the boy was telling the truth. A little voice inside of Michael told him that he needed to protect the lady that had gone into the restroom. So he told Dave he didn't think his sister was in there because his 'friend' just went in and he was waiting for her. He said this 'friend' didn't feel very well and she may be in there awhile.

Susan could hear the two men talking outside and kept quiet. She wondered whom this other voice belonged to, that said his 'friend' was inside. Could it be the man she had just asked to please help her? Perhaps she couldn't trust him either. If only someone would come to her rescue, she prayed.

Michael still puzzled over what had taken place, continued to wait for the unknown lady in the restroom. Finally the confused teenager went back to Susan's car.

Dave got into the car and tried to start it but it would not start. He looked up and noticed a man standing in front of the car with his hands on the hood. No matter how hard Dave tried to start the car, it just would not go. The young man behind the wheel wondered whom this man might be, standing in front of the car. Where did he come from and what did he want? Somehow Dave felt that if this man would just go away the car would start. As long as the man stood there Dave seemed frozen behind the wheel. He could not back up because Mr. Lane's car was right behind him.

Inside the station, the manager had been listening to the radio about a stolen light blue car, an abductor and a lady with him. The car and the boy that had just stopped by perfectly fit the description given on the radio but he never saw the lady. Nevertheless he quickly called the police when Dave went into the men's restroom, inside the station. Dave had paid for the gas and went back to the stolen car. The manager watched the boy go into the car. He looked bewildered as he saw the boy just sitting there as if his hands were glued to the steering wheel. The manager could not see the man standing in front of the stolen car, with his hands on the hood. He could not understand why Dave did not try to drive away.

The police sirens could be heard coming down the road. The station manager, Mr. Lane, and Susan knew that help was on the way. Susan slowly opened the restroom door. Surely by now it would be safe to come out, she hoped. To her amazement she stood face to face with the man she had asked to please help her. The thoughts of a second abductor entered her mind. Thankful that the police had arrived, she quickly walked over to her car.

Susan was surprised to find it still there with Dave sitting inside as if in some sort of a trance. Just as Michael followed Susan to her car, he noticed a man standing in front of the car. The man appeared to be the same one he had met earlier, standing on the road. The stranger of the road looked at Michael, waved his hand, smiled and then disappeared. No one could see him except Michael and Dave.

Mr. Lane told Susan she could trust him, even though they had never met before. Susan wondered just who was this man that had introduced himself as Michael Lane and why had he taken a sudden interest in her? He appeared to have a special glow about him that she couldn't help but notice. Something inside of Susan told her that she could indeed trust this man.

The police handcuffed the young man and proceeded to question Susan King about what had just happened. Michael continued to stay at Susan's side through all this. Susan didn't know why, but somehow she felt a sense of relief just knowing this man, Michael, stood by her.

The handcuffed boy seemed frightened and Susan could not help but feel sorry for him. Dave told the police he longed to feel needed and wanted, by his so called, new gang of friends. To belong to this 'gang' he had to rob somebody and steal a car. Three boys from this gang drove him to the rest-park and demanded that he steal a car from there. When the opportunity to rob Mrs. King and steal her car presented itself, he decided to carry out the plan his three 'friends' commanded him to do. Dave thought by doing this that the gang members would be impressed of his actions and let him become a part of their group.

Dave went on to say that he didn't know where his parents were. He had lived with his grandparents as long as he could remember. Dave continued on, saying that his grandparents were Christian people and always took him to church but were getting older with old-fashioned ideas. He wanted to do something more exciting than going to church. After spending sometime with this gang, he became involved in drugs and couldn't break away from them. Dave realized what he had done was wrong.

The young man knew he should give himself up, especially after listening to Mrs. King talk, sing and pray the way she did in the car while they were driving, but he was afraid. Dave knew that God was trying to talk to him, but he didn't want to listen. Then when he saw some man standing in front of the car and the car wouldn't start for any reason at all, somehow he knew that God had His hands on the car.

The police said they would have to take Dave to the police station and turn him in for theft and abduction. He could face a jail sentence if Susan pressed charges against him. If Dave was guilty then he would have to pay the penalty. Susan thought of her own son, Erick, and hoped he would never do anything like this some day.

Michael's eyes went back and forth from Susan to Dave. There seemed to be something special about both of them that tugged on his heartstrings. Just what it was, he did not know. Michael could almost see in this boy, Dave, an unusual resemblance of his own life. This lady, Susan seemed so calm through all she had just been through. Michael knew she had a special character about her that not many people have. He wondered what the future held for both of these two people that the stranger of the road suddenly put into his life.

Michael sensed that both Dave and Susan needed help. The stranger of the road told Michael that he was to help the lady in distress at the station, so he decided to do what he could to help her. The police would take care of

Dave.

Susan had been told that her children were at a police station about seventy miles north of where they now were and that they were being well cared for. The police also told Susan that her daughter gave them the name and address of her parents in Indiana. They had been notified of what had taken place and were on their way down here to be with the children, just in case something should happened to their daughter.

Susan signed some papers stating that Dave was indeed the young man who had abducted her, along with her car, then she was released to go. Susan was very anxious get back to her children. Surely they were frightened and wondered what had become of their mother by now. If all goes well, in about two hours she should be reunited with Heidi and Erick. The policeman called ahead to where Susan's children were, and notified them that Mrs. King would soon be on her way there.

Even though Susan seemed calm through all this, Michael did not think she should drive the seventy-five miles by herself. Then he had an idea. Michael asked the station manager if he knew of someone who would be willing to drive his service wrecker and tow Mrs. King's car to the place where her children were. He then would be willing to drive his car, take the lady with him, and follow the wrecker with her light blue car in tow. That is, if Susan would agree. The station manager said he was just ready to close for the day. But he would be willing to offer his services, for a small fee, plus the gas to drive the wrecker.

Susan didn't know for sure if she should accept this offer. After all, she never met this man before now. The police told Susan that she could trust the station manager. He had a two-way radio in his truck so he could communicate with the police, should he have occasion to do so. Susan could have rode in the wrecker with the service manager but decided not to. Anxious to be reunited with Heidi and Erick, she agreed to ride in the car with Michael. Just as soon as the station would be locked up for the day, they would all be on their way.

Still feeling sorry for Dave, Susan said she decided not to press charges against the boy. The police said Dave would still be arrested and have to serve a limited time in jail, even though only sixteen years of age. The boy would be taken to the jail closest to his grandparent's home.

Just before the police took Dave away, the boy, with tears in his eyes, looked at Michael and then at Susan and said, "I'm sorry, so sorry, for what I have done. Please forgive me." Then they were gone.

Susan King turned to Michael and said, "I'm sorry, too. He really isn't a bad boy. What he needs is love and the right friends. I wish I could help him somehow. This will surely be hard for his grandparents."

"My heart goes out to the boy as well," replied Mr. Lane. "The way the boy trembled, I knew he had to be afraid. Somehow, I too, feel sorry for Dave's grandparents. It will be difficult for them when they find out what their grandson has done. It can't be easy for the elderly couple to raise that boy, with all the world had to offer in the way of drugs and gangs."

By now the station manager had locked his place of business. He notified his wife to let her know why he would be coming home late. Susan's car had now been hooked up behind the wrecker and the three were finally on their way.

As Michael and Susan drove down the highway following her car in tow, they talked about her children and about their past. Susan somehow soon felt at ease, this time, riding in a car with someone she had never met before. The two soon found out that both were Christians who loved the Lord dearly. Susan told her driver about her husband, Keith, who went to be with the Lord and how much she and the children missed him. Michael said he had not yet found the right mate for him and had never been married. Someday if the right girl comes along, he would like to get married, if it is in God's plan for him to do so.

Michael went on to tell Susan that his mother gave him up for adoption when he was a baby and he never knew her. The only parents he ever knew were the ones who adopted him. They, too, were fine Christian people and he loved them dearly.

In talking with one another, Michael and Susan were surprised to find out that they both were from Indiana, growing up in communities about twenty miles apart. Michael Lane had been to southern Kentucky on business and was on his way home when suddenly a stranger on the road temporarily delayed his plans. He then proceeded to tell Susan about this stranger. Susan had not seen this stranger, even when he stood in front of her car, preventing Dave from driving away. Susan agreed with Michael that the stranger must have been an angel sent on a mission from God.

It was nearly dark by the time the wrecker, the light blue car in tow behind it, and Michael with his passenger, arrived at the police station where the two children were waiting. After releasing the car, Michael paid the station manager for the use of the wrecker and for his services. Then the man headed back to the little town where so much had happened just a few hours ago.

Anxious to see her children, Susan ran into the police station. Michael followed quickly behind. By now Susan's parents had arrived as well and greeted her with open arms. She saw her two precious children fast asleep on reclining chairs each with a Teddy Bear in their arms. Susan woke up Heidi and Erick and the happy reunion brought tears to the eyes of everyone in the room, including Michael.

Susan introduced Michael to her parents and told them she didn't know what she would have done without him. She said he was definitely 'heaven sent.'

Susan and her parents decided to take the children and go to a nearby motel for the rest of the night. This had been a long hard day for everyone and they all needed a good night's rest.

Michael and Susan said good-bye and with tears in her eyes she gave him a hug and said, "I'll never be able to repay you for all you have done for me. The Lord will have to do that for me. May God bless you, and I thank you for being my stranger on the road.

Somehow the two felt as if they had known each other for a long time. Michael said he would try to keep in touch with her, especially if she should happen to move back to Indiana. They would only be about twenty miles apart. Susan said she didn't know what the future held in store for her and her children. She would let God decide that for her. Susan and her parents thanked the policemen for taking such good care of the children and for the Teddy bears. Then they left the station and headed for the motel.

Michael Lane headed his car north towards southern Indiana, where he had one more business meeting before heading home. He couldn't pull his thoughts away from the young woman whom he had met that day. It was late and he had trouble staying awake. He decided to pull off at a truck stop and get some coffee to help keep him awake. After buying the coffee he went back to his car and noticed someone sitting in the passenger's seat.

As Michael approached his car he was surprised to see the same stranger of the road sitting in his front seat. Michael got in his car and the two men took off down the highway together. Feeling as though he could trust this stranger, Michael actually seemed relieved to have someone to talk to. The stranger told his driver that after his business meeting in southern Indiana, he should go back and visit Dave in jail. The man then told Michael that Dave needed a big brother to help him. After giving Michael the directions to the jail where Dave was held, the stranger suddenly disappeared as Michael looked in awe at the empty seat beside him.

Mr. Lane had in his mind to check up on this boy, Dave one day, but not so soon. He had hoped first to look up Susan's parents and try to see her again. For some reason she kept coming into his thoughts. Just the thought of seeing her again warmed his heart. But the stranger had told him to change his plans and go see Dave instead. Michael knew the stranger was right. Susan had her parents to look after her and the children. Dave just had his elderly grandparents. This boy certainly did not need the friendship of the gang members that set him up for the crime he had just committed.

Mr. Lane checked into a motel and had a good night's rest. The business meeting went as expected for Mr. Lane the following day. That morning he had prayed he would make the right decisions concerning Dave. He still would rather go home now that his meeting was over with, but the stranger of the road had told him to go find Dave. He wanted another sign to be sure he really was to talk to this boy. Then as he sat in his car again he opened his Bible and his eyes fell on I John 3:17. It said, "But whoever has this world's goods, and sees his brother in need, and shuts up his heart from him, does the love of God abide in him?"

Michael knew a brother could be anyone who had a need and certainly this boy, Dave, could use a big brother, just like the stranger said. Michael Lane loved the Lord and he felt as if he was again being put to the test. This Bible verse verified the fact the he had to help this boy.

Once more Michael turned his car around and headed back to the Kentucky hills. He passed the city where Susan King had been reunited with her children. That was the last time and place he had seen this lovely lady.

After following the directions the stranger had given him, Michael finally reached the jail where Dave was held. What if the authorities wouldn't let him visit this young man he had come to see? What if Dave refused to see him or talk to him? The stranger of the road instructed him to come here so surely God will open the door for him.

It so happened to be visiting hours when Mr. Lane arrived at the jail. The jail keeper told Michael that Dave's grandparents were with him in the security room. The man asked Michael if he was Dave's minister. Michael told him that he was on a mission, that God had sent him here to talk to this young man in jail. The jailer let Michael join the grandparents. Upon entering the room, it appeared to him that the elderly couple seemed quite distressed and Michael felt very sorry for them.

Dave looked on in disbelief as he saw Michael Lane step into the room. The first thoughts that entered Dave's mind were that perhaps Mrs. King had decided to press charges against him after all. But when Dave saw the compassionate look on Michael's face he somehow felt that this man was here to help him and not to hurt him.

The grandparents looked at Mr. Lane and then at their grandson. They were amazed to see such a resemblance in these two men. Michael introduced himself as Michael Lane from Indiana. Then he explained to the elderly couple how he had just recently come to know their grandson, Dave.

The puzzled grandfather looked at Michael and said, "Is your name really Michael Lane? Do you really live in northern Indiana? Are you about thirty years of age?"

The grandmother looked at her husband and said, "Are you thinking the same thing I'm thinking? If all this is true, then God has finally answered our prayers."

Michael spoke up kindly and said, "What are you two talking about? Will you please tell me what's going on?"

Dave and Michael listened very intently as the grandparents proceeded to tell their story. Thirty years ago their daughter, Marci, had a baby boy she named Michael. Being very young and not married, she didn't want her baby. At the time the grandparents were not able to care for the infant boy either so they both agreed that he would be given up for adoption. A fine Christian couple, by the name of Lane, from northern Indiana adopted the infant boy. They never saw him again. Then fourteen years later their daughter Marci came home with another baby boy, she had named David. She didn't want him either and left him with her saddened parents. Then she took off and had not been seen or heard of since.

As they had often wondered about their first grandson, the grandparents decided to try to keep David, and raised him by themselves. It had not been easy. They took him to church and tried to bring him up to love the Lord. Then David became involved with this gang and they could no longer control him. All they could do was to turn their grandson over to the Lord in prayer and ask that he would someday change his ways and come back to church. They never expected him to turn out this way.

Michael Lane could not believe all that he had been hearing. So this was why the stranger on the road told him to get in touch with Dave. Could this boy really be his younger brother? A brother he never knew he had? Could these dear elderly people really be his grandparents? God works in mighty mysterious ways, but he never imagined anything like this happening to him.

Tomorrow, Michael decided, he would go to the local courthouse to see if the records there would confirm what he had just been told. In the meantime he would try to gather more information from Dave. He wanted to know more about this elderly couple and his real mother, if indeed what he had been told was true.

Dave said he hoped Michael really was his big brother because he never knew his father and he hoped the two of them could possibly now become friends.

Visiting hours were over and the four said their good-byes to one another. Michael promised Dave he would be back to let him know what he had found out about their past and possibly about their mother, if indeed they were brothers. Having no reason to doubt them, Michael seemed inclined to believe the story the grandparents had told him. And the more he looked at Dave the more he could see the resemblance between the two of them.

The grandparents insisted that Michael spend the rest of the day and night with them. They were convinced this man was their grandson whom they hadn't seen for thirty years. They wanted to get to know Michael better and what better way than for him to spend the night with them.

Michael followed them to the meager home they leased, in the beautiful blue grass hills of Kentucky. It wasn't a fancy home by any means but it had all the facilities needed and it appeared to be very neat and clean. Michael could sleep in David's room. The warmth of this fine elderly Christian couple filled the house with a special love. Michael noticed a picture of a lovely young lady on the bookshelf. The grandmother told him it was Marci, David's mother and perhaps now his mother as well.

The young lady in the picture looked so pretty. Why, he wondered, did she ever leave her parents, hurting them in the way she had? Where could she possibly be now? He had so much he wanted to find out. Everything had happened so fast, ever since he first met the stranger of the road!

The next morning, Michael went to the courthouse and found out what he wanted to know. He went back to the elderly couple's house and knocked gently on their door. The grandmother opened the door only to find Michael Lane standing there grinning from ear to ear.

He handed her the bouquet of flowers he had just purchased and said, "My dear grandmother, may I come in? The records show that I am indeed your grandson."

The elderly women threw her frail arms around Michael as the tears ran down her wrinkled cheeks. She took an old handkerchief from her apron pocket and wiped her eyes. Standing just inside the door, Grandfather heard the good news and began singing the song, "Praise God from Whom all Blessing Flow--." Then he said, "You are indeed a heaven sent blessing. Welcome home, my boy!"

Everything had been happening so fast that Michael hardly knew what to do next. After having a long talk with the grandparents he never knew, he asked them if they would consider moving to Indiana to be near him. He told them he knew of a lovely retirement home close to where he lived and he would love to have them live there. He would make all the arrangements if they would be interested.

"But what about David?" asked Grandfather. "We can't just leave him here alone, not now, when he needs us the most?"

"He won't be alone, not anymore," replied Michael. "You see, I checked into that as well. Dave doesn't know it yet but I paid his bail. The sheriff said he would place him in my custody if the fines were paid. So from now on, I take full responsibility for the boy. I will be my brother's keeper. As part of the agreement, the authorities said Dave would have to be placed in a Boys' School for one year. There is one not too far from where I live. The arrangements have already begun to have him transferred there and we will be able to visit him. So what do you two say about all that?"

Since the elderly couple had no one else to look after them or David, they decided to accept Michael's offer. They had nothing to lose. Grandmother said she felt like Ruth in the Bible. They had just read the story that morning after Michael went to the courthouse. She had reference to the two verses in the first chapter in the book of Ruth, which says, "Entreat me not to leave you, or to return from following after you: for where you go, I will go. Where you lodge, I will lodge: your people shall be my people, and your God my God. Where you die, will I die, and there will I be buried. The Lord do so to me, and more also if ought but death part you and me."

Mr. Lane arranged for a moving truck to pick up the grandparent's and Dave's belongings within two days. He had already called and found out there was an empty duplex available for them to move into. While they were busy packing their belongings, Michael went to visit Dave. The authorities knew of Michael's intentions and told him if Dave does anything wrong that Michael would be held responsible. Somehow Mr. Lane felt that Dave would not cause him any trouble.

Upon arrival at the jail, Michael was taken to the cell where David had been kept during this time. There he found the young man reading the Bible his grandparents brought to him the day before. He had been reading the third chapter in the Gospel of John. Tears began flowing down his cheeks when he looked up and saw Mr. Lane standing there.

Michael said, "Come on, Brother Dave, let's go home. I've always wanted a brother and now the Good Lord has given me one. From now on we'll be pals, you and me. No more gangs, okay, Pal?"

"You mean you really are my brother, Michael, you really truly are?" questioned Dave, with the tears streaming down from his eyes.

"Yes," replied Michael. "You are placed in my custody from now on and we're moving away from here. I'm taking you and 'our' grandparents back to Indiana with me tomorrow."

The young man threw his arms around his big brother and said, "Alright! But I'm so sorry for all the trouble I've caused everyone, please do forgive me. I want God to forgive me, too."

"You are forgiven," replied Michael. "You want to know something? God works in mysterious ways. If you had never stolen Mrs. King's car, the stranger of the road perhaps would not have brought us together in this most unique way. Come on, Brother Dave, let's go home."

The grandparent's house had never been so happy as the four united family members shared this last special night together before departing for Indiana.

A month later, school had started with Dave now enrolled in Boy's School. He seemed to be adjusting quite well in his new surroundings and was determined to straighten out his life. He grew very fond of his big brother and looked forward to his visits, along with his grandparents. Someday, Dave wanted to be just like Michael.

The boys' grandparents were settled in their retirement home and they just loved it. Michael visited them often and together the three of them would go visit Dave when ever possible.

One day as Michael Lane drove home from work, he again saw the stranger of the road standing near a large tree by the side of the road. The stranger motioned for Michael to stop. Once again the man got into Michael's car and the two started down the road together.

"What is it this time?" asked Michael, knowing there must be another mission waiting to be accomplished.

The stranger told him where there was a large lovely house for sale about fifteen miles from where he now lived. He suggested that Michael purchase it.

"It sounds great, but why should I buy that big house?" asked Michael.

"Even when Dave is out of Boys' School the two of us will never need a place that big. You must have something else in mind. Right?"

The stranger told him that Susan King lived in that area, that she and her children had decided to stay in Indiana. They do not plan to return to Tennessee. He went on to say that even though Susan is with her parents, she still feels quite lonely. The stranger then gave Michael a paper with the directions to the church that Susan, her children and parents attended. Then he disappeared.

Here I go again, thought Michael. But the thought of possibly seeing Susan again warmed his heart. He had been so excited about finding out his identity, getting his new grandparents and brother settled that he had temporarily put Susan out of his mind.

Meanwhile, Susan King found a job in the same town where her parents lived. She and her children moved from Tennessee to Indiana in time for the children to enroll in school for the coming year. They would be living with her parents until Susan found the right place to raise her children. Heidi and Erick were delighted to be with their grandparents and near their cousins.

Several days later, Michael visited the church where Susan attended. She seemed surprised, yet happy and delighted to see Michael Lane again. He asked if he might take her out for Sunday dinner. She agreed, and Heidi and Erick went home with their grandparents.

As they sat at dinner together in a nice cozy restaurant, they had much to tell one another about the events that had taken place since the day they had first met. They felt as if they had known each other for a long time. Soon Michael and Susan were seeing each other almost weekly.

Several weeks later Michael again went to see Susan at her house. He fell in love with her children and they with him. He asked them if they would like to go for a ride out into the country. The four of them soon were on their way to the big house that the stranger of the road told Michael he should consider buying. He drove up the lane and stopped beside the lovely old country house. He stepped out of his car and asked them to follow him. They all proceeded to the front door of the house. He unlocked it and they went inside.

"Wow!" said the children together. "What a house!"

"Do you like it?" asked Michael.

"Yes!" the two replied together. Then they looked at their mother and said, "Mommy, can you buy this house for us, please?"

"I'm afraid that's out of the question. We could never afford this lovely house," answered their mother. "Besides it's too big for the three of us."

"But not too big for the four of us," said Michael softly. Then he knelt in front of Susan and the children. He took Susan's hands in his and asked her to marry him. They could all live in this house together. When Dave is out of Boys' School he would also live with them and attend the local High School.

Heidi and Erick chorused together, "Yes, Mommy, say yes, we want Michael to be our daddy!"

Susan admitted that ever since she first met Michael there seemed to be something special about this man that attracted her to him. She said she had been praying that if she should ever marry again that God would send the right man at the right time. Susan said the right time and man had finally arrived.

She looked at her children, then clasping Michael's hands said, "Yes, Michael, I will marry you if you are sure you want me, and my children.

Michael put his strong arms lovingly around Susan and said, "Remember you will also get my younger brother, Dave, in this deal. But with God's help we'll all be just one happy family."

"Yippee!" cried the children. "We get a new daddy and a new house. Yippee!"

The next week Michael and Susan drove to the Boys' School to visit Dave and told him the news of their coming marriage. Dave hugged Susan and said, "I knew there was always something special about you, but I never, ever thought you would be my sister-in-law some day. Wow! Things just keep getting better and better."

The day of the wedding arrived. Susan's parents loved Michael and were happy their daughter could again find someone to love and be loved. She looked beautiful as she walked down the aisle on her father's arm, dressed in an off white linen suit. Her sister preceded her as maid of honor. Dave, out on a one day's leave, attended his brother as best man. Heidi and Erick also were in the wedding party. It was a lovely ceremony and everyone seemed so happy!

The elderly grandparents wished somehow the boy's mother could see them now. Surely she would be proud of them. They continued to pray everyday that their daughter would one-day return to them. Even though they no longer lived in Kentucky, surely someone there would tell Marci where she could find her parents, if she ever came back to look for them.

Michael's adopted parents, his grandparents and Susan's parents, her sister and brother's families and others congratulated the happy couple as they celebrated their wedding with a small reception. Then the two left for a few days on their honeymoon. Heidi and Erick stayed with Susan's parents while their mommy and new daddy were away.

The children were very excited about moving into the big farmhouse in just a few more days. They had already begun to pack their toys and other belongings.

The new Mr. and Mrs. Michael Lane and children had now settled into the big house and were adjusting very well. The weeks passed by, one by one. Soon Dave would be out of Boys' School. He would then come to live on the farm with the Lane family.

By now, Dave had truly repented of the crime he had committed and had given his heart to the Lord, while in Boys' School. He had realized he was a sinner, taking seriously what the Bible said; "All have sinned and come short of the glory of God." He wanted to spend eternity in heaven and not in hell.

Since he asked Jesus into his heart, he now desired to be baptized. He would regularly attend church with Michael, Susan and the family, once he lived out on the farm.

Dave would still be on parole another year but with God's help he would try to stay out of trouble. The Bible says, "Greater is He that is in you than he that is in the world." With God now on his side, Dave wished to help other teens that were on drugs and would try to win them over to Christ as well. They needed a second chance also, just as he had been given.

David's grandparents were so happy that God brought Michael into their lives and for the new change they now saw in David's life.

It was two weeks later and Dave now lived on the farm. The following Sunday he hoped to be baptized in church. That day had now arrived. Before his baptism he stood before the church and gave a testimony of his faith and new experience with Jesus Christ. He also spoke about the crime he had committed. Then he mentioned the unusual incident that brought him and the brother, he never knew he had before, together. As the congregation listened to his story, many were wiping tears from their eyes.

Just as the preacher was about to baptize Dave, a faint quivering voice from the back row softly said, "May I say something, please?"

Everyone turned around to see who had spoken. There on the back row, just inside the door, sat a middle-aged lady, who appeared to be quite frightened. She looked like the last rose of summer as tears ran down her cheeks and onto her soiled wrinkled dress.

The congregation became so quiet you could have heard a pin drop. Who was this lady, and where did she come from?

The lonely lady stood up and said, "As I stepped up to the door of the church I heard this beautiful singing. It has been a long time since I attended church anywhere. Then I heard the song "Now Wash Me and I Shall be Whiter than Snow." Something drew me inside this church so I slipped into the back bench. I didn't want anyone to know I was here. But after hearing what the young man had just said, I realized I missed out on so much of my life." She took a deep breath, wiped her eyes, then continued speaking, "You see, I was the one who abandoned David and Michael when they were babies. I am their mother. The responsibility of raising children scared me and I wanted to be free and do my own thing. Now I know I was wrong. I realize I have made many bad decisions and I know I am a sinner. If my boys reject me, I understand because I rejected them once myself, but more than that, I know now that I rejected God."

The tears were still flowing from Marci's tired eyes as she said, "Mom, Dad, I know you are sitting up front. I'm sorry, so very sorry. Please forgive me and I want God to forgive me, too." Then the lady slowly walked up to the bench where her parents were seated.

By now there was not a dry eye in the church. The minister stood and listened as the woman told her story. Michael's new grandparents stood up and recognized their daughter, Marci. Soon the three reunited adults were embracing and sobbing tears of sweet sorrow. Michael and Dave just looked at each other, in unbelief of what was happening. This was the first time they had ever seen their mother, since she had left them as infants. If what she had just said was true, then she really must be their mother. The boys did not know exactly what to say to her.

The women looked at the preacher and then at her parents. She mentioned to them how she had been raised up by Christian parents. But as time went on she rebelled, as David said he did when he became involved with the wrong gang. She, too, had become a part of the wrong crowd that almost destroyed her life. She went on to say that she felt like a prodigal daughter and mother, who is now ready to come back home and change her life around. If her family does not want her now, she would understand, because of the way she has treated them in the years gone by. Regardless, she still wanted to commit her life to Christ and start over again, as her son has now done. Marci continued to say if she would be a burden to her family here, then she will return to St. Louis, where she had just come from, and try to start over a new life, there.

The woman then hugged her parents and sons and said, "I'm not worthy to be called your daughter and mother, but I want you to know, I'll always love you. Please forgive me before I say good-by and leave here." Then Marci turned around and with her head lowered in shame she walked towards the back of the church.

Finally the minister spoke up and asked the woman to please sit down. He said before anybody leaves, they better proceed with Dave's baptism. After all, that is what they are here for. After that he would be more than willing to talk with her, and the family involved.

Hesitantly the woman stayed and watched her son's baptism. Somehow Marci had the desire to do the same thing, but there were so many things in her life she needed to make right. She felt so ashamed of her past life. After the baptismal ceremony was over, Marci's family gathered around her.

Michael Lane's adopted parents felt sorry for this woman who had given birth to the boy they had raised. The elder Mr. Lane said the house their son used to rent from them is vacant again, now that he has moved into the big house. If this woman wants to rent it she could do so.

Susan's father spoke up and said he needed another clerk in his store. If this lady wanted the job he would be willing to hire her.

The minister said God always needs more people to fill His church. Marci would always be welcome to attend, for as long as she wanted to come.

Finally the woman's mother spoke up and said, "We sure could use a daughter again. How about it Marci? We welcome you back home with open arms. We will always love you, no matter what you have done in the past."

Michael and his brother, David, exchanged glances. Then after talking to each other Michael spoke up and said, "We're thankful you came back into our lives. We also both welcome and forgive you. Just as Christ forgave us our sins, He can forgive you, too. Life on earth is too short not to be at peace one with another. Welcome back--Mother."

Soon the whole congregation approached Marci one by one, making her feel welcome. She had never felt such love and warmth since she left her parent's home years ago.

Finally almost everyone had gone home except for the distressed woman, her parents, Dave, the minister, and the family of Michael and Susan.

Marci, still wiping her eyes, said she wanted to repent of her sins and ask Jesus to come into her heart. Soon they were all kneeling in prayer as the woman made a commitment to Christ. But her walk with the Lord was just beginning.

Michael Lane asked this woman, who claimed to be his mother, how she ever found them here in this church.

Marci said she had been driving to Indiana to meet an old acquaintance of hers. She had stopped to get gas for her car. After paying for the fuel she got into her car only to see a man sitting in the passenger seat beside her. She immediately became frightened but the man seemed so calm and kind. He told her to drive north and she did. He told her that the day of Grace could soon come to an end. All those who have not given their heart to Jesus Christ will be lost for all eternity. Marci said she doesn't even remember the roads she had been driving on because she was so taken in by what this man had been telling her. She said that he told her to follow his advice, otherwise she may never, ever see her parents or sons again.

Marci wiped her eyes again and said, "Suddenly the man disappeared and the road I was on somehow led me to this church. As I stepped out of the car and heard the beautiful singing coming from inside the church, something told me to go inside. I know it had to be an angel of the Lord giving me one more chance. And now here I am, so sorry, so unworthy, and so ready to surrender my all to Christ."

"The Stranger of the Road!" Michael exclaimed. "Thanks be to God, the Stranger of the Road brought our family together. If it had not been for this messenger sent from God, Susan and I would not have met. I never would have known I had a brother, nor would I ever have met my real grandparents and mother. Thanks be to God for the Stranger of the Road!"

Later that night, as they all walked out to their cars, Heidi and Erick cried, "Look, look, over there!"

To everyone's surprise they saw the Stranger of the Road once more, walking away from the church, down the road, as if satisfied that his mission had now been accomplished. Then just as before, he disappeared into the dark of the night, and they never saw him again.

THROW OUT THE LIFE-LINE

Three teenage cousins were spending the day together with their parents and families at a lake cottage in Northern Indiana. The girls loved to swim. Rochelle, the oldest of the three, had training to be a lifeguard.

About six thirty in the evening the three girls, Rochelle, Nicole and Rachel, decided to take the row boat out onto the lake and try their skills at rowing. They had gone canoeing before and thought it would be simple to row a boat. They planned to be out just for an hour. Their parents were aware of their plans.

The three girls had fun rocking on the waves caused by passing speedboats. That is, they had fun until Rachel suddenly leaned over the side of the twelve-foot rowboat and decided to feed the fish. That's right; her evening meal suddenly came up, and where else could she put it but in the water?

Rachel, not feeling very well from motion sickness, suggested they go back to the cottage for fear she might next lose her dessert overboard.

The girls were having so much fun until now, that they had forgotten to watch the time. They had drifted and rowed out towards the other side of the lake, farther than it would take them to get back to the cottage in one hour's time.

Nicole noticed the sky getting really dark in the west and also suggested that they row the boat back towards the cottage. The winds began to blow causing white caps on the water. Each girl put on her life jacket in case they might encounter a storm. The small boat reeled to and fro on the white-capped water. Soon the girls were rowing the boat with all their might.

Suddenly they hit a snag! The wind had blown them against some hidden stumps and they were wedged among them. Off in the distance they could see a red light on top of the small lighthouse near their cottage. When a storm would approach, the lighthouse had this special red light glowing on top of its tower to warn boaters of an on-coming storm. The girls knew they had to free the rowboat from the stumps and head for the lighthouse as soon as possible: but how?

What if the electricity would go off because of the storm? They would not be able to see any lights along the shore except for a possible flashlight beam or car headlight blinking here or there in the distance. Would they be able to find their way home?

The winds became much stronger, tossing the girls about in their boat, as if they were sitting in a little toy. It rocked and slapped helplessly against the hidden stumps. And yes, by now Rachel lost her dessert in the water.

An occasional crack of thunder frightened the girls. The lightning did help the girls to see what was going on around them, but they knew they were in great danger of lightening striking their helpless craft on the water. This storm came up so fast. When they left the cottage there was no sign of an approaching storm. Now they were like sitting ducks on the water.

The girls were reminded of the story in Matthew 28, where it says how Jesus once calmed the tempest of the sea. They knew that He could calm it for them now. The three teenagers began to pray for their safety, and kept their eyes on the lighthouse in the distance. If only their dads were here with them, they would know just what to do. The girls knew that Jesus, their heavenly Father, was with them and surely He would send someone to help them.

If the waves became any higher the water would soon come into the boat, then what would they do? Without a bucket they could not even dip out water, should that happen. The oars seemed almost useless in this storm.

The frightened girls knew their parents would be concerned for their safety. Rochelle, an avid swimmer and the brave one of the bunch, decided to go into the water and try to free the boat away from the stumps. An old rope lay coiled on the floor of the boat. Rochelle tied one end around her waist. The girls tied the other end of the rope securely around the cross board seat in the middle of the boat. Once in the water, the waves tossed Rochelle about like a struggling fish. Frantically she used her feet to push against the slimy stumps and the strength of her arms to shove the stranded boat away. Rochelle was thankful she had brought her life jacket into the boat and not just a life cushion. The jacket kept her head above water while she struggled to free the restless boat. The lifeguard training she had in school came in very handy.

Rachel, still not feeling well, knew she had to help do what she could.

Nicole and Rachel, were very concerned for their cousin, Rochelle, out there in the rough waters and knew it must be difficult for her to see what she was trying to do. They were so thankful for the rope that kept their cousin from drifting away. It truly was a lifeline. With a prayer on their heart, the two girls each took an oar and tried to help push the boat away from the stumps. The cousins knew they had to work fast. If they couldn't free the boat soon it would beat against the stumps so hard that possibly a hole could develop in its side. Then it would take on water for sure.

The teenagers worked frantically to free the helpless rowboat and at the same time tried to keep their eyes on the lighthouse in the distance. Rachel said that Jesus was their lighthouse and if they would just keep their eyes focused on Him, He would surely calm the waters and lead them safely home.

While in the water, Rochelle thought she heard what sounded like a duck going, "Quack, quack," but thought it couldn't be. Surely a duck would not be out in this storm. Nicole and Rachel thought they heard it also. Sure enough to their amazement, just a few feet from the lodged boat, all three girls saw a little duck bobbing up and down on the waves around them. They couldn't imagine what a duck would be doing out there in this storm.

It was as if this big bird was trying to tell them something. Every time Rochelle would push the boat away from the stumps the duck would go, "Quack, quack; quack, quack." But as it did so, to the girls it sounded like a voice saying, "You can, you can." So every time the duck quacked, Rochelle pushed on the boat and Nicole and Rachel pushed with their oars. The girls kept hearing this voice saying, "You can, you can," and yet there was no one around except the duck.

Rochelle, now quite exhausted, decided to use one of the oars for support in the murky waters, and at last freed the boat from between the stumps. While doing so, a gust of wind and a big wave took the oar from her hands and it slapped against a stump breaking the oar in two. For a moment Rochelle thought her rope snapped, but it didn't. At last the boat was safe and free! Nicole, pulled on the rope, reached over the side and helped her brave cousin climb wearily into the boat. It was raining now and the wet, frightened girls knelt in prayer in the middle of the boat, holding hands as they thanked God for freeing their little rowboat. They asked God to safely guide them back to the lighthouse and their cottage. They knew they had to keep their eyes upon the beam of the lighthouse.

Once the boat was freed and away from the stumps, the little duck continued to stay close by, always swimming just a few feet ahead of the girls and their boat. Even though it was almost dark and at times hard to see the bird, they could always hear the "Quack, quack; quack, quack" of the duck as though it was telling the girls to follow it towards the lighthouse. But to the girls it still seemed to say, "You can, you can."

The girls had not taken any flashlights with them because they had hoped to be back before dark. But now darkness had settled in and without any light on board, no one would be able to see them in their distress, no one but the little duck.

As the teens knelt in prayer, Nicole suddenly felt something under one of her knees. Reaching down she picked up a small box of matches. Where they came from, no one knew. No one had noticed them before.

Rachel said, "It is an answer to prayer. God must have dropped them from the sky." The other two agreed.

Rochelle suggested they light one match at a time in hopes someone would see them. A little light goes a long way in the darkness. Nicole took off her sandals and fixed a little windbreak to protect the tiny flame from blowing out. Rachel held her hand slightly above it to keep the rain off their little flickering light. With the one oar they had left, Rochelle and Nicole took turns trying to row the little boat towards the lighthouse. The girls were wet, cold, tired, and frightened, and for some reason Rachel was rather hungry.

Now that darkness had set in, the winds finally subsided. One by one Rachel lit the matches, as the girls struggled feebly for the lighthouse with their little boat and one oar. They kept their eyes focused on the lighthouse. If no one came to help, they knew it would be quite a while before they would reach the shore across the lake, but they kept on going. The duck continued to lead them, and they could still hear a soft voice say, "You can, you can." They did not know just how but somehow they knew they would make it.

Then the trio began to sing the song of "Throw Out the Life-line across the dark wave." All three of the girls had given their hearts to Christ, repenting of their past sins, and were living in His love. They knew Christ was their Lighthouse and only hope.

Rachel said, "Surely, if God can walk on water He can walk with us now and bring us safely to shore somehow. After all, He is our Lifeline as well, and a shelter in the time of storm! Didn't He provide the duck for us, and the matches, little as they were? Surely He can provide a way for us to return safely to shore."

Suddenly, while they were desperately trying to row their little boat, they saw ahead of them a beam of light and heard the motor of an approaching watercraft.

The girls had just lit their last match and were singing as loudly as they could. What if, Rochelle thought, just what if the oncoming craft failed to see them and collided with their little boat! Then the cousins stopped singing and on the count of three together they yelled, "Please, somebody, please help us!" Soon a water patrol boat carefully pulled along side of them. Two men in the boat questioned the girls to make sure they were okay and to see if they were the girls reported missing by their parents.

The thankful, shivering girls told the two patrolmen who they were and what had happened to them, and also told them about the little duck and the matches. The police didn't believe their story about the duck and shined their light all around the girls' boat, but the duck was nowhere in sight. The girls looked at each other in amazement, wondering where the duck had disappeared.

Nicole said, "God must have dropped the duck from the sky like He did the matches. Now that it isn't needed any more, He must have taken the friendly bird back to shore somewhere."

The patrolmen just shook their heads in bewilderment at the girls' stories about the matches and the duck being sent from heaven. The men tied a lifeline to the twelve-foot rowboat and now with tears in their eyes the girls were finally being towed in the direction of the lighthouse across the lake and were going home.

The teenagers thanked the Lord for sending help to them. At last a Lifeline of hope would bring them home. As they neared the lighthouse they began to sing, "Brightly beams our Father's mercy, from His lighthouse evermore; but to us He gives the keeping of the lights along the shore." They were indeed glad to be near, and to see, the lights of shore!

After reaching the shore, the wet, shivering girls climbed out of their little boat, happy to be back on land and near home again. Rachel asked the patrolmen how they found them out in the dark night. The men told the girls they saw the small, flickering lights of the matches and the breeze from off the water carried the sounds of the girls voices as they sang, "Throw Out the Life-line! Someone is drifting away." The patrolmen knew if they kept their eyes on the little light in the drifting boat and their ears tuned to the singing they heard, soon the light of their own boat would reveal where the drifting girls were.

The girls, happy to be back with their parents, told them about the incidents of the matches and the duck. All agreed that they had to be sent from God. The girls said they would never go out in a boat alone again without an older adult. Even though they were thankful for the matches, they said they would always make sure they had a flashlight and an extra oar or two, regardless of whom they go out on a boat with from now on. You never know when you'll need them.

Friend, Jesus is our lighthouse and if we always keep our focus on Him, He will guide us through any storm that may come our way. He is the Lifeline that will take us through the trials of life and bring us safely to His home in heaven someday, if we completely focus on Him. The girls kept their eyes and ears focused on the lighthouse and the little duck. The patrolmen kept their eyes and ears focused on the girls and the light of the matches. We need also to continuously focus on Jesus as the light of the world and listen as He gently calls us to come to Him.

Jesus keeps His eyes focused on us and is always there when we need Him. In Isaiah 43 verse two it says, "When you pass through the waters, I will be with you: and through the rivers, they shall not overflow you." As surely as Jesus was with the girls in the waters which did not overflow them, He will be with all who call upon His name.

The last line in the chorus of the song the girls sang says, "Throw out the Life-line! Someone is sinking today."

Dear friend, if you are helplessly sinking in the sins and cares of this world, please reach out to the Lifeline of hope Christ has provided for you through His shed blood on the cross. He can calm your soul as He calmed the waters, giving you peace beyond measure. You will be so glad you did!

TRIANGLE OF LOVE

Rob Baker and his seven-year-old daughter, Maria, lived with his mother in a big house in the country hills of Southern Indiana. Rob's wife passed away when Maria was just three years old from the dreaded illness of cancer. His father had also passed away several years ago, leaving his mother alone in their big house, so Rob and Maria moved in with her. The job Rob had took him away from home for two or three days a week. Rob didn't want to leave Maria with just any baby sitter. The elder Mrs. Baker was lonely in her big house, so she was glad to have her son and only grandchild move in with her. She enjoyed looking after Maria and Maria loved her grandmother very much.

Every Sunday they would go to a little country church and every night that Rob was home he would kneel at Maria's bedside. Holding hands, they would pray together and thank God for their many blessings.

One night as they knelt in prayer, Maria prayed that she might be able to someday have a pretty new mommy. Oh, she and Granny got along just fine, but her friends in school and church all had pretty, young mothers to take them places. With Granny's arthritis, it was getting harder for her to get around. Rob was surprised to hear his daughter ask this favor from God. He had never really given too much thought of getting married right away because he still thought of his dear wife so much.

When Maria was through praying, she asked her daddy if he thought he could find a pretty mommy for her. The little girl assured her daddy that no one would ever take the place of her real mother. But what if something should ever happen to Granny Baker, then who would take care of her when daddy was away from home?

Rob really hadn't given that too much thought until now, but he told

155

Maria he would pray about it. If his young daughter was to have a new mommy, God was going to have to reveal to him the right person, because he would not marry someone just because she was pretty on the outside. She must be a God-fearing woman, one who would be willing to move in with them in their big country house, and someone who would love Maria as well as he himself. From that night on Maria and Rob continued to pray that perhaps God would find a new wife and mommy for the two of them if it was to be His will.

Nothing was said, however, to Granny Baker because they did not want her to think that she wasn't useful anymore. In fact, Granny also had told Rob that he should start thinking about Maria's future as well as his and that perhaps he should get married again when the right person came around.

Rob wondered why all of a sudden the idea of marriage was thrown at him. Was God trying to tell him that perhaps he should give this some serious thought?

A few days later Rob again left for his business trip to Chicago. On the plane he happened to sit beside an elderly man who was on his way back to Chicago from Cincinnati where he had visited his ailing sister. In talking to this man, he found out that he was a retired minister and a fine Christian man. Being a widower, he lived with his daughter, who was a schoolteacher near Chicago.

Rob told this man that he, too, was a widower, with a seven-year-old daughter. He asked the elderly gentleman if he ever considered getting married again. The man said he thought he was too old to think of getting married any more unless God had other plans for him. Then Rob told him how his daughter and his mother thought he should seriously think about marriage again, but up until recently he really had not even thought about it. He would do so only if God provided a nice Christian lady to fulfill the duties of being a wife and instant mother at the same time. His daughter was his first obligation and he did not want to do anything that would hurt her. So Rob would be very particular in finding the right helpmate that could be the third party in his triangle of marriage, and God would have to find her for him. The other two points of the triangle would of course include he himself and, most of all, God at the top.

The elderly gentleman asked Rob about his age. Rob told him he was thirty-seven. It was soon time for the plane to land, so the elderly man quickly wrote something on a piece of paper and handed it to Rob just before they left the plane. As they were leaving the plane, the retired minister told Rob that he would be praying for him. Then he disappeared in the crowd, and Rob never saw him again.

Once in the taxi and on the way to his hotel, Rob remembered the paper that the elderly man had given him and he realized he didn't even know the man's name. When he opened the paper, he was surprised to find the address of a lady written on it, and that was all it said. Rob thought perhaps the man might have written his name on it, but he hadn't. Then Rob remembered something the elderly gentleman had told him on the plane. He said: "WHEN GOD CLOSES A DOOR HE ALWAYS OPENS A WINDOW." Something inside of Rob seemed to tell him that he had to find out whom this lady might be, the one whose address had been written on the piece of paper.

Once inside his hotel room, Rob looked through the pages of the phone book to see if her phone number might possibly be listed. The address of this lady, Rosanna Palmer, was in a suburb of Chicago. Evidently, if she had a phone, it was an unlisted number because Rob could not find it in the phone book.

In the dresser drawer of his room Rob found some hotel stationery and, after praying for God's guidance, he decided he would write to this lady, Rosanna. Rob wondered if she could be the daughter of the elderly man who gave him her address. He also wondered what she looked like and how old she might be. Then he remembered that the elderly gentleman had asked Rob about his age. Perhaps he wanted to find out if Rob was near the age of this woman, Rosanna.

Rob thought of his daughter, Maria, back home with his mother and wondered if they were still praying that Maria might someday have a new mommy. Since God makes no mistakes, Rob felt that God had placed the elderly retired minister on the seat next to him on the plane for the purpose of introducing him to this lady. Rob wrote to her strictly by faith, telling her about the gentleman who had given him her address. If she did not want to write back to some stranger she had never met, that would be okay, but somehow Rob felt in his heart that he would hear from her.

A few days later Rob was back home with Maria and the elderly Mrs. Baker. He cherished the moments he could spend with his daughter.

That evening as Rob again knelt by Maria's bedside, she thanked God for bringing her daddy safely home. Once again the little girl asked for a new mommy because Granny's arthritis really seemed to be bothering her that day and Granny hadn't been able to take her to the park to play with her friends. The mothers had taken their children on a picnic and swimming party at a lovely park about five miles from where the Bakers lived, in the beautiful hills of Southern Indiana, and Maria couldn't go. Rob did not tell Maria or his mother about the letter he had written to this person whom he had never met. But he did tell Maria that she could pray for a new mommy. If it were to be, God would provide one for her at the right time.

In writing to Rosanna, Rob did not give her his home address but instead gave the address to the office of his employment. Not that he didn't trust his mother with his mail, but what would she think if suddenly he would be getting letters with a woman's address on them? How would he explain to her about writing to someone he had never met? There was also a chance that he would not even receive a letter of reply from this lady. Rosanna was such a pretty name and somehow Rob had the faith to believe that he would hear from her.

The next week Rob again flew to Chicago on a business trip. He thought of renting a car and driving out to the suburb where Rosanna apparently lived. Rob wanted to see if he could find her, but then he thought he had better wait to see if she first answered his letter. Why, he wondered, was this person whom he had never met suddenly in his thoughts so much of the time. What did she look like? Did she have dark hair or light hair? Was she tall or short, thin or chubby? Did she wear glasses? Rob tried to put this unknown person out of his mind, but he could not.

When Rob again returned home he went straight to his office instead of going directly home. He started going through his stack of mail and was pleasantly surprised to find a letter from Rosanna. Right away he opened it and noticed the beautiful handwriting throughout the letter. Rosanna explained that the elderly gentleman seated next to him on the plane, who had given him her address, was indeed her father. Mr. Palmer, Rosanna's father, had not told her that he had given her address to Rob until she received her first letter from him. Rosanna also was surprised to receive a letter from someone she had never met. She thought if her father liked this young man he had met on the plane, then she would take a chance in answering his letter and wait and see what might happen. And that was the beginning of a friendly courtship strictly through faith, via mail only.

When Rob felt that he knew a little more about Rosanna, he told his mother and his daughter that he had a new lady friend but had never met her. He told them that they had been corresponding with each other for four months now and he had never even talked to her. Rosanna relied completely on the Faith of God to bring them together if it was to be His will. It would all be in

God's hands. These two separate people did not even know what each other looked like. Rosanna had verified to Rob what her father had said about her being an elementary school teacher. She also said that she had been married about five years ago and that her husband had been killed in a small airplane crash. Up until now she would not let herself get involved with another male friend. Rosanna, like Rob, relied on the Faith and Trust of God to control the present and the future days of her life.

Maria seemed very excited to think that her daddy finally had a new lady friend. Rob assured Maria that just because he was writing to this person, she should not believe that they might get married. He told Maria that once he had met Rosanna perhaps he would find out this lady would not be someone he would want to be his wife or Maria's mother.

Maria begged her daddy to take her to Chicago so she could meet her and then she could tell if this lady would be a good mommy or not. Rob said that perhaps in a few weeks they could take a little trip to Chicago, just the two of them, and try to spend some time with their new unseen friend.

By now Rosanna's letters were coming to Rob Baker's house and Maria, taking the return address from Rosanna's letters, also began writing to her, unknown to Rob. Maria wrote and told Rosanna that she needed a new mommy and would she please come to live with them. Rosanna assured Maria in a letter that it was not that simple, but that she should continue to pray that God's will be done in all of their lives.

Then one day Rob received a letter from Rosanna stating that her aunt in Cincinnati was very ill. She and her father, the elderly Mr. Palmer, would be going there to see her the following weekend. Her father would be staying there for a week but she would have to go back home to teach school again on Monday. Upon going back to Chicago from Cincinnati on the plane there would be a short lay over at the Indianapolis airport, and perhaps if it would work into Rob's schedule they could meet at the airport for the first time, even if it was just for a short time.

Rob lived an hour's drive from the airport. He was used to making this trip, as he often did when his job took him away on business, and he would usually fly out of this airport. He seemed excited about the opportunity to finally meet this secret admirer. Maria begged her daddy to let her go along and he agreed to have her go with him to meet this person for whom she had been praying for, for so long.

There was a restaurant at the airport and Rob thought the three of them could have a brief lunch together before Rosanna had to catch her next flight back to Chicago. Rob told Maria that she should not expect to find that Rosanna was the beautiful lady she had been dreaming of to be her new mommy. Perhaps they might find out upon seeing Rosanna that this was not the kind of person they would want to live with. Maria told her Daddy that she had a dream about a lady who was to be her mommy. She was very pretty and God had told her this lady would soon come to live with them. Rob wondered if God could possibly be trying to talk to him through his little girl? Would Maria be able to recognize Rosanna at the airport if indeed God did reveal Rosanna to her in a dream? They would soon find out.

Rosanna told Rob what time she would be at the airport and that he would recognize her by the red silk rose she would be holding. All the way to the airport Maria had many questions for her daddy. Rob himself wondered what was in store for him and his little girl. And what about his dear mother, should he happen to get married again? He couldn't put her out of the house. A small summerhouse stood behind their big house. It had three rooms in it that perhaps could be fixed up for his mother, should he marry again. Then he thought of his first wife and wondered if this was what she would want for him and Maria. Surely she would not want Maria to be alone without a mother. God seemed to be truly working in a mysterious way. What a unique way to meet the lady who just might be Maria's new mother and his new wife.

Rob could feel his heart beating fast as they entered the airport terminal. He was sure Rosanna would know them due to the fact that there are not too many men alone at the airport with a little girl at their side. Rob felt he knew a lot about Rosanna from all the letters that they had been writing the past four months, but he still did not know what she looked like. And then he saw her! This lovely young lady with soft light brown curls embracing her radiant face. Their eyes met each other and Rob thought surely this must be Rosanna! As he looked down at Maria to see if she, too, had noticed this lovely person, the young lady disappeared, and Maria had not seen her.

Then Rob saw another young lady coming towards him holding a red rose and his heart sank. This lady had a lovely smile but she was poorly dressed. It appeared as if her hair had not been washed for some time and she was short and rather heavy. Maria saw her also and told her daddy that this was not the lady they were supposed to meet. He didn't know what to say. He kept looking around the terminal for the lady with the soft brown hair and lovely eyes he had first seen. Meanwhile the lady with the rose asked him if he was Rob Baker and if the little girl was his daughter, Maria, and he assured her they were. Then Maria asked her if she was the lady that God sent to be her new mommy because she held the silk rose.

Maria said if she was, she didn't look like the lady she had seen in her dream. Embarrassed at what his daughter had just said, Rob asked the young lady if her name was Rosanna. She evaded answering him by saying she didn't have much time before she had to catch her next plane and she wanted to eat a bite before her next flight home.

Then the young lady handed Maria the rose she was holding and Rob politely asked her to have lunch with him and his daughter there at the airport. Maria whispered to her daddy not to worry because this was not the lady God had for them but they had better go eat with her anyway. If this wasn't Rosanna, who could she be? Also, why was she carrying the rose, Rob wondered? And like Maria said, where was the real Rosanna?

When they stepped inside the restaurant, Rob saw the same lovely young lady he had previously seen. For a moment her pleading brown eyes met his. But then she turned away and looked towards the man sitting across from her. Rob thought that this could not be Rosanna because she had a gentleman with her. Just then Maria saw this same lovely young lady and told her daddy this was the person she had seen in her dream. And before Rob could say anything, Maria went over to the young lady, already seated, and asked her if she was the real Rosanna. Was she the one God had sent to be her new mommy? An embarrassed, blushing Rob came over to the table where the young woman and gentleman were seated and apologized for what his daughter had just said.

His apology was accepted and the young lady said that she was indeed Rosanna Palmer. The lovely young lady went on to explain that she had met this other couple on the plane. They were also on their way back to Chicago, and she decided she would really test Rob's faith. Rosanna thought if Rob would be kind enough to have lunch with the lady Rosanna had given her rose to, then she would know that the young man she was about to meet was indeed sent from God. Rosanna thanked the chubby young lady for meeting Rob with the rose in her hand, and also her husband who had been sitting with her. Rosanna told the waiter that she would pay for the couple's lunch. The short lady, with the straggly brown hair, thanked Rosanna for letting her be helpful and for buying their lunch.

What Rosanna had just done really impressed Rob. He seemed to be overtaken by the kindness of this lady he had written to for so long and was finally now able to meet for the first time!

The time at the airport went quickly by. Rosanna would soon be catching her flight back to Chicago. Maria asked her when she was going to come live with them and be her new mommy. Rob and Rosanna were both somewhat embarrassed, but as their eyes met somehow they knew that this would not be the end of their relationship.

Rob now had Rosanna's unlisted phone number and he would call her every time he was in Chicago. He even rented a car and would go see her whenever his job allowed. It wasn't long until Rob knew, in his heart, that Rosanna was the one for him, according to God's will, and soon they were making plans to be married.

Neither Rosanna nor her father liked living in the big city and the thought of living in the quiet hills of Southern Indiana thrilled her; but what about her father? Would he continue to stay in Chicago by himself or would she be able to find a place for him to live, close to her, once she and Rob were married? One weekend Rosanna and her father, Mr. Palmer, went to visit Rob, Maria and Granny Baker and to see the big house where she would soon be living.

Mr. Palmer and Granny Baker hit it off together and found out they, too, had much in common. The elderly gentleman loved the hills of Southern Indiana as much as his daughter did, or was it that they loved the ones who lived in those hills? Mr. Palmer had not known Granny Baker as long as his daughter had known Rob, but by faith he was going to ask the elderly woman to marry him. Granny happily accepted. Together they fixed up the old summerhouse where they would soon be living. They would leave the big house for Rob, Rosanna and Maria. It seemed to Mr. Palmer that God had now opened a window for him as well as for his daughter. Maria said she didn't know she would be getting a new Grandpa, too, but she liked the idea. Granny Palmer, as she was now known, seemed so happy that she almost forgot she ever had arthritis. She and her new husband are now enjoying their new home and life together. Also, Mr. Palmer fell in love with Maria. He now had the grandchild, he always hoped for. Maria loved him as well. And now they are all just one big happy family.

As for Rob and Rosanna, who of course are now married, they often think back of the letters they wrote to each other. They were thankful that God worked through Rosanna's father, by him giving Rob her address on the plane. They were thankful also that Rob had the courage and faith to write to Rosanna. And they were especially thankful that little Maria continued to pray and have faith that God would find her a new mommy. Rob and Maria both fell in love with Rosanna, for which they were all thankful.

Rosanna would be teaching at the same school where Maria attended, because one of the former teachers had just retired. She would be home when Maria would be home in the summer time and be there when Rob would have to go away on his business trips. The three of them got along so very well together, because Christ dwelled among them.

Maria's prayers had now changed to prayers of thanksgiving, thanking God for answering her prayers for a new mommy, and a new grandpa as well. Rob and Rosanna continued to have faith that God would direct their future life as he had directed the past. Their marriage was by faith thus creating a beautiful union of hearts with Christ at the head of their family.

If we put our trust and faith in God He will do wonders in our lives, too. Why not give him a chance to do just that?

Marriage is a three-fold Union of Hearts. If you are married or perhaps thinking of getting married some day, imagine a triangle, if you will, and put yourself, as Rob did, on one of the bottom points of the triangle. Now visualize your spouse or life's companion at the other point on the bottom of the triangle, as Rosanna did. Most important of all put God on the top point of the triangle. You can easily see that when both married partners, together on the bottom of this triangle, walk more closely towards God, who is on the top of the triangle, their life together as husband and wife will also be brought closer together. This should create a LOVE TRIANGLE that should, by God's Grace, never be broken!

Why not begin a LOVE TRIANGLE in your home today, by putting God at the top, yourself at one point on the bottom and your spouse and or family members at the other point of the triangle? Then encourage each one in your household to begin a closer walk with God and see if you are not all brought closer together in a wonderful triangle with God's love wrapping around your whole family. You are encouraged to read I Corinthians 13 in the Bible, putting the word LOVE in the place of Charity.

God

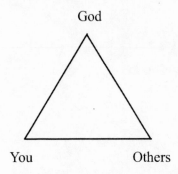

You   Others

THREE LITTLE SISTERS

Kenyon Wayne, a widower in his early thirties tried his best to raise his three young daughters. After the death of Kenyon's wife, he and his little girls went to live with his mother in the suburbs of a large mid-western city.

Kenyon's mother, Verena, a widow herself, lived in a large older house in the city. There was plenty of room for all of them in this big two-story house. She took the family in so the girls would have someone to care for them and to keep house for her son while he was at work.

Kenyon's three daughters, Karen, age nine, Anita, age eight, and little Gretchen, age five, were his whole life. Mr. Wayne worked as a maintenance man in a nearby hospital. His meager income seemed barely enough to support his precious daughters and himself.

Ever since Kenyon's wife died during the birth of baby Gretchen, the young man was determined to keep his little family together. He had thought about working two jobs but decided it was more important to be home with his girls in the evenings, now that his wife was gone. Kenyon would sacrifice the luxuries of life just to spend time with Karen, Anita and Gretchen. The two older girls barely remembered their mother; Grandma Verena was the only mother they really knew.

Kenyon was a Godly man, who loved and lived for the Lord. He could always remember his parents taking him to church, as a child. Likewise every Sunday, you would still see Kenyon, his mother and girls attending church together. The three young sisters loved to go to Sunday school. During the week you could hear them singing the songs they learned in church. Often the girls would line up their dolls and teddy bears and pretend to be in Sunday school. The two older girls loved taking turns being teacher to their silent audience.

Karen, the oldest of the sisters, had soft, curly, brown hair like her mother. Two dimples accented her pleasant disposition. Anita had lovely long blond hair and blue eyes like her daddy. Little Gretchen, like her older sister, had brown curly hair and deep brown eyes that sparkled as she talked.

One day Karen decided to ride the bicycle she shared with her sister, Anita. Bobby, an ornery neighbor boy who lived around the block from the Wayne family, threw a stick into the spokes of the front wheel of Karen's bicycle. It caused Karen to tumble to the ground. In doing so she badly scraped her left leg and arm as she fell on top of the bicycle. Bobby ran away, laughing at what he had done. Gretchen, with her brown curly hair waving in the wind, had been following Karen a short distance behind, peddling her little red tricycle as fast as her short legs could go. She was trying to keep up with her sister and saw the boy throw the stick into the bicycle spokes.

Karen was thankful this happened on the sidewalk and not on the road, where she sometimes rode, otherwise a car could have hit her after she fell. With tears in her eyes the oldest sister managed to stand up on her feet. She looked down at her hurting leg and saw that it was bleeding.

Brushing the brown curly hair out of her teary eyes, Karen stood her bicycle up. Why, she wondered, did Bobby do this to her?

Gretchen said, "You'll be all right, Karen, I know you will. Please, don't cry."

Slowly the two sisters started for home. Karen, walking with a limp, pushed her bicycle closely behind Gretchen, who peddled her little red tricycle slowly in front of her sister. When they arrived home, Grandma Verena carefully washed Karen's injured leg and arm, putting band-aids where needed. They were thankful her injuries were not serious. Grandma reminded Karen that in time the bruises would be gone and you would not be able to tell she had ever fallen.

Two days later after school, Karen, and her sister Anita, were again going around the block. This time they were on roller skates. Their little sister, Gretchen, followed behind on her little tricycle. Suddenly Karen doubled over and fell to the ground. She said her side hurt so badly she could not stand up. Little Gretchen got off of her tricycle and sat on the sidewalk beside her sister.

Gretchen looked up to her sister with encouraging sparkling eyes and said, "You'll be all right, Karen. Don't be afraid, I'm here with you."

Meanwhile, Anita, her long blond hair softly flowing behind her, skated home as fast as she could go for help. Grandma immediately tried to locate her son at work to notify him that something had happened to Karen.

Mrs. Hirshey, Bobby's mother, who lived across the street from where Karen lay on the sidewalk, was just coming home from work and happened to see the young girl fall. Instead of calling the grandmother first, the lady quickly ran into her house and called the EMS. Before Grandmother Verena could get to Karen, Mrs. Hirshey had gone over to the young girl lying on the sidewalk to see what had happened. The lady noticed the bruises on Karen's arm and leg. Without even asking Karen how she received those bruises, thoughts of child abuse ran through this lady's mind. Little did Mrs. Hirshey realize that it was because of her son, Bobby, that Karen had these bruises.

Finally Grandma and Anita arrived at Karen's side after notifying Kenyon that something had happened to his daughter. There, around the block, Grandma saw Karen lying on the sidewalk with her roller skates still on. The girl, with her dimpled, teary cheeks, seemed to be in a lot of pain.

Beside her on the sidewalk, sat little Gretchen saying, "Please don't cry. Jesus will help you, Karen. The Bible says Jesus made sick people better and I know He will make you better, too, if you are sick." The youngest sister reached over to Karen and brushed the soft, brown curls away from her face.

The EMS had arrived and insisted on taking the sick girl to the hospital for observation. The attendant thought it might be Karen's appendix. Grandma, seeing Karen in so much pain, agreed that the girl needed medical attention as soon as possible. Grandma could not just leave Anita and Gretchen, but she did not want to send Karen off by herself either. Finally she told Anita to be brave and take her little sister home and stay there until their daddy arrived. He should be there very soon. So Grandma Verena, in her gingham dress and soiled apron, rode in the EMS with her granddaughter, Karen, to the hospital.

Anita tried hard to be brave. She took hold of Gretchen's dimpled hand and the two little girls started out for home. Before they arrived home, they met Bobby, the boy who had thrown the stick in Karen's bicycle spokes two days earlier.

"It just serves her right!" said Bobby. "Karen deserves to have something wrong with her."

Anita looked at the boy and said, "Karen does not deserve to be sick or to be treated the way you are treating her. Please let her alone!"

"So you think you are better than I am. Well, we'll see about that!" said Bobby as he adjusted the glasses on his dirty face. Then he gave Anita a hard shove, knocking her down onto the sidewalk. The boy laughed and took off running.

"Here, take my hand, Sister," said little Gretchen, as she tried to pull Anita to her feet. "Bobby is a naughty boy. I wonder if he loves Jesus. He doesn't act like he does." The little girl, with pleading eyes, looked up at her sister and saw the tears in her eyes. She said, "Don't cry, Anita, you'll be okay. I know you will." Gretchen reached up to her sister and stroked her long blond hair. Then the two girls slowly walked back to their house.

Just as Kenyon pulled the car into the driveway he saw his two daughters as they were walking hand in hand up the steps that led to the porch in front of their big house. Kenyon hurried out of the car and put his arms around the girls. The young father saw that his daughter, Anita, was limping and noticed the bruise on her leg. Anita told her daddy that she had been pushed down by the same boy that threw a stick into the spokes of Karen's bicycle a couple of days ago. Kenyon took the girls into the house. He checked Anita's leg and after seeing that she was not seriously injured, put a band-aid on the girl's leg.

Anita and Gretchen told their father all about Karen and how sick she appeared to be. Anita said that Grandma rode in the ambulance with their sister to the hospital. Then Kenyon and his two daughters got in their car and drove to the same hospital, where Kenyon was employed, to be at Karen's side.

Sure enough, Karen's appendix was badly inflamed. The doctor said it needed to come out before it ruptured. Mr. Wayne gave permission for the operation, which lasted a little over an hour.

The doctor came to the waiting room and told Kenyon that all went well with the surgery and Karen should be just fine in a few days. The doctor then asked if he could briefly examine Anita and Gretchen. Kenyon looked puzzled and said the girls were okay and didn't need to be examined. The doctor insisted and said he had orders to examine them.

The doctor looked Gretchen over and found nothing wrong with the child. Then he examined Anita and found what he had suspected. There he saw a big bruise on her leg covered by a small band-aid. The bruise was similar to the one he had noticed on Karen's leg. Now he was sure that Mrs. Hirshey had told him the truth. The girls were being physically abused. The doctor proceeded to tell Mr. Wayne that he had no other choice but to take the two older girls away from him and his mother. The doctor believed that one of the two adults in the Wayne household had been beating the girls.

Mrs. Hirshey, a welfare caseworker, had spotted the bruises on Karen's arm and leg when she saw the girl doubled over on the sidewalk two days earlier. It was then that she surmised that the girls were being abused. Mrs. Hirshey told the doctor that the bruises she saw are similar to those of other abused children. The determined lady had quickly received a court order to have the girls removed from Mr. Wayne's home.

Kenyon and his mother, Verena, were completely speechless as to what had just taken place. They couldn't believe what they had heard! Surely this was all some kind of a dream and had not really happened.

Anita, in her pretty multi-colored, flowered, dress, hung tightly to her daddy and cried, "That's not true! Daddy and Grandma never beat us! It's all Bobby's fault. Daddy, don't let them take me away! Please, Daddy, please hold me tight!" She pulled up the hem of her dress and wiped the tears from her eyes.

Kenyon and the grandmother both agreed with Anita that they have never ever abused the girls. He tried to explain to the doctor that the bruises were caused by falling: due to the mischievous acts of Mrs. Hirshey's son but the doctor would not believe him.

Little Gretchen began crying and said, "Daddy is right, I saw Bobby throw the stick at Karen's bicycle and I saw him push Anita down. Jesus knows we're telling the truth, Doctor, we really are! You can't take my sisters away. You can't, you can't!"

The doctor still would not believe the Wayne family who by now were all in tears. "I'm sorry," he said. "The law is the law. Once a month the caseworker will be coming to your house, Kenyon, to examine your youngest daughter. If any bruises are found on her, we will take her away as well. I don't make the rules, I just follow orders."

Then the doctor went on to say that Karen should be out of the recovery room by now. He told the family they would be allowed to spend just one hour with her, then they will have to leave. Anita would be allowed to stay with Karen until the foster family arrives. They will be coming shortly from another nearby city to pick Anita up and to also visit Karen. Mr. Kenyon and the grandmother are to be gone by the time the foster parents arrive. The doctor continued to say that he was sorry, but he must do all he can to keep the two girls from further abuse. He assured Mr. Wayne that the sisters would be kept together and not separated. Then he walked out of the room.

Anita and Gretchen were crying as they held tightly onto their daddy's hands. Verena tried to be brave and not cry but tears were coming from her eyes as well. The grandmother took an old handkerchief from her apron pocket and wiped her weary eyes. Kenyon also fought hard to keep back the tears but he could not. The sick girl lying in her hospital room was not yet aware of what would soon be taking place.

As Kenyon, his mother Verena, Anita and Gretchen stepped into Karen's hospital room, the young girl reached out her hand. Mr. Wayne took his daughter's hand, brushed her hair out of her eyes, then broke into tears again. The two younger sisters clung tightly to their grandmother. Still in unbelief of what the doctor said, Kenyon sat at his oldest daughter's bedside and slowly began to tell her that she would not be coming home after being dismissed from the hospital. Instead she and Anita would be placed in a foster home together. It was very difficult for Kenyon to explain all this to his children. He told his family he would do everything in his power to get the girls back home as soon as possible. At least Karen and Anita would stay together and he was thankful for that. Mr. Wayne told the two girls that no matter where they go he will always be their daddy. He said thoughts of them would always be in his heart. He went on to say that he loves them very much but Jesus loves them even more and He will take care of them.

Little Gretchen, with tears in her dark brown eyes that were not sparkling now, looked at Karen lying in the hospital bed. Between whimpers of crying the youngest girl said, "Jesus will help you and He will watch over you just like Daddy said. He will, I just know He will."

Karen, now crying as well, said, "It's all Mrs. Hirshey's fault, because of her son. Bobby said his mother told him to copy my answers for the test we had the last week of school, because she didn't have time to help him study. I told Bobby I would not give him the answers because that's not fair. Then he failed the test. He has been picking on Anita and me ever since."

"So that is what happened! Bobby's mother is the caseworker for the welfare department. She is the one who is taking my girls away from me! Well, I won't let her, you can be sure of that!" said Kenyon who seemed very upset and rightfully so. "Karen and Anita, you may have to go for a few days, but rest assured you will soon be back with Grandma, Gretchen and me."

Just then the head nurse came into Karen's room and said, "Mr. Wayne, your time with your daughter is up. You have to leave now. Anita is to remain here with Karen until the foster parents arrive. If you cause any trouble, Mr. Wayne, you could lose your job here. Also, I might add, when you come to work, even though your daughter is here as a patient, you cannot come to visit her. When you leave here today, that is the last you will see of her unless a miracle happens." And Kenyon did indeed pray for a miracle.

Kenyon hugged his two older daughters and they wept bitterly in each other's arms. With tears running down their cheeks, Grandma Verena and Gretchen hugged them as well. The two older girls held very tightly onto their daddy's hands. They did not want to let go. The nurses could hear the girls crying clear out in the hallway. Finally Kenyon broke loose from his two sobbing young daughters, then he, Verena and Gretchen sadly left the hospital room leaving Karen and Anita behind. They would all now begin to pray for the miracle the nurse mentioned.

As they were leaving the room Gretchen turned back and saw Karen bury her head in her pillow as Anita held her hand. The little girl still with tears in her eyes said, "Jesus will take care of you, I know He will." Then out into the hallway the sad little girl went, trying to be brave as she followed her daddy and grandmother out to the car.

For Kenyon this was the hardest thing he had to go through, even harder than losing his wife whom he dearly loved and missed. She had been so sick and after her death she no longer had to suffer. Kenyon knew that his dear wife went to be with Jesus when she died. He knew someday he would be able to see her again. He now also placed his daughters in Jesus' hands, but this was different.

It was so very hard for the young father to leave his daughters behind, not knowing what kind of people would be taking care of them. Would they be Christian people, he wondered? Would they take the girls to a good Bible believing church? Would they continue to instruct them as he had? Would he really be able to get them back in a few days? All these thoughts and more came into his mind as he drove home. His mother sitting beside him, and Gretchen still whimpering on the back seat of the car, said very little to one another.

When the heartbroken, incomplete family arrived home they were again reminded of Karen and Anita. Upon seeing their toys, bicycle, clothing and so forth, they once more broke down in tears. Kenyon concerned that the separation of Karen from her family might slow her healing process still could not believe what had happened.

Gretchen ran up to the room she shared with her sisters. She grabbed their teddy bears and with one in each arm the youngster knelt beside her sisters' double bed.

"Dear, Jesus," Gretchen prayed, "Please, take care Karen and Anita. Please, help Karen to get better and to be strong. Help Anita not to be afraid. Please, help the people where they will be staying, to be kind and good to my sisters. You know I will miss them very much, so bring them home soon. My bedroom will be so empty without them. Daddy's heart is breaking and so are Grandma's and mine. Please, Jesus, help us all to be strong, Amen." Then the little girl climbed up on the bed, her two older sisters shared, and cried herself to sleep, still clinging to their two raggedy teddy bears.

Kenyon, still very upset, called his minister and informed him of what had just taken place. The minister's son was a fine Christian lawyer. Kenyon knew he could depend on this young lawyer for help. The minister called his son and the two men immediately went over to Mr. Wayne's house where they had a long talk together.

When Gretchen woke up, she went into the living room where her daddy and the two men were discussing the situation. She crawled up onto her daddy's lap, rubbing her sleepy eyes. Gretchen looked at the other two men and said, "It's all Bobby's fault! Mrs. Hirshey's son is not a very nice boy. Jesus will help my sisters; I know He will. I hope He helps that naughty boy, too. He needs help and so does his mother."

The little girl, with sparkling brown eyes that made you melt when you looked at her, then went on tell how Bobby had thrown a stick into the spokes of Karen's bicycle wheel, causing her to fall. Gretchen said she saw the boy do it. And he also pushed Anita down causing her to get the bruises on her leg, like Karen had received when she fell.

The lawyer and the minister both knew that Mr. Wayne would never abuse his daughters. From the lips of this little girl they now knew what had happened. They could tell by the look on Gretchen's face that she was telling the truth. The lawyer said he had trouble with Mrs. Hirshey before. She was a woman who could not be trusted. The young lawyer said he would do everything he could to get the two older girls home as soon as possible.

A few days later Karen was dismissed from the hospital and joined her sister, Anita in the foster home. At the home where the two older girls were staying, Jesus truly was on their side, just like Gretchen said He would be. Mr. Lee, the husband of the foster couple, and Mrs. Hirshey were brother and sister, but the girls did not know that.

The girls found a large assortment of stuffed animals in the bedroom they shared together. The second night after Karen had been dismissed from the hospital the two girls lined up all the animals along one wall in their bedroom. Then they played Sunday school like they often did at home, with their dolls and teddy bears again being their silent audience.

Mr. and Mrs. Lee heard the girls singing and went to their room to see what the two sisters were up to. You see, no one had ever sung like that before in the Lee household. Mr. and Mrs. Lee quietly stood in the doorway leading to the girls' room and watched their foster children. The couple was amazed as they listened to the singing. As Karen and Anita sang the songs they had learned in Sunday school, they were letting their little lights shine even in this difficult situation. The two girls were also telling Bible stories to the stuffed animals lined up along bedroom wall. Mrs. Lee had a lump in her throat as she watched these young innocent girls.

Suddenly Anita noticed the foster parents standing by the door. The girl, with lovely long blond hair, asked if they would all be going to Sunday school the next Sunday. She said their daddy always took them to church. The couple looked at each other knowing that they had not been to church in years. Mr. and Mrs. Lee said they would think about it. Karen thanked Mrs. Lee for all the pretty clothes that she bought for the girls and said the dresses would be very pretty to wear for church. In fact the girls had never seen such pretty clothes before.

The hearts of Mr. and Mr. Lee were also being touched at meal-time as well, when the girls bowed their heads to give thanks for the food they were about to eat. The foster parents had gotten away from this privilege of saying Grace a long time ago. Karen asked Mr. Lee to read the Bible like their daddy did after supper, while they were still seated around the table. Mr. Lee looked down and said that he would try to find his Bible and perhaps sometime he would read to them. In his heart he really did not want to read it because he felt guilty and yet he knew that he should.

The next night, the girls asked Mr. Lee to please come to their room and pray with them before they go to sleep. They told Mr. Lee that their daddy always prayed with them at night. The man seemed embarrassed but hesitantly agreed to do so. There was something about these two girls that seemed to melt his heart. He pulled up a chair to the edge of the bed the girls had been sharing, the last few days. There he listened as the young girls began to pray.

Karen prayed first. "Dear Jesus," she began, "Please be with Daddy and Grandma and my sister, Gretchen. Please don't let Mrs. Hirshey take Gretchen away, too. I miss Daddy so much! And please forgive Mrs. Hirshey's boy, Bobby, for trying to cheat with my papers at school. Forgive him for making Anita and me fall and getting bruised so his mother would take us away. Dear Jesus, I know you love the boy like you love me. Please help him not to be mean anymore. Thank you, Jesus, for helping me to get better from my operation, but I sure wish I could be home with Daddy. I love you, Jesus, Amen."

Mr. Lee sat spellbound as he heard the words of this lovely innocent young girl. Her dimpled face almost seemed to radiate as she prayed. He couldn't believe that Karen even prayed for his own sister, Mrs. Hirshey, and her son, Bobby. Could it really be that Karen was telling the truth?

Did his nephew really cause the bruises on the girls' legs? Perhaps the one who abused the girls, after all, was his own nephew and not their father or grandmother. He always knew that Bobby was a spoiled boy and his mother would do anything he wanted her to do. Now perhaps this time they had gone too far!

Then Mr. Lee looked at Anita, with her lovely blond hair and blue eyes accenting her face as she lay on the soft pillow beside Karen. He listened to her as she said her prayers. Anita began, "Dear Jesus, I miss Daddy, Grandma and little Gretchen so very much. I'm sure they miss us, too. Gretchen said you would take care of us and I know you will. Please, take care of Daddy, Grandma and little sister at home. And take care of the foster parents in this home. I know you love them too, Jesus, like you love all of us and even Mrs. Hirshey and her boy Bobby. Please help them to love you, too. And help Karen and me to be good girls so we can go home soon. I know you will help Daddy because his heart must be breaking like my heart is, because I miss him so much. You know Daddy hasn't done anything wrong. Dear Jesus, you took our mommy away from Daddy once; please don't take us away from him now. I love you, Jesus; please help me to be a good girl. Amen." Then Anita looked right into Mr. Lee's eyes and asked him to tuck her in bed like her daddy always did.

Mr. Lee just couldn't resist and suddenly he took both girls into his arms. With tears in his eyes, he said, "I have never seen such faith in this man, Jesus, as you two girls have. He must really be a special friend that you can talk to Him the way you do. Your daddy must be very special also. You know something else, girls? For some reason I cannot explain, I really believe your story. Perhaps you did not know that Mrs. Lee is my sister, but I now think that God used her to send you girls here to us. When my sister and I were children we always went to church, but after our parents died, we both drifted away. It took both of you to show me that I need to go back to church and learn more about Jesus." With his arms still around the girls he went on to say, "If you girls are still here on Sunday we will go to church and Sunday

School. What do you say, girls, would you go with Mrs. Lee and me?"

"Oh yes," they both cried together, "We would love to, but we wish we could go to church with our daddy, sister and grandma. It must be hard for them to go to church without us."

Mr. Lee took a big handkerchief from his pocket, wiped his eyes and said, "Tomorrow is Saturday and the Welfare office is closed but I'm going to see if I can locate my sister, Mrs. Hirshey, and see if you two girls can go home where you both belong. We have had several foster children in our home in the past but never anyone as precious as you two girls. I will really miss you when you're gone, but you belong with your father."

Just then Mrs. Lee entered the room, also with tears in her eyes. She had been standing outside the girls' bedroom door and heard every word spoken. She agreed with her husband by saying, "God truly must have sent the girls here." What a strange way for God to get their attention, she thought. How hard it must have been for Karen, Anita and their father to be separated from one another. But it was God's way of getting through to this couple that they needed to get their lives together Spiritually and serve the Lord. How Mrs. Lee longed for the faith that these two young girls have shown while staying at their house. Yes, the girls definitely need to go home and she and her husband definitely need to go back to church, beginning Sunday.

Mr. and Mrs. Lee both hugged the girls, tucked them in bed and told them good night. The thought of perhaps going home soon made the girls so happy that each one planted a big kiss on the cheeks of their foster parents. Then the Lees left the room.

"Gretchen said Jesus would take care of us," repeated Anita once more as she looked at her older sister cuddled next to her. "I think He is going to take care of Mr. and Mrs. Lee, too. Do you suppose somehow Jesus will let Daddy know we may be coming home soon?"

"It was a terrible thing to be taken away from our family, but if we helped the foster parents to go back to church then maybe God did want us here for a little while," replied Karen with her eyes half closed. "I know what we are going through is hard for all of us but just think of all Jesus went through when those mean people nailed Him on that awful cross. But now, because of that He is in heaven and so is our mommy. Yes, somehow I think Daddy can feel that we may be home soon."

The girls had single beds to sleep in now, but ever since they had come to this foster home they both shared one single bed together. It helped to make them feel closer to each other since they were not at home in their own bed.

Anita was careful not to get against Karen's tummy, where she had her surgery. Finally the two sisters, with their arms around each other, drifted off to sleep.

The next day, Mr. Wayne and his lawyer friend went to see Mrs. Hirshey. The lawyer told the woman how Gretchen witnessed everything her son, Bobby, had done to Karen and Anita. He said he was sure the bruises on the girl's legs were caused because of her son's unruly behavior and not by their father's abuse. The lawyer went on to say that perhaps it is her son that needs to be in a foster home and not Mr. Wayne's daughters.

Mrs. Hirshey was very restless and upset. She did not want to believe the lawyer's story. Then her phone rang. It was her brother, Mr. Lee, from the neighboring city, calling to say the girls, who were entrusted in their care, need to go home to their father. He told his sister she had made a bad mistake and should admit it. Mrs. Hirshey could not believe her brother had turned against her also.

Finally the woman admitted that she had been wrong. Her son didn't like the Wayne girls and often told his mother it was Karen's fault he received bad grades in school because she would not give him the answers to their tests. Mrs. Hirshey, always too busy to help her son with his homework, had told Bobby to get help from someone else. When Karen refused to help him cheat, the boy made up stories about the Wayne girls. Bobby had told his mother that Mr. Wayne beat his girls. Mrs. Hirshey had believed her son. But now after hearing her brother's story she admitted she made a bad mistake and the girls should be released to their father. Mrs. Hirshey, afraid that Mr. Wayne might press charges against her, said she was sorry and begged his forgiveness. She said her son, Bobby, would be disciplined for what he had done. Mrs. Hirshey promised that she would also try to spend more time with Bobby.

Kenyon Wayne told the woman that everyone makes mistakes. He said he would forgive her for the all the anxiety she put him through by having his girls taken away from him. Then he told her that, most of all, Jesus would forgive her as well. Kenyon said Jesus loves everyone, including her and her son, no matter what they have done. The father, of the three little sisters, said no charges would be pressed but he had one request. It was that Mrs. Hirshey and Bobby start attending a good Bible believing church regularly, beginning tomorrow. The lawyer agreed with Mr. Wayne's decision.

Mrs. Hirshey admitted that she and her brother always went to church as children. Later she became too involved in her own activities and career to take the time to go to church. She, like her brother, now realized she had made a mistake and had been missing out on time she could have spent with her son. She agreed to go to church with Bobby, beginning tomorrow, whether the boy wanted to go or not. Then she gave the lawyer the necessary papers that were needed to have Karen and Anita released to their father. Kenyon could go pick up his daughters yet that day.

Kenyon stood up. With his hands on his hips he looked at Mrs. Hirshey and said, "If taking my two girls away from me will bring a change of heart to you and your brother then I suppose it was worth it all, though it has been very hard for all of us."

Finally the lawyer, standing beside Kenyon bowed his head and began to pray. "Dear Lord," he said, " thank you for giving these people a change of heart. Because of the faith of two young girls who in their innocent ways let their little light shine for those around them, lives have been changed. We all need to repent and be sorry for our sins and ask God's forgiveness. Please help us, Lord, where we have done wrong, to do this. And also I thank You that little Gretchen had faith enough to believe in prayer, asking that You return her sisters home again. Please help us all to have the faith of a child. And please, dear Lord, help Mrs. Hirshey, her son, Bobby, her brother and his wife, Mr. and Mrs. Lee, to come to know You as their Lord and Savior as Kenyon and I have. Help us all to put our trust fully in You. We just thank You that Karen is doing well from her recent surgery and that the two girls could stay together. You know, Lord, this has been very hard on the Wayne family and I thank You for giving them the strength and courage to endure. May You help us all to be a beacon for You to those around about us, Lord. Again thank You for hearing and answering the prayers offered in behalf of the Wayne family. We praise You and love You. In Jesus name, Amen."

Mrs. Hirshey had not heard a prayer like this in years. She stood, wiped her eyes, and again confirmed her commitment to start going to church the following day.

The three adults once more said good-by, each one thanking the other for the way everything turned out. A rejoicing Kenyon, thanked the young lawyer for going with him to Mrs. Hirshey's house. The young father then went home and told his mother and youngest daughter the good news!

A few minutes later Kenyon, Grandma Verena, and Gretchen left for the big city where Karen and Anita were staying. Little Gretchen, with her brown curly hair bobbing around her face, sat in the back seat of the car holding her sister's faded teddy bears as well as her own.

The little one, looking between the three teddy bears with her brown eyes sparkling more than ever before, said, "Daddy, I knew Jesus would help my sisters and bring them home again. Jesus heard me when I prayed for them and I'm sure they prayed for us, too. Don't you think so Daddy?"

Kenyon agreed with Gretchen. Then he said, "Through prayer Jesus can work miracles. We must be very thankful that Jesus heard all of our prayers once again."

It was later in the afternoon by the time Mr. Wayne pulled up to the Lee residence where his two older daughters had been staying since Karen's operation. Through a window Anita saw the family car pull up into the drive way and she cried, "Daddy's here, Daddy's here!"

The two girls ran out to their daddy, who by now had stepped out of the car. They threw their tender young arms around his neck. Then they hugged Grandma Verena and their little sister, Gretchen. Everyone cried tears of joy. Gretchen went back to the car and brought out her sisters' old raggedy teddy bears, and gave each of the girls their own bear. Karen and Anita, who ran out of the house each with a new stuffed animal under their arms, suddenly dropped their new toys, and replaced them with their old raggedy bears. They thought the bears never looked so good.

What a joyful reunion Mr. and Mrs. Lee witnessed from their front porch. The foster parents agreed that this family truly had real love one for another. It was the kind of love they longed for and wished to have.

Mrs. Lee walked out to the car and told the two girls that they could each go back to the bedroom they had been sharing and pick out a dress to take home with them. She told little Gretchen that she could go pick out a stuffed animal to take home. The little girl, not wanting to replace her old teddy bear, said she would take the soft furry kitten Anita had just dropped on the sidewalk. The two older girls thanked the foster parents for everything. The girls once more gave Mr. and Mrs. Lee a big hug and again planted a big kiss on their cheeks.

The reunited Wayne family happily returned home, thankful to be together again. They looked forward to all going together to church the next day as a complete family once more.

Mr. and Mrs. Lee, thankful they had the privilege of caring for Karen and Anita for a few days, vowed to start a new life, serving the Lord as the Wayne family has been doing.

Mrs. Hirshey also thankful that her eyes had been opened promised to take her son, Bobby, to Sunday school and church. She, too, wanted to start life anew hoping to find the love, faith and happiness that the Wayne family had.

So because of the faith and assurance of three children who believed Jesus would help them, others were touched and given the hope of living a better life.

Friend, why not put your faith and trust in Jesus as a little child. He can answer your prayers giving you peace, love and contentment beyond measure. He can help you through the trials of life.

The Bible says in Psalms that, "Out of the mouth of babes and infants you may have your strength ordained." Just as the three young sisters had faith to believe Jesus would somehow hear and answer their prayers, you too, dear friend, can have faith and strength to believe Jesus will answer your prayers. Why not call on Him today? You will be glad you did!

TRUE FRIEND

Just by looking at Sarah with her long, silky blond hair and sparkling blue eyes, you would think she might be the envy of all her classmates, especially of the girls, but not so. You see Sarah had a physical handicap. She had one leg that always wanted to turn inwards. It seemed as though even surgery could not correct this condition and she had to wear a metal brace to keep her leg straight. Without the brace, she walked with a very noticeable limp. At times, the young girl didn't know which was worse, to limp or to wear this brace.

All through grade school, the children called her "Iron Leg," which hurt her more than wearing the brace itself. As a result of this, Sarah often withdrew from her classmates and you would see her alone during recess and the lunch hour. The children didn't realize how cruel they were to her. Being crippled was difficult enough to live with, but to be rejected by classmates hurt Sarah even more.

Sarah usually wore jeans to school to cover her leg brace but there were times when she would wear a long dress or skirt and then the children would really make fun of her.

Sarah soon grew to become a lovely young teenager and her parents and older brother and sister loved her deeply but how she longed to be loved and wanted by other teenagers like her.

Then in the summer when Sarah became fifteen, her father received a transfer in his job and the family moved to Benton, a city in the neighboring state. The parents knew it would be hard for the children to change schools during their high school years, so they prayed for their children to have the strength to cope with their new surroundings. Sarah hoped perhaps she would be accepted by her new classmates and would no longer be called "Iron

Leg."

The first day in her new school, many students noticed that Sarah walked with a slight limp, even with her brace on and they soon labeled her as "Limpy." It didn't matter that she had beautiful long blond hair, sparkling blue eyes and a pleasing personality, the students still seemed to ignore her.

Within a day or two Sarah realized that Benton High had a lovely swimming pool and a great swim team for both girls and boys. How she wished she could participate in that event! With her handicap she thought it would be out of the question to even so much as inquire about it. Besides, no body would want her on their team, she thought.

The school where Sarah attended before coming to Benton did not have a pool, but her father often drove her to a nearby city where they had a WMCA with a nice pool. There she would be allowed to swim for physical therapy. She would remove her leg brace and once in the water, her dad, an avid swimmer himself, could hardly keep up with his lovely daughter. Sarah always looked forward to spending this time with her dad.

Then came time for the first football game of the season. Sarah went to the game with her older brother and sister. The three of them went up on the bleachers and sat with Benton High's cheering block.

Sarah's brother and sister seemed to be adjusting well in their Junior and Senior years, respectfully, in this new school. They did all they could to help their younger sister but often they were busy with their own activities.

Sarah happened to sit next to Carissa, a charming teenager who seemed very popular among the students. Her boy friend played on the football team. Before the game started everyone stood and joined in singing the National Anthem. Carissa stopped singing and listened to the lovely voice next to her. And seated not too far away from them, the school's choir director also stopped singing as Sarah's lovely voice echoed through the bleachers. The song was over before Mrs. Ashley, the choir director, could tell where the lovely voice came from.

Carissa noticed that Sarah had some difficulty as she climbed up onto the bleachers and sat down next to her. Now she discovered something else about this new girl who walked with a limp. It was her lovely voice that rang out like a clear bell, not loud or piercing, just beautiful singing!

Suddenly Carissa, who sang in the high school choir, turned to Sarah and asked her if she ever thought about singing in the choir.

Sarah said she hadn't thought too much about it, for various reasons. Carissa told Sarah that she, herself, sang in the choir and they could surely use such a lovely voice as hers. She also told Sarah that the girl, who sang some of the lead parts in the school musical productions, had moved away this past summer. They needed someone to replace her. Sarah told Carissa all about her handicapped condition and she didn't think the other choir members would accept her.

By the time the football game had ended, Carissa and Sarah had become friends. But Carissa's other friends were envious of the fact that she spent so much time paying attention to this new girl, "Limpy," as they now called her. Carissa remembered the Sunday school lesson from last Sunday where they were instructed to, "Do unto others as you would have them do unto you." For some reason Carissa felt sorry for this new girl and wanted to be kind to her because Jesus would want her to be. Sarah may have a physical handicap but she certainly made up for it in her singing, and she seemed like such a pleasant girl to be with.

Carissa found Mrs. Ashley, the choir director, and introduced Sarah to her. Mrs. Ashley said, "So this is the girl with the lovely voice!" Then she asked Sarah if she ever had voice lessons. Sarah told Mrs. Ashley she hadn't, that her voice just came as a gift from God. The choir director asked Sarah if she would like to sing in the choir. Sarah said she didn't know what to say for fear of the choir members not accepting her because of her physical disability. Mrs. Ashley said she would be willing to try and adjust Sarah's class schedule, if possible, the following Monday so she could sing in the choir.

Sarah's brother and sister encouraged her to, "Go for it." Surely the other students would accept her once they heard her sing, they thought. Over the weekend, Sarah talked to her parents about singing in the choir. It would mean giving up her study-hall time. A little voice inside of her kept saying, "You can do it, Sarah, go for it." Sarah's parents had been praying that their daughter would somehow be accepted in her new school. Now, perhaps this would be an answer to their prayers, if Sarah would agree to become a part of Benton High's choir. After prayerful consideration, Sarah agreed.

Mrs. Ashley met Sarah the first thing Monday morning to see what she had decided to do. She was delighted indeed as the lovely girl with sparkling blue eyes told the director she would like to try singing with the choir. She just hoped the students would accept her.

It was then arranged for Sarah to adjust her schedule for choir. When fourth period came, Sarah timidly walked into the choir room and was greeted by the popular girl, Carissa. Sarah asked her new friend how she knew for sure that she would be coming to choir. Carissa said a little voice told her over the weekend that, "Sarah will do it; she will go for it. And now here she is!" Sarah was so glad to have at least one friend in choir. Mrs. Ashley, thrilled to see Sarah also, soon introduced her to the class.

The sopranos sat on one side of the choir with the altos beside them. Mrs. Ashley placed Sarah with the sopranos in the second row beside Carissa, who sat in the middle, at the beginning of the alto section. Sarah realized Carissa was a very popular girl, a girl that everyone wanted to have around. Carissa had a very pleasing personality that you couldn't help but like, and Sarah would try her best not to be a burden to her. At the same time she longed for Carissa's friendship but she didn't want her to give up her own friends just because of her.

Carissa told Sarah not to worry about her other friends because God would take care of that situation. "With the sweet personality she has, Sarah will soon have friends," Carissa thought. "Just wait and see."

Sarah thought of the Bible verse her father read to her the night before where it says, "One that hath friends must show himself friendly." She would try her very best to be friendly to everyone, even to Carissa's friends who seemed jealous of her because of the attention Carissa was now giving to her.

This popular girl, Carissa, realized Sarah was seeking her friendship. She could have shunned her like the students in Sarah's previous school had done but she didn't. Instead, here was this new girl sitting next to Carissa in choir, and she would do her best to make her feel needed and wanted even at the expense of perhaps losing her own friends. "Or," the thought crossed Carissa's mind, "were they really ever my friends? If as the Bible says: 'A friend loveth at all times,' and they ignored her just because of Sarah, then perhaps they really weren't her friends after all. If she was in Sarah's shoes she would want someone to be kind to her as well."

After choir was over, Mrs. Ashley thanked Sarah for coming and all the students left the room except for Carissa, Sarah and another student, Adam, a junior, who also sang in the choir. Adam told Sarah he attended some of her brother's classes and he had been watching and admiring her as she sang during choir. He asked if he might carry her books to the next class. Sarah didn't know what to say as she looked to Carissa standing nearby. Carissa told Sarah it would be okay, she could trust Adam.

Sarah couldn't believe her ears! A boy actually asked to carry her books. Her heart fluttered as she walked down the hall with Adam, while students looked on in amazement. Perhaps God really was going to open a new door for her after all! Adam and Carissa continued to be her friends while others still shunned her.

One day during choir practice, Carissa told Sarah she wouldn't be spending much time with her in the next several weeks. Sarah's heart began to sink as she thought Carissa finally was getting tired of her and would be spending time with her other friends again. But Sarah soon found out that wasn't the case. Carissa explained to her why. It was because she swam on the girls swim team and they would be having swimming practice almost every night after school. Sarah asked if she would be allowed to come watch her swim sometime and Carissa guessed she could. A couple of days later, Sarah stayed after school and went with Carissa to the pool. All the girls except for Sarah, who still wore her leg brace, went into the water. Sarah wished she would be able to join the girls as she watched them swim. The same little voice that Sarah heard before began to talk to her again, telling her, "You can do it, Sarah, go for it!" Before she realized what she was doing, Sarah asked the coach if there were any extra bathing suits that were not in use. The puzzled coach said, "Yes, they are in locker number ten in the dressing room."

Sarah came out of the dressing room without her brace and limped to the edge of the pool. Suddenly all the girls stopped swimming and looked at Sarah as she stood there with one leg turned in. It was very noticeable with just her swimsuit on. The girls looked at one another and said, "Just because she can sing doesn't mean she can swim, too!" Then the girls looked at Carissa to see what she was going to do about "Miss Limpy," now sitting at the edge of the pool. Ignoring what the other girls said, Carissa went over to Sarah and helped her into the water.

Soon Sarah began to swim, using her strong arms and good leg, with her long blond hair floating along like wings on the water. And swim she did indeed, with Carissa right beside her all the way. The other girls began to swim again but to their bewilderment, Sarah surprisingly out swam them all. The coach looked on in amazement. When Sarah finally came out of the pool the coach asked the girl where she learned to swim. Sarah told the coach that her father took her swimming for therapy in the WMCA where they used to live. Being in the water with her father is how she learned to swim.

The coach asked Sarah if she might consider being on the swim team, even with her handicapped condition. Sarah said she would love to but she was afraid the other girls would make fun of her and wouldn't want her on their team. Besides, she would have to talk to her parents about it first.

And then it was as if a miracle happened! Soon the whole swim team gathered around Sarah. Carissa, with tears in her eyes, gave her a big hug and said, "Sarah, all the girls want you to be on the swim team!" Soon they were all chanting together, "You can do it, Sarah, go for it!"

Sarah couldn't believe what she was hearing! She looked first at the coach, then at the girls. She then turned to her dearest friend, Carissa and asked her why the girls all of the sudden wanted her to be on their team. Carissa, just as surprised as Sarah, told the bewildered girl that during the time she swam beside her in the pool, a little voice kept saying to her, "With God all things are possible." After she saw how fast Sarah could swim she began praying that God would reveal to each girl on the swim team how much Sarah needed their friendship and what a great asset she would be to the team. "From then on," Carissa said, "God took over."

The girls told Carissa and Sarah they had been wrong for behaving the way they did and they were sorry. The coach was delighted as to what was taking place and said, "Indeed all things are possible with God and now if Sarah would agree to swim with us, it may be possible to have a winning team again!" Then the coach looked at the bewildered girl and said, "Go for it, Sarah, you can do it!"

Sarah knew her parents would be thrilled to have her on the swim team. Besides being good physical therapy for her leg, it would greatly boost her self-confidence, like it did when Mrs. Ashley asked her to sing in the choir. She couldn't wait to tell her parents and Adam what had just taken place. To her it was indeed a miracle, another gift from God.

From then on, Carissa's friends never shunned, or turned their backs on her again, but saw in her a special trait that made them want to be more like her. Carissa's popularity continued to grow and so did Sarah's. The crippled girl gained new friends every day, just because a true friend, Carissa, really cared.

And now Adam, the boy who seemed to be taking an interest in Sarah, had some more good news for this lovely girl whose blue eyes were sparkling more than ever. He told her he had a cousin, Rodney, who owned a Christian recording studio. Adam told him about Sarah and her beautiful voice. Adam's cousin wanted Sarah to audition for recording. Rodney hoped to record some of her favorite Gospel songs with background music, and make tapes to sell. The profits would all go to her. With Adams help, Sarah agreed to do this.

Sarah's parents also found out about a new orthopedic specialist in a nearby big city. With this doctor and their faith in God, they now had a hope of having their daughter's crippled leg straightened.

As time went on, Sarah's parents saw a great change in their daughter. Her leg was operated on and she finally could walk without a brace. Sarah and her parents thanked God every day for giving her new friends and a new outlook on life. Sarah never became proud but remained the same sweet girl she always had been before. The girl, whom no one noticed before she moved to Benton, was now loved by everyone. Sarah knew if she became proud she could lose her self-esteem and her friends, because the Bible says, "God resists the proud but gives grace to the humble." She always wanted to remain humble. Sarah thanked God for answering her prayers to be able to walk without her brace but even more so for sending Carissa to be a true friend indeed, in the time of need.

To be a true friend one needs to obey the great commandment found in the Bible in Matthew 22:39, "Thou shalt love thy neighbor as thyself." Also in Proverbs 17:17 it says, "A friend loveth at all times." The kind of love Carissa had for Sarah certainly became an unselfish love.

We can all gain new friends if we practice the commandments above. Why not try it, friend, "You can do it, go for it!"

TRUE CHRISTMAS SPIRIT

About a week before Christmas, Jeff Collins went to the department store to find a nice religious card for his mother. Jeff, raised in a Christian home, knew well the true meaning of Christmas. Going to the area where the Christmas cards were displayed, Jeff looked disappointed as he saw very few cards about the Birth of Christ. Jeff noticed a young lady nearby, also looking for cards. He said, "It seems so sad. It's almost like the first Christmas when nobody had any room for Jesus, except in some place where you wouldn't expect to find Him. What few religious cards they do have seem to be hid behind other cards, as if the store clerks are ashamed to put Christ first. It's almost impossible to find the true spirit of Christmas in the stores anymore."

The young lady standing beside him continued to look at the cards and said aloud, "I can't believe what I just heard. This man said he could not find the spirit of Christmas in the stores anymore. Why, that's silly. I see it everywhere. See that big Santa that's all lit up over there? He sure looks spirited to me. And these Christmas cards have lots of spirit in them. Here's one with Santa and his reindeer, this one has a cute snow man, and here are cards with Christmas trees, fireplaces and lots of presents around them."

After purchasing some of these cards for her friends at work, the young lady walked past the toy department. She said to herself again, "Why just look at all these toys children will be receiving. They'll surely feel the Christmas spirit when they open their presents again this year! I don't know why that gentleman thought there is no true Christmas spirit. He's probably one of those religious fanatics who do not believe in Santa Claus. The stores would be awfully drab at Christmas time without the decorated trees, Santa and his reindeer and all the glitter that goes with it." After going to the jewelry department, but not finding anything she liked, the young lady went outside.

Jeff Collins, still standing outside in the softly falling snow, was looking at all the decorations the town had put up. He thought to himself, "The decorations are pretty, but there is not one thing out here that depicts the true meaning of Christmas in the birth of Christ." Then looking up at the snow, he saw a break in the clouds and said aloud, "There, there it is I see it!" And as he stepped backwards, still looking up, he bumped into the same young lady he had seen a few minutes ago, looking for Christmas cards.

"Why don't you watch where you're going instead of sticking your nose up in the air?" the young lady said rudely.

"I'm sorry, Ma'am," said Jeff, still looking upward, "but don't you see it up there?"

"See what?" asked the young lady. "I see lots of pretty decorations and that big Santa all lit up over there. That must be what you were looking at."

"No," said Jeff. "I was trying to look past all this glitter to see if I could find the true spirit of Christmas, when through those clouds I saw the most beautiful bright star shining, but now it's gone."

"So what's so special about some silly old star anyway? We can see them year around, but Christmas is just once a year," said the young lady. Then looking right at Jeff, she said, "Aren't you the man that was looking for some kind of an old fashioned Christmas card a few minutes ago in the department store. Didn't I hear you say that you can not find the Spirit of Christmas? Wake up, Man, and listen!"

"Listen to what?" asked Jeff, disappointedly.

"All this lively Christmas music they're playing outside tonight." And she began to sing along with the words, "'Santa Claus is coming to Town.' That song surely puts you in the Christmas spirit, doesn't it?"

"Those songs they're playing do not have THE TRUE CHRISTMAS SPIRIT either," said Jeff, sadly.

"Say," said the young lady, pulling her lovely fur coat tighter around her to protect her from the snow and cold, "don't I know you from somewhere? Haven't I seen you before?"

"Perhaps you have," said the young man. "My name is Jeff Collins."

"Jeff Collins? The Jeff Collins from Central High that never went to dances and parties because you were too good to join us! It sounds like you're still too good if you can't find any Christmas spirit to suit yourself," the young lady responded. "Instead you find one little star and ponder on that."

"Now that you seem to know who I am, I suppose I should know you, too," said Jeff, looking at the young lady. "You look like someone I should know, but I'm not sure."

"Sally Smith is my name," said the young lady. "My name was so common, and there were so many Smiths, that I was always trying to change myself and make myself different."

"Yes, Sally Smith," said Jeff, "now I remember. We never knew when you were going to be a blond, brunette or red head in school. And the clothes and jewelry you wore were really way out. I should have recognized you, but with your lovely fur coat and with your hair now black, and all that stuff on your face, it was hard to recognize who was really behind it all."

"So what's wrong with a little make up?" asked Sally. "I take it you don't like it?"

"It's just like all this Christmas glitter," said Jeff. "It hides the true meaning of Christmas, and I want to think that all your make up and glitter isn't the real Sally either."

"Maybe you're right, Jeff, maybe there is more than meets the eye with Christmas and with myself," replied Sally. "But tell me one thing, what did you see in a lone little star above all this Christmas glitter?"

"It was so depressing to me when I didn't see anything here in town about the true meaning of Christmas. I could not even hear a Christmas carol over the loud speakers, so I looked up and was about to ask myself, what is happening to our little town in America? Then through the clouds I saw a glimmer of light. It was a star, and a very bright one, that reminded me of the Star of Bethlehem," answered Jeff.

"You really do believe there's more to Christmas than all this glitter, don't you, Jeff? You are still different, just like you were in high school," said Sally. "You're still old fashioned. To me Christmas is Santa Claus, parties, glitter, and presents. I even buy my own presents, that way I get what I want!"

"Do you buy gifts for others as well?" asked Jeff.

"No, why should I? Others don't buy for me either," answered Sally.

Jeff looked at Sally and said, "Do you know, it is more blessed to give than to receive? The greatest gift of all times was given on the first Christmas day."

"My, but you are old fashioned," said Sally. "My boss is giving me a Christmas bonus and I'm going to buy a new fur coat. I never did like this old one I bought last year. And I'm going to buy a new diamond necklace to wear to our company Christmas party. Say, Jeff, why don't you come as my guest and I'll show you some real Christmas spirit?"

"No, thank you, Sally, that wouldn't be for me," answered Jeff.

"I didn't really think you would accept my invitation. You're still refusing to go to parties and have a good time, aren't you, Jeff?" said Sally.

"It's just not my way of life," he replied. "Besides, don't you feel guilty spending all that money on yourself for diamonds, fur coats and all those things?"

"Why should I feel guilty? There is no one who cares about me that I should buy gifts for," said Sally, looking a bit sad. "My parents were both killed in an auto accident when I was just three, and my aunt, who never married, raised me, or tried to. That's why I always fixed up the way I did because I wanted to be somebody, not just a plain Smith orphan girl."

"I'm sorry to hear that, Sally, and that you feel this way about yourself," replied Jeff. "But tell me, do you really believe all there is to Christmas is Santa Claus, parties and presents? Don't you ever go to church and hear about the true meaning of Christmas? Don't you ever read your Bible?" Looking across the street to the Coffee Shoppe he said, "It's rather chilly out here, Sally; let's go into the Coffee Shoppe and have some coffee or hot chocolate, okay?"

Sally agreed and together they crossed the street, went into the Coffee Shoppe, and sat down at a booth, across from each other.

After giving their order, Sally said, "You know, Jeff, I don't even own a Bible. My aunt always said religion was old fashioned and for sissies. She never took an interest in such things, so neither did I. Oh, she did take me to church on Easter occasionally to show off our new clothes and I do remember hearing them talk about some man called Jesus. But I never had time for church; it seemed like a waste of time. You said you've been trying to find the true meaning of Christmas, Jeff. Just what does Christmas mean to you?"

"This Jesus you said you once heard about, I'm sorry you never had time for him," said Jeff. "He is what Christmas is all about. God sent Jesus, His Son, to be born to the Virgin Mary and her husband Joseph. Jesus was to be King of all Kings and was sent to earth to live and die for us so we can go to heaven some day if we do His will."

"I suppose," said Sally, "this Jesus, if he was to be a king, was born in a big palace with great honor and fame."

"No," said Jeff, "quite the opposite. Mary and Joseph had gone to Bethlehem to pay their taxes along with many other people. When they got there, all the rooms were full, so the innkeeper said they could spend the night in the stable."

192

"You mean with animals, cows and chickens?" questioned Sally.

"Yes, and that's where Baby Jesus was born. His bed was a manger full of hay," said Jeff. "In the field nearby there were shepherds watching their sheep and a great host of angels came down from heaven and told the shepherds to go worship the Baby Jesus in Bethlehem."

"Angels," said Sally, "you really believe in angels, too? I thought they were just a decoration to put on top of a Christmas tree."

"Yes, Sally, I do believe in angels," said Jeff. "After Baby Jesus was born, a bright star appeared in the sky above the place where the infant Jesus was. Three wise men, who studied the stars, saw this unusually bright star and followed it to where Jesus dwelled. There they, too, worshipped Him and gave Him gifts of gold, frankincense and myrrh. The star I was looking at outside reminded me of this star of Bethlehem. It is the only thing I saw tonight that was close to the real meaning of Christmas."

"So that's why you were looking at that star," Sally replied. Then the young lady went on to say, "That little baby, that poor little baby, born in a stable with animals and laid on a manger of hay for his bed! If I had been there I might have given him my fur coat. Imagine, a King born in a stable!"

"But that's not all," said Jeff. "When this same Jesus grew up to be a man he told people to love one another, obey His commandments, and love and serve him so that we could have the hope of living in heaven someday, if we repent of our sins."

Holding tightly to her coffee cup, Sally said, "I'm afraid I haven't been very good about obeying those commandments."

"But there's more," said Jeff. "Some men were very jealous of Jesus and wanted to kill Him so they beat Him, spat on Him and put a crown of thorns on his head."

"Oh," cried Sally, "that sounds terrible!"

"Then," said Jeff, "they nailed Him to a cross where He died for our sins so that we wouldn't have to."

"Oh how cruel," said Sally with tears in her eyes. "You mean He died for me, too?"

"Yes," replied Jeff, reaching across the table and putting his hand over hers. "But there's still more; the best is yet to come. After Jesus died and was laid in a tomb that had been sealed with a great stone, an angel of the Lord rolled away the stone. The angel told Jesus' followers that He arose from the grave and is alive again so that we, too, can live."

By now Sally was really interested in what Jeff was saying. Wiping the tears from her eyes, she said softly, "You really believe this Jesus arose from the dead?" Her hands were still cupped under Jeff's.

"Yes," answered Jeff, kindly.

"I'm glad He's alive again," replied Sally. "These angels you mention must be for real. First they tell the shepherds that Jesus is born in a stable and then an angel tells people Jesus has risen and is alive again. Jeff, I want to know more about this Jesus."

Jeff continued to tell Sally that God loved us so much that He gave His only Son to die on the cross and shed His blood for our sins so that we wouldn't have to die for them. And that it was God who raised Jesus from the dead. He is now in heaven where we can go, if we will live for Him and accept Him as our Lord and Savior.

Sally was beginning to understand and said, "You mean the first Christmas God gave His Son to mankind so that we can go to heaven, and that was the greatest gift of all to man? Christmas isn't about Santa Claus after all, is it?"

"That's right," said Jeff, reaching into his pocket and handing a small book to Sally. "Here is a New Testament for you to take home so you can read the whole story for yourself. The Christmas story is recorded in the first two chapters of the Book of Matthew and in the second chapter of Luke."

"Oh, thank you, Jeff," said Sally. "You know, I like the story about the Wise Men because they gave gifts to Baby Jesus. They could have kept the gifts for themselves, and they were expensive gifts too, even gold."

Then as she picked up the Testament she noticed a folded paper sticking out from between the front cover and first page. Thinking that it might be something that Jeff wanted to keep, she unfolded it gently to see what it was, and her eyes fell upon the words, FORGOTTEN AT CHRISTMAS.

"What does this mean?" she asked Jeff. "Who's forgotten at Christmas? Is it Baby Jesus? And where does this poem come from? Did you write it, Jeff?"

"No," replied Jeff. "My mother wrote it last year when she, too, realized that the true meaning of Christmas is becoming harder to find in the hearts of people, who seem to be replacing Jesus with Santa Claus."

Jeff picked up the paper and began reading the poem aloud to Sally:

"FORGOTTEN AT CHRISTMAS"

'Twas the night before Christmas, and all through the town,
Not a creature was stirring; no one was around;

Except for the night watchman checking the stores
Making sure all was fine behind the locked doors.

When what to his wondering eyes should appear
But a poor, lonely man, kneeling down in fear
Because of what has happened to people on earth,
Who were filled with gaiety, laughter and mirth.

The lonely man noticed the toys in a mess.
They had been picked over; for presents, he guessed.
He glanced at the clothes that had been tossed about
By shoppers who thought they just couldn't do with out!

Then down the aisle his eyes met Santa so tall.
So this is what people really want after all!
Oh, what has happened to people on earth?
They really HAVE forgotten their Savior's birth!

With this he sobbed and did sorrowfully cry
While the night watchman on him continued to spy.
Up from the floor he pulled this poor man with a bound.
On him no identification was found.

He was ready to handcuff him and take him to jail!
When he awoke from his dream, ashamed to tell
That in the hands of this poor man,
WERE THE PRINTS OF A NAIL!

Then Jeff gave the poem back to Sally because he had another copy at home.

"That poem has so much meaning, Jeff. It makes me feel guilty and ashamed, too," Sally said sadly, looking down at the Testament she held tightly in her hands. "And I, too, feel as if I'm coming out of some kind of a dream. A dream I don't want to go away. You remember the necklace I said I wanted? Guess I really don't need it after all. You know something else, Jeff? I don't need another new fur coat either. In fact," said Sally humbly, "I don't need this one I have on. There are other coats in my closet I can wear.

I think I'll just sell this coat and give the money to some needy family. The Welfare Department and Salvation Army are always saying, "Help the needy at Christmas," and that's what I plan to do. Certainly I am not needy, in fact, maybe I've been a little too greedy."

Jeff looked with surprised pleasure at the young lady sitting across from him and said, "That would be nice, but are you sure you want to do this? You know that the meaning of Christmas and giving has to come from within and not just an outward showing."

"I'm beginning to understand all this, Jeff," said Sally. "Because of you, this is going to be my first real Christmas. Recently I bought a big Santa panel to put on my front door. There were also panels of the Three Wise Men holding gifts. I'm going to discard Santa and buy the one with the Wise Men instead and put that on my door. I wonder what my aunt and my friends at work will think. Oh well, for some reason it really doesn't matter anymore."

"You know," replied Jeff, "I think you really do understand the true meaning of Christmas after all."

"Thanks to you, Jeff," said Sally, as she finished her coffee. "If you hadn't stood outside looking up at that star we never would have had this conversation. It was that star that brought us together. Because of that you led me to know the true story of Jesus and what Christmas is all about. I really want to know more about Jesus. I'm going to start going to church and I'm going without my fur coat!"

"I'm really glad to hear you say that," said Jeff. "God does work in mysterious ways and I, too, feel He has led us together."

"How can I ever thank you for showing me the true way?" asked Sally, with a look of great appreciation.

"Don't thank me; thank God," said Jeff, pleadingly.

"You really aren't old fashioned after all; in fact, I'd say you are more like an angel," Sally replied.

"Me, an angel!" chuckled Jeff. "I don't think so, but why do you say that?"

"Because," said Sally, "angels must be messengers of God. Didn't you say it was an angel who told the shepherds about Jesus' birth and didn't you say an angel announced that Jesus was risen from the tomb? And now you have been a messenger or angel that God has sent to me. My eyes have finally been opened and this is the happiest day of my life! For the first time I feel like I really am somebody, because God made me somebody and has given me a New Hope in life and in myself."

"Sally," Jeff said lovingly, "I'm just thankful I had this opportunity to talk to you and get to know you better." Jeff looked at his watch and went on to say, "Some friends from church and I are going Christmas caroling in a few minutes. How would you like to join us and be my guest?"

"I, go Christmas caroling? I've never done anything like that in my whole life! You really want me to go and sing songs I've never sung before?" asked Sally.

"Yes," said Jeff. "God will give you the words to sing and put a new song in your heart."

"I'd love to go," she said anxiously. "If you really want me to go and if you think your friends will accept me."

"Yes, Sally, they'll accept you gladly," said Jeff lovingly. "I'd really like to be a part of your first real Christmas, if you'll let me."

"You already are," said Sally joyfully. "For the first time in my life I feel good and warm inside and not because of my fur coat, but a different kind of warm feeling. Do you suppose it is THE TRUE CHRISTMAS SPIRIT after all?"

"Yes, I do," replied Jeff, as they walked outside into the soft falling snow.

"I can't wait to tell my friends about my new experience," said Sally excitedly.

"Listen," said Jeff as they walked down the street together, "hear that singing off in the distance?"

"Yes, I hear it, it sounds so beautiful! What is it?" asked Sally excitedly.

"It's the carolers," he answered. And eagerly the two of them went into the night together. Soon they were joining the other carolers singing, "Silent Night, Holy Night," a night that truly changed the meaning of Christmas in the heart of one more soul because someone else cared enough to share the "TRUE SPIRIT OF CHRISTMAS" with others.

TWIN TROUBLE

Reah and Renae were twin daughters born to a fine Christian couple. Renae, the first born, was a beautiful baby with lots of golden blond hair and beautiful dimples. Reah, born soon after Renae, and by no means identical to her twin sister, had red hair like her grandmother. Her ears did not lay nice and flat along the side of her head, as did Renae's, but stuck out beneath her short red hair.

The parents loved their twin daughters very much and treated them as equals. The girls were taken to church every Sunday. As soon as they were old enough, they went to Sunday school, where they loved to hear and sing of the stories of Jesus. Reah had a beautiful voice and she could really sing. Because of that Renae was often envious of her twin sister's singing.

For some reason Renae liked to tease Reah and make fun of her as they were growing up. Renae called her sister "Red Head" and "Big Ears," but Reah would just pretend she didn't hear what her twin sister was saying.

The twins had an aunt who lived several hundred miles away and she didn't get to see the girls very often. For their eighth birthday their aunt sent them one coloring book and a packet of one paper doll with clothes. Evidently their aunt thought one girl would want the color book and one the paper doll, but Renae wanted both of them. Renae said she couldn't color next to "Big Ears," so she tore out half the pages of the coloring book and gave them to Reah. Then she took the paper doll, laid it on a plain piece of paper, and traced around it, making the ears of the doll extra big, and colored the hair red. Renae then gave the homemade paper doll along with half of the original paper doll dresses, ones she didn't particularly care for, to Reah, so they would each have their own doll.

Reah with her sweet, kindly attitude said nothing and accepted the torn out coloring pages and homemade paper doll. The little girl then traced a new paper doll with smaller ears and colored the hair not quite so red. She even made extra dresses and colored them beautifully.

Reah's hair was beginning to turn into a lovely golden red color with soft natural curls. It had now become long enough to cover her protruding ears. Her green eyes accented her radiant face.

Renae's hair was like the hair of a Barbie doll, long, straight, thick and beautiful. Her blond hair, blue eyes and dimples were the envy of her classmates and she knew it. Renae always seemed to be proud of her appearance.

The twins' parents often wondered how the two girls could be so close, yet so different. One was so self-centered and the other was so sweet and humble. They tried their best to change Renae's attitude, but it only seemed to make matters worse.

When the girls were asked to help with the household chores, Renae always pouted and fussed around, making excuses to get out of work because she didn't like to get dirty. On the other hand, Reah always did her chores willingly, usually singing as she did so, which aggravated Renae even more. Reah loved to sing and had a beautiful voice for a young girl. She often had been asked to sing solos in school and church programs. A jealous Renae would make sure she, herself, would get the lead part in any plays that were given at school.

Renae's outside appearance was indeed very attractive, but inwardly she was still selfish and proud. Renae would often frown because of her attitude towards others. Renae made new friends quickly, but she seemed to lose them just as quickly. On the other hand, Reah, who was not nearly as pretty as her twin, was a beautiful person on the inside. Her radiant face glowed so that when you saw her you knew there was something special about her that everyone loved.

Both girls were quite intelligent in school, but Renae did not like to study. When no one was looking, she often copied her sister's homework. But one day it caught up with her. Reah became sick with the flu and had to stay home from school for three days. She was too sick to do her homework. Renae liked to daydream, as usual, and hadn't paid much attention to the oral discussions in class the day before Reah got sick, thinking she could always copy her sister's homework again. Now in school without her sister, Renae was on her own. The pretty blue-eyed, blond twin always liked to be on her own and away from Reah, except for her school and homework.

The twins' teacher had suspected for some time that Renae was copying her sister's homework because their answers were always so much alike. Now she would put her to the test while Reah was absent. Each child was to write the answers to the questions she would be giving them on a clean sheet of paper with their name on it. The questions were about yesterday's oral discussion. The first two questions were simple ones and Renae had no trouble with them, but after that she could no longer write the correct answers. So she glanced across the aisle to the boy beside her, copying his answers. The boy saw what Renae was doing, so he answered all the rest of the questions incorrectly. He had never liked Renae because she always thought she was better than anyone else and would call him "Fatso" because he was on the chubby side. He didn't care if he did fail the test; he wanted to get even with Renae and now was his chance to do so.

The test was over and the papers were handed in and graded. Renae thought to herself that she could get along quite well without Reah. She was thrilled that she could copy someone else's answers. And she didn't have her sister to compete with while she was home sick with the flu. Renae did not think that she possibly might get the flu as well.

Over the lunch hour the boy, who had always gotten good grades, went to the teacher and told her why he had written almost all of his answers wrong. It was because he thought Renae was copying his answers. Even though the teacher told him he should not have done it, she said she would excuse him this time because she, too, wanted to see if Renae copied someone's answers in Reah's absence.

The teacher called Renae's parents and told them how their daughter had cheated in class. Because of this, Renae would not be able to be in the Christmas play. The twins, now thirteen years of age, were both to be in the play. Renae was to be Mary, the mother of Jesus, and Reah, one of the angels.

When Renae came home from school, her mother had a long talk with her about cheating. Mother reminded her daughter what the Bible says in Numbers 32:23: "Be sure your sins will find you out." Renae's cheating had been found out and she would now have to suffer the consequences. She would not be allowed to play the part of Mary. And besides not being in the play, she had to write a letter of apology to her teacher and to the boy she had copied the answers from. Renae would have to take another test after school when the other students went home.

Renae thought if she could not be in the play, her sister shouldn't be either, and she would see to that somehow! But the next week when Reah was better and back at school, Renae came down with the flu and she had to stay home. Of course, she blamed Reah for the flu she now had. While at home recuperating from the flu, Renae figured out a way she could keep Reah from being in the play. Her twin had now been chosen to be Mary, the part Renae was to have. Renae did not want Reah to be Mary in the play.

Reah and her parents wondered why Renae always seemed to be so hateful. The beautiful blond had so much pride in herself and at the same time always belittled her sister, Reah. The family read the Bible and prayed together and did their best to have peace and harmony in their home, but Renae was always stirring up trouble with her bad attitude.

Once over the flu, Renae carried out her plans to prevent her twin sister from being in the Christmas play. These plans would soon bring her a change of heart.

Since they lived in the sunny South, where it was warm the year around, the girls usually rode their bicycles to school. Renae always started out first because she didn't want to ride along side of "Red Head." On this one particular morning, Renae told Reah to go first because she had to go back in the house for something. Reah started out and was two blocks from home when she came to a stop sign at an intersection the girls went through every day on their way to school. Reah applied her brakes, but she couldn't stop. Instead, the twin with the wavy auburn hair slid out into the intersection and right into the path of a car. Fortunately, the car wasn't going too fast but, never the less, it collided with Reah, throwing her over the hood of the car and out onto the pavement!

By this time Renae had started out on her bicycle and saw that something had happened down at the intersection. She did not realize her sister had been seriously injured until she arrived there and saw Reah's broken bicycle lying on the road in front of the car. When she saw Reah lying lifeless on the road, she quickly rode her bike back home and tremblingly told her mother what had just happened.

After calling the girls' father, Renae and her mother quickly went to the scene of the accident. By the time they arrived at the scene, the ambulance and police had been called and were already there. Renae looked at the bicycle and then at her sister. Renae began to sob pitifully, saying it was all her own fault. If she hadn't messed up the brakes on her sister's bike, this wouldn't have happened. Renae had hoped that her sister, Reah, might just have a minor fall or perhaps a sprained ankle so she wouldn't be able to be in the play. Renae had no idea the terrible thing she had done to her sister's bicycle would end up in a tragic accident like this!

Reah was taken to the hospital where she laid unconscious for several days with a broken arm and leg. For the first time, as Renae saw her sister laying in the hospital, she actually felt sorry for her and didn't want to leave her. She kept thinking of what her mother had told her, "Be sure your sins will find you out!" Now they had and she felt terrible!

Reah's arm and leg had been set and put in a cast. The doctors assured the family of the injured girl that once she got over the bad concussion she had received from hitting her head on the road she should be okay.

Every day after school Renae would go to the hospital and talk to her twin sister. She would tell Reah about the day's activities, while holding her weak, limp hand. Renae pleaded for Reah to please open her eyes and talk to her. Renae told the girl lying silently on her hospital bed how sorry she was for the way she had behaved in the past. With tears in her lovely blue eyes, Renae said she wanted to make it up with her sister, if she would only get better.

One day after school Renae again went to the hospital, as she had been doing every day since Reah's accident, to sit by her sister's bedside. She buried her blond head in her arms, resting them on her sister's bed next to the girl's unconscious body. She wept bitterly and prayed that Jesus and her sister would both forgive her for what she had done. Then she promised if Reah could be made well again she would never again call her "Red Head" or "Big Ears" or cheat on her schoolwork. She would also do more than her share of the chores at home. And she wouldn't even care if Reah always played the part of Mary in the Christmas play. "Please, Jesus," she prayed, "make Reah all better again!"

A ray of sunshine shone softly through the window above Reah's bed. As Renae looked up at her sister, she noticed for the first time just how beautiful her sister's hair really was. It seemed to glisten, bringing out the golden auburn colors even more. Renae actually wondered why she never noticed how lovely her sister looked before.

Renae, again resting her head in her arms, suddenly felt a soft hand on her blond hair and an unsteady voice softly said, "Renae." Renae, afraid to look up, thought perhaps a nurse had come and was going to tell her to leave because she was crying and talking so much. But then she heard it again, the same soft voice calling her name. She looked up and Reah's hand was reaching for her hand. As the injured girl's eyes half opened for the first time since her accident, she faintly smiled at Renae and softly said, "I forgive you, my sister." Renae, with tears running down her dimpled cheeks, put her arms around Reah and told her how much she loved her and how she had missed her at home and at school.

For the first time Renae also noticed her sister's lovely green eyes and how beautifully they accented her hair. Again, she wondered why she never noticed her sister's eyes before. Then Renae realized it was because she had thought so much about her own appearance that she never saw the beauty of her twin sister.

The twins' mother had also come to see Reah. When she saw what was taking place between her daughters, she just stood back by the door. With a silent prayer and tears in her eyes she thanked God for answering her prayers, not only for Reah's health to return but also for Renae's change of heart. The mother thought how sad it was that it had to take an accident like this to bring her daughters closer together. God has a purpose for everything and she knew God had a hand in her daughters' lives as well.

After that day, Reah began to recover quickly and before long was back home. Renae was now the one helping Reah, by bringing her school books home and helping her get caught up with her homework. Neither of the girls would be in the Christmas play. But both agreed, along with their parents, that they had the best Christmas ever, because of Reah's recovery and Renae's change of heart, giving her a deeper love for her sister and others than she ever had before.

Renae learned it is what is on the inside of your heart that counts, not the outward appearance. She memorized I Peter 3:3,4 from the Bible and never forgot it, daily putting the verses into action. The verses are as follow: *"WHOSE ADORNING LET IT NOT BE THAT OUTWARD ADORNING OF PLAITING THE HAIR, AND OF WEARING OF GOLD, OR OF PUTTING ON OF APPAREL; BUT LET IT BE THE HIDDEN MAN OF THE HEART, IN THAT WHICH IS NOT CORRUPTIBLE, EVEN THE ORNAMENT OF A MEEK AND QUIET SPIRIT, WHICH IS IN THE SIGHT OF GOD OF GREAT PRICE."*

WELCOME HOME

A life of uncertainty lay ahead for Stan and Cynthia Neuen and their two children, Jonathan, or Jonny as he was called, almost ten, and Sandy, age seven. The family would soon be leaving their small rented home in the country. Mr. Neuen found a job in the big city of Cleveland and hoped to move his family there.

For the last ten years Stan had worked for a dairy ranch in central Ohio. When the owner of the ranch passed away, the ranch and all the cattle were sold to settle the estate. The new owner had other plans for the farm and Stan lost his job. He did not seem too concerned since he already had a new job lined up. Hadn't God always provided for them in the past and would He not provide for them again?

The last night before leaving the farm, Stan and his young son, Jonny, sat outside on the old porch swing. It was a beautiful clear night. The stars seemed to shine brighter than ever as they looked down from the heavens.

Jonny said, "Daddy, if the bottom of heaven is this pretty, what does the other side look like?"

Stan told his son, "Heaven is the most beautiful place there is. It is by far more beautiful than any place on this earth! See how the stars twinkle? I like to think that for every person on earth, there is a star up there that watches over us."

"There's the big dipper, Daddy," said Jonny. "Look at that bright star over there. Could it be the North Star? Perhaps that's the one that is watching over me."

Mr. Neuen said, "You know, Son, I like to think that the morning star is the one that watches over me. Though it shines all night, it seems brightest in the morning. When I go out to milk the cows in the morning, I often look for this star. Did you know that in the last chapter of the Bible, Jesus says He is the bright and morning star? On the mornings when I can see this star, it seems to remind me that God is once more in control for another day."

In the first chapter of Genesis it says, God made the stars and set them in the firmament along with the sun and moon to give light upon the earth and to rule over the day and night. Stan and Cynthia trusted in God and believed in Him as the Creator of the heavens and the earth.

"It's getting late, Jonny," said the boy's father. "We better go see if our two girls need any help inside."

Upon entering the house they found Mrs. Neuen packing the last box of grocery items to be moved to the city tomorrow. Little Sandy had just finished putting her few toys in an old pillowcase before getting ready for bed. Soon the family settled down for their last night on the farm.

Early the next morning Cynthia went to awaken the children so they could eat an early breakfast. Jonny was not in his room. Where could he be so early in the morning, Mother wondered? The family planned to leave soon after daybreak. They had a four-hour drive to the city. Cynthia told Stan she didn't know where Jonny was and breakfast soon would be ready. Father went out to look for his son and found him sitting on a fence post near the big barn.

"Mother has breakfast ready, Son," said Father. "Is something wrong?"

The young boy with tears in his eyes, said, "This is I the only home I've ever known, and I just had to say good-by. I wanted to find the morning star to see if it will send us on our way, because I won't ever be back here to see it again."

"The morning star will be in Cleveland the same as it is here but with all the lights of the city we may not be able to see it." Father replied. Then he went on to say, "Let's go eat breakfast. We have a big day ahead of us."

After breakfast, Stan read to his family from the Holy Bible. Then he prayed, asking for God's protection on the highways.

Little Sandy seemed anxious to go to the city. The children had never been there before and to the little girl it sounded exciting. For once she hoped to have some playmates living close to her. Sandy wasn't afraid to go because as long as she was with her parents she knew everything would be okay. They had said Jesus would be with them where ever they go. If her parents trusted in Jesus then she could trust her parents. Isn't that just the way we, as children of God, should trust in our Heavenly Father?

The Neuen family climbed into the moving truck they had rented and started out, with their seven-year old car in tow behind them. All four were seated closely together in the front seat of the truck. Jonny turned around for one last look at the farm. His dream was to one day become a farmer. He loved the country and now he had to leave it.

Stan and Cynthia had mixed emotions as well about leaving the home they started out in, after they were married. The job Stan had accepted would be a challenge for him. He would be working in an industry that manufactured farm equipment. It would be a whole new field of work for him. After his job in the great out doors on the farm, he would be working inside a factory all day.

Cynthia would also miss the farm. She always had plenty of fresh milk, and a big garden to raise food for her family. She wondered if she would ever have a garden again. Who would their new neighbors be? Would they get along with them, especially Jonny and Sandy? They would be living in an apartment house, about three miles from Stan's place of employment. Hopefully, if all goes well, they would one day be able to purchase a home of their own.

The Neuens had no other close relatives to turn to, except Stan's Uncle Ted, who lived somewhere in the hills of south-eastern Ohio, close to the Ohio river. Uncle Ted owned and worked in a coal mine for years. Stan could have had a job in the mine years ago. But since he had a severe case of pneumonia when he was sixteen, the doctor advised him to stay out of the mines. He really enjoyed working out in the fresh air and was glad when the opportunity to work on the farm came along, just before his marriage to Cynthia.

By the time they reached the edge of Cleveland, the sun was well up in the sky. The traffic had really picked up with cars flying by as if on some kind of a racetrack.

"Daddy, where are all these cars coming from?" asked Sandy. "This road is so wide and there are so many cars on it, I'm afraid we're going to have a wreck! What if someone hits our car we're pulling behind this big truck? Is it still back there, Daddy? Can you still see it? How soon will we be at our new house?"

"It won't be long now, and we'll soon be there, Sandy," answered Mr. Neuen. "Yes, the car is still behind us. I can see it in the big mirrors beside the truck. See those tall buildings over there? They are close to where I will be working. Our apartment is not too far away."

The little girl clung tightly to the doll she had been holding all the way, as if to protect it from the hustle and bustle of the traffic.

"Sandy," said Mother, "there is a verse in the Bible that says, God will give His angels charge over us to keep us in all our ways. Try to think that for each one of us here in this truck there is an angel hovering over us, protecting us from all the traffic flying by. You can't see the angels but if the Bible says they're out there then I believe they are really there, don't you?"

"Yes, I guess so," replied Sandy. "But I bet some of the angels have trouble keeping up with all the cars as fast as they are going."

"The angels have it all under control, I'm sure," responded Mrs. Neuen.

Then Jonny spoke up, "That's really neat! The angels watch over us during the day and the stars watch over us at night!"

"That's a good way to put it, Jonny," said Mr. Neuen. "We need never fear for God is always near. Now, who made the stars and the angels?"

The two children answered together, "God and Jesus."

"That's right," said Father. "The city will never be so busy that the angels can't watch over us nor will the lights of the city ever be so bright that the stars will cease to shine. We may not always see them, but they will always be there."

"Look," said Mother, "here is the street to our apartment. It looks like a nice neighborhood. Since we know no one here, children, you will be staying at our apartment the rest of the day, unpacking your things as we bring them in."

The two children replied together, "Yes, Mother."

"Here we are at last," said Father. "Welcome home."

There were three other families in the apartment building, where the Neuens would be moving too. As they pulled into the driveway, the neighbors one by one, came out onto the sidewalk to meet the new comers.

It was Saturday and most of the neighbors were home. One man immediately came up to the big truck and offered to help carry in the furniture the family brought with them. Stan gladly accepted his offer and in a couple of hours the truck had been emptied. It just so happened that this kind, helping neighbor worked for the same company this rented moving truck belonged to. He even offered to go with Stan to return the truck and bring him back home. Stan wanted to pay him for his help and kindness but the man wouldn't accept anything.

By nightfall everything had been put away in the Neuen household. The children arranged their small bedrooms as Cynthia put away the last of the kitchen items. They had three bedrooms upstairs and a bath. Downstairs there was a kitchen, living room, utility and a half bath. The rooms all needed to be painted or papered. The curtains were gray and dingy and needed laundered. The landlord said they could fix it up at their own expense. For right now the Neuens were just glad for a place to stay.

In the days to come the children made friends with others in the neighborhood. Sandy was especially happy to find a playmate, a little girl her own age, in the same apartment building they lived in. Jonny found some friends too, but he still missed the farm. Mrs. Neuen also met the ladies in their building and they all seemed friendly enough. Stan tried to adjust to his job but it was difficult. He, too, missed the farm and the quiet, calm, serenity it offered, compared to the hum, drum of this big city.

Life went on, with the children now enrolled in a nearby school. Cynthia would be taking care of a neighbor's five-month old baby during the day while the mother worked. The extra money would help to buy groceries because there appeared to be no room for a garden. All their food would have to be purchased. Also their car needed new tires and other repairs. The old furniture they moved from the farm, needed to be recovered or replaced and the children were outgrowing their clothes. Stan and Cynthia also needed to replace their farm clothes with something more suitable for city life.

For several mornings Stan and Jonny both tried to find the morning star but the city lights around them were too bright and they could not see it. Cynthia kept reminding the children to stay close to home and not wander too far away. The city had much to offer the children and it may not always be good for them. She especially warned them to stay away from strangers and prayed daily that the angels of the Lord would truly watch over her family.

Just when everything finally seemed to be going a little better for the Neuen family, they received some bad news. The company Stan worked for was going to close its doors almost immediately and file bankruptcy. Stan had no idea his job would be in jeopardy when he agreed to work there. Times were getting tough with jobs hard to find. There were layoffs in many other industries as well.

They had been in the city now for eighteen months and six months ago the landlord raised their rent. It was hard to save any money for emergencies. The mother of the baby Cynthia cared for, had also been laid off. Now this mother would be taking care of her own little one. So that meager income would also stop for Cynthia.

Stan and Cynthia prayed and asked Jesus to please help them and guide them in the way they were to go. It was fall and cold weather would be just around the corner. They would not have enough money to pay their heat bill let alone the rent. Just when they thought things were going to be better in the city they were getting worse. On the farm Cynthia had been able to raise enough food to preserve plenty for the winter months, and there was always plenty of fresh milk and eggs. Now everything had to be purchased.

The family had been attending a small church down the street from where they lived. The folks there were also beginning to have financial struggles and couldn't offer much help.

Then two days before Thanksgiving, the landlord informed the Neuens that if they could not pay last month's rent, along with this months rent, they would have to move out. Where could they go? They had no family, except for Stan's Uncle Ted and they weren't even sure exactly where he lived. For all they knew, he probably still lived along the Ohio River somewhere, working in a coal mine.

Stan and Cynthia sat down with their children that evening and told them they would be leaving Cleveland on Thanksgiving Day. They would head south, to somewhere along the Ohio River.

"But I like my friends and my school here," cried Sandy. "I don't want to leave!"

"Some Thanksgiving this will be!" pouted Johnny. "I really don't want to move either, now that I have made some new friends. But if we can move back to a farm, I'll go."

"Right now, children, we are not sure where we'll be going," replied Mother. "But God will provide a place somehow, I know He will."

"You mean we don't even know where we're going to live?" cried Sandy again.

"No," answered Father. "Just as your mother said, God will provide as He has always done in the past. You do believe that, don't you?"

The children didn't know what to think. Mr. Neuen took the Bible and opened its tattered pages before the family went to bed. He read from chapter four in Philippians. It said, "Be careful for nothing: but in everything by prayer and supplication with thanksgiving let your requests be made known to God. He shall supply all your needs according to His riches in glory by Christ Jesus." Then he prayed, asking for God's guidance to take them wherever He would have them to go.

Father said not to worry because he is sure God has a better plan for them, one that they don't even know about. Right now, they just need to have faith to trust in Him.

The next day the family started packing all they could into the old car. Mostly things like clothing, dishes and food. They couldn't afford to rent a truck to move their old furniture. Besides, the landlord said if they left it there, they wouldn't have to pay the rent they owe. It would be rented as a furnished apartment to someone else, even with the furniture in need of repair. The appliances belonged to the apartment anyway, but the bedroom, living room and kitchen furniture belonging to the Neuens, would all be left behind.

It was a sad day indeed, when after Thanksgiving breakfast the Neuens once more started out, this time for an unknown destination. Cynthia packed enough food for a little Thanksgiving lunch and supper to be eaten somewhere in the car. Other food items were jammed into the trunk with the rest of their belongings. The blankets were taken inside the car and laid across the seats, just in case the family would have to spend the night in the car somewhere.

They drove all day and finally came to a small town along the Ohio River. They really had no money for a motel because they needed it to buy gas to keep the car going. Besides, it was Thanksgiving Day and the motels probably were not open anyway. About one hundred miles back they had a flat tire and that took extra money for repairs. They were just thankful to find a service station open that was willing to repair the old tire. How Stan would liked to have stopped somewhere along the way and treat his family to a nice Thanksgiving meal at some restaurant, but that, too, was out of the question. Besides not having the money to do so, most restaurants were closed for the Holiday anyway.

Mr. Neuen said somehow this town where they had arrived looked strangely familiar to him. He remembered it as the place where he and his father used to come on occasion; when he was a young boy, like Jonny. He remembered bringing his Uncle Ted to the train station here and picking him up again when he went away on one of his business trips.

Jonny told his family that day that he no longer wanted to be called, Jonny, but Jonathan. He reminded his parents that he is now eleven years old and no longer a little boy. So his parents and sister agreed to call him Jonathan, the name he wanted to be called.

Then Mr. Neuen had an idea. Things were pretty quiet in town since it was Thanksgiving, so he drove past the old train depot to see if it might still be in use. He saw no one around and it appeared to be permanently closed to trains. Then he drove over to the fire station that was open, and went inside.

Jonathan asked his mother why Father went into the station. Mother had an idea what her husband was up to but she just said, "Wait and see, children."

Father came back out to the car where his restless, tired and hungry family, were waiting. Then he drove off towards the depot. When they arrived at the old brick building he stopped the car and said, "Welcome home."

"You mean we're going to stay in the train station?" exclaimed Sandy. "That sounds exciting!"

"We don't even have any furniture, or beds to sleep on. We'll have to sleep on the floor!" murmured Jonathan. "But this is Thanksgiving and I'm just thankful we won't have to sleep in the car."

"You mean we can actually stay here tonight?" asked Cynthia. "But surely we can't stay without paying someone for using the building, and we haven't much money. Somehow, though, I feel the Good Lord has led us here for a reason. He has never let us down yet. He will provide."

Mother, Jonathan and Sandy looked on in amazement as they got out of the car and Father pulled out a key from his pocket. He went to the side door of the depot, unlocked it and once more said, "Welcome home, family, and Happy Thanksgiving!"

The Neuens went inside and found the heat and electricity still on and the restrooms still in use. There were twelve rows of long benches inside that the family could use as beds with the blankets they had brought along.

Cynthia, with tears in her eyes, looked at her husband and asked, "How did you ever manage to get this place for us? It almost looks like a church in here and it makes me feel so humble."

"Isn't the Lord just wonderful, Cynthia?" Stan said as he hugged his wife and children. "When I went to the fire station and told them our situation, I asked if there is a possibility we could spend the night in the old depot. A kindly man by the name of Rodney, said we could and he gave me the key to unlock the door. He said we could stay here until we find somewhere else to go. There is even a hot plate in here for us to use. It is my understanding that a group of people from this community bought this old depot and fixed it up to be used for a little church. Rodney, the fireman, and his wife attend services here.

"God surely is wonderful! He always provides in our time of need," said Mother. "Now let's get our things in from the car, and eat the rest of the lunch I packed for today. I'm sure everyone is hungry."

So the family, thankful for a temporary place to stay, unloaded the items they needed and sat down on the old church benches to eat the rest of their peanut butter sandwiches, carrot sticks and apples. Father suggested they first hold hands together and sing, "Praise God From Whom All Blessing Flow." Then he thanked God for providing this shelter and the food they were about to partake of.

Then almost before he could say, "Amen" there was a knock on the side door. There stood Rodney, the fireman, with a box of food. He said his family had plenty of food for their Thanksgiving dinner and had all this left over. His wife wanted the Neuen family to have it. There was even some left over turkey and pumpkin pie in the box.

Little Sandy ran up to the kindly man, gave him a hug and said, "You must be a Thanksgiving angel! Thank you, thank you!"

Jonathan said, "Sir, I am so hungry I could eat a bear, but this turkey will do just fine. But why are you doing all this for us? You wouldn't have to, you know. You don't even know who we are. We're just some strangers in the night!"

Rodney said, "Have you ever heard of the commandment where Jesus says, we are to love our neighbors as ourselves? Well, right now you're in our neighborhood and if I was in your shoes I'd appreciate some help. Also the Bible says in Corinthians that, 'Every man according as he purposes in his heart, so let him give; not grudgingly, or of necessity; for God loves a cheerful giver.' Now according to the purpose of my wife and I, we want to share this with you, so just enjoy it, my boy, just enjoy it!"

Stan introduced his family to the fireman and with tears in his eyes said, "Thank you and God Bless you!"

The family sincerely thanked the man for the gift of food and for the shelter over their heads. Stan said he would begin looking for a job tomorrow and a place to live so the family won't have to impose on this little church congregation.

The fireman assured the Neuen family they could stay until Stan found a job and he himself, would help try to find some kind of work for him. Rodney knew Ted Neuen, Stan's uncle, but didn't even think, at the time, that he might be related to Stan so he never mentioned him. In fact, unknown to Stan, his Uncle Ted, was one of the men who donated money to help buy this old depot so it could be fixed up and used for a church.

The fireman left and the family enjoyed their Thanksgiving dinner. It tasted much better than their peanut butter sandwiches would ever have tasted. Once more Stan bowed his head and thanked the Good Lord for their abundant blessings. He felt so unworthy of the fireman's kindness. Perhaps some day he can repay him for everything.

It had been a long day and everyone seemed tired. The blankets were laid out on the benches and each one, with their own pillow, would soon be ready to go to sleep. Mother said, "I don't know if I feel like we're in a train station, with the tracks and trains still running outside, or in the solitude of a church. Since this depot is now a church, I'm sure God's presence will be with us here, as well as anywhere. The angels surely were watching over us again today."

Father picked up the Bible and began reading Psalms 103. He began, "Bless the Lord, oh my soul and all that is with in me, bless His holy name." He continued reading and when he came to the fourth and fifth verse he repeated the words that said, "Who crowns you with loving kindness and tender mercies; who satisfies your mouth with good things." Continuing on further he again stopped at verse seventeen, repeating it as well. "But the mercy of the Lord is from everlasting to everlasting to those who fear Him, and His righteousness unto children's children."

He read on, ending the chapter with verses twenty through twenty-two. "Bless the Lord, you His angels, that excel in strength, that do His commandments, heeding the voice of His word. Bless the Lord, all you His hosts; you ministers of His, that do His pleasure. Bless the Lord, all His works in all places of His dominion: bless the Lord, O my soul."

"Surely," he said, "God must have led us to this place where the angels were indeed hearkening to the voice of His word, sending this fireman as a minister of God to help us in our time of need. In Hebrews chapter one it says, "The angels are ministering spirits, sent forth to minister for them who shall be heirs of salvation." It is my prayer, children, that we will all be heirs of this salvation."

Jonathan and Sandy each said their prayers, thanking Jesus for their safety on the highways, for their wonderful Thanksgiving meal, and for this special "house of rest."

Soon everyone settled down the best they could on the narrow, hard church benches. The streetlights gave just enough light through the north windows that they could see shadows inside.

Suddenly Sandy screamed, "There's something moving on the floor over here!"

Mr. Neuen, using his flashlight, saw a little mouse eating some of the crumbs left from their evening meal. "It's only a little church mouse," he chuckled. "He must be hungry too, and wants a Thanksgiving feast. I guess we can share our fallen crumbs with him, can't we?"

"Welcome home, little mouse," said Sandy as she clung to her doll, while trying to stay on the bench. "You have some new guests in your house. Now if you don't mind, while you finish your supper, I'm going to sleep."

Soon all was quiet as the Neuen Family finally went to sleep each wrapped in their blankets on the old narrow pews. Twice during the night, the walls of the old depot rumbled as a train passed by waking its visitors. But they soon went to sleep again, trying not to turn over for fear they might end up on the floor. At one time Jonathan thought of sleeping on the floor where he would have more room to move, but since he saw the mouse he decided to stay on the hard narrow bench. The floor had no carpet and the benches had no padding so either place would be uncomfortable. He wasn't going to complain however, because he had a pillow, two blankets and a warm place to sleep.

Early the next morning Cynthia got up, went into the restroom, and dressed for the day. How she longed for a good hot bath. But she was thankful for a sink where she could at least bathe in such manner. Then she began looking through the box of food she brought from Cleveland, for something to fix her family for breakfast. Stan, anxious to go out and look for a job, even if it meant working in a coal mine, was also up and about.

After noticing that Jonathan was not in the building, Stan went outside to see what his son might be up to. He saw him across the railroad tracks, standing between some trees and he quietly walked over towards him. There on the other side of the trees, down a small ravine, Stan saw the awesome sight of the beautiful Ohio River. They both stood in amazement as they looked down on the majestic river. The early morning lights were still reflecting on the water.

Suddenly Jonathan exclaimed, "Dad, look over there!" And he pointed to the clear blue sky above the river, "It's the morning star! I haven't seen it so bright since we left the farm and went to the city. You were right, Dad, God does follow us wherever we go and that star will watch over us just like it did on the farm. It's so beautiful out here, Dad. I know you loved the farm where we used to live, but why did you ever leave this area?"

"Because I had pneumonia when I was a teenager and the doctor said to stay out of the mines. After my parents passed away, I left this area and got a job out on the farm. Yes, it is beautiful here. I didn't realize how much I had missed it until now. It has been years since I've been here," said Father. "The morning star was with us all the time in the city, too. It was just harder to see, because of all the lights."

Father continued, "We better go inside. Mother has breakfast ready and I must go look for work and a place for us to live. How would you like to go with me today, Son?"

"I'd like that very much," said Jonathan as they crossed the tracks back to the old converted church building. Off in the distance they could see and hear another train rumbling down the tracks. It was carrying carloads of coal from the mines near by. The trains came through several times a day.

After breakfast, Stan, along with Jonathan, set out in search of a job. The sun shone brightly for the day after Thanksgiving. The air was fresh and crisp. Mother and Sandy decided to go for a walk to try to find the local school. On Monday the children should be enrolled in school here, that is if Stan found a job. Surely God will hear their prayers and supply their needs by providing a job for her husband.

The day soon came to an end. Mrs. Neuen and her daughter had found the school, but Stan didn't find a job. Without a job they would not be able to pay rent for a place to live. Times were tough even here along the river, and Stan hoped he wouldn't have to work in a mine, but he may have no choice.

That evening Mother fixed supper with some of the food from the box they brought with them from Cleveland. Their food supply was running low. If her husband didn't find work soon, she may have to go look for a job as well.

Once more they settled in for the night and thanked God for their warm shelter and for their evening meal. Stan had faith to believe somehow his family would be provided for. Just how or when he did not know. Again that night the little church mouse came looking for a handout. Although he did not find as many crumbs as the night before, he went away satisfied.

Before breakfast the next morning, Jonathan again went outside to see if he could find the morning star. Right away he noticed it was cloudy and he couldn't see any stars; but what he did see, surely must have been sent from heaven itself! There near the door of this old depot sat a box of food with a note that said, "Welcome Home." The box was heavy but he managed to carry it inside.

His parents couldn't believe their eyes! No one really knew they were here except for Rodney, the fireman. Surely he didn't bring this welcomed box of food again. Or did he? After breakfast, Stan would go find out.

The pancakes Mrs. Neuen fixed on the little hot plate, tasted better than the dry cereal they would have had. There was no refrigerator in the building so they couldn't have any milk or perishable food items, even if they could afford them.

The children loved the pancakes, which could be made by just adding water. There was a small jar of maple syrup also included in the box and by the time breakfast was over the syrup was gone. Cynthia found a container of powdered milk in the box of food that could be mixed with water for cereal another day. But today everyone wanted pancakes, with real maple syrup!

After breakfast the family decided to clean the building they have been staying in and move their items, not needed, to the storage room. Tomorrow would be Sunday and they wanted everything to be in order for the church services that would be held there. The Neuens were eager to attend church in this building they now called home. They were anxious to meet the people who let them stay in their little converted church building.

About mid morning the family went outside just to enjoy the cool crisp air and to discuss what to do next. Across the tracks sat an old park bench where one could just sit, relax and enjoy the view of the Ohio River. They decided to do just that and were fascinated by watching the tugboats as they slowly moved down the wide river.

They no sooner sat down on the bench when they heard the sound of an approaching train in the distance. For some reason Stan turned and glanced at the nearby intersection and railroad crossing. A car, with a man sitting inside, appeared to be stalled on the tracks. The signal was now flashing and the gates were coming down as the train drew near.

Stan said, "Cynthia, that car is not moving! I just can't let that man sit in his car. He'll be killed! I'm going after him!"

"No, Stan," cried his wife, as she put her hands up to her face. "You'll both be killed!"

"Daddy, don't do it! Daddy, please, no," the children cried together!

By now some other town folks had noticed the stalled car sitting on the tracks with the train fast approaching. All felt so helpless in this dreadful situation. Everyone seemed to be frozen in fright as to what might happen next.

The train engineer saw the stalled car and immediately applied the brakes. He knew the train would not be able to stop in time to avoid hitting the car.

Stan ran under the gates and to the car sitting on the tracks. The elderly man inside seemed to be in a daze. Stan opened the car door, grabbed the gentleman and quickly pulled him away seconds before the locomotive hit the back of the car, swinging it around like a toy, completely demolishing it. Just a few seconds later, Stan, and the man in the car, would both have been killed!

Almost in shock, Stan recognized the elderly man as his Uncle Ted whom he hadn't seen for years. The ambulance soon appeared and the dazed man, after being loaded onto a stretcher, was whisked away to a hospital in a near by town. He apparently had suffered a light stroke and upon seeing the oncoming train went into shock.

"It's unbelievable," said Stan in a quivering voice to Rodney, the fireman, as he stood the scene of this almost fatal tragedy. "I can't believe that the man I just rescued was my Uncle Ted!"

"Yes, it is unbelievable," said the fireman. "Unbelievable how you risked your life to save someone you didn't even know at the time. You will surely be rewarded."

The train finally came to a stop. After assessing the situation, the engineer, thankful that no one was killed, couldn't thank Stan enough for his bravery.

The Neuen family and others gathered around Stan, who was still trembling from what he had just done. Finally, with a quiver in his voice, he quoted

John 15:13, "Greater love has no man than this, that a man lay down his life for his friends." Then he went on to say, "I had no idea who was in that car but I knew I had to help him. Christ laid down His life for me. The least I could do was to help this man who miraculously turned out to be my Uncle Ted." He looked at the fireman and said, "You, too, sacrificed your building and Thanksgiving meal, and a box of groceries for our family, again, this morning. You helped us when we were in need and I had to help the man in the car."

"As for the box of food this morning, Mr. Neuen, that came from your uncle," replied the fireman. "You see, when I told him we had some tenants living temporarily in the church, he asked what he could do to help. I told him about your family, your need for food, shelter and a job. Ted came to town this morning, bought the groceries and left them at your door. He had some other errands to run then he planned to stop by and welcome you home. What a way for the two of you to meet!"

"How did he know who I was? Did you tell him my name?" quizzed Stan.

"Yes, because he wanted to know who was living in his church. He seemed delighted to think that his nephew came back home." Rodney, the fireman, continued on, saying, "About two years ago your uncle and his wife became Christians, then she died of a sudden heart attack, leaving him all alone. He never had any children. Since then he became more and more interested in our little church project and donated money to keep it going. He is a mighty fine Christian man who sincerely loves the Lord. Until now, our little church family was all he had."

Stan, happy to hear about his Uncle Ted, informed his family that they would be going to the hospital right away to see him. Stan wondered if his uncle realized it was his nephew that saved him from being killed, when he pulled him from the car seconds before it was hit by the train.

When they arrived at the hospital, they were allowed to spend a little time with Uncle Ted. As Stan stood by the bedside of the elderly gentlemen, the uncle reached for his nephew's hand and in a trembling voice said, "Welcome home, Son. Thank you for saving my life."

"But how did you know it was I?" quizzed the nephew. "You were in such a daze I didn't think you knew me."

"The doctor just told me a man with the same last name as mine saved my life." Still quivering the elderly man said, "I knew you were in town and there is no one else around here by the name of Neuen. So it had to be you. Welcome home, my boy, welcome home."

The stroke didn't seem as bad as expected. In fact, the doctor said he could go home in a couple of days if he had someone to stay with him and care for him.

Uncle Ted looked at Stan's family whom he had never met before. He asked Mrs. Neuen if she was a nurse. She told him no, but said she would be more than willing to come take care of him if he wished her to do so.

Then Uncle Ted looked at the children and said with a twinkle in his eye, "How would you like to have me for a grandpa?"

The children seemed delighted, because they never remembered having a grandpa before.

The next day the Neuen family went to church in their temporary home. They had much to be thankful for, especially thankful that Uncle Ted and Stan's life had been spared.

In the days that followed many things happened. Uncle Ted was dismissed to go home. He asked Stan and his family to come live with him on his farm up on the hill. Stan would manage the farm and the small coal mine at the edge of the farm. He wouldn't have to work underground, just be in charge of the men who worked down in the mine.

Needless to say the family was elated. The first night on the farm Uncle Ted, and his four new tenants, gathered in prayer around the old kitchen table and thanked the Good Lord for answering all of their prayers. Uncle Ted said he had been praying, since his wife died, that somehow the Good Lord would find his nephew and bring him home again. Stan agreed that God's plan was far better than he could have ever hoped for. He praised God for bringing him and his dear family here where they were delighted to be. This was far better than living in Cleveland, the other farm, or anywhere else on earth.

Uncle Ted hugged his nephew and said once more, "Welcome home, Son, this is your home from now on, for as long as you want it, that is, if you'll have it. There's only one string attached, I go along with the farm, so you'll have to take me, too."

The family chuckled and agreed to stay on the farm. The children were enrolled in school and Sandy soon found new playmates living just a short distance down the road. Jonathan especially enjoyed the farm and fell in love with Uncle Ted's horse. He would learn to ride it before long.

Mother would again have a garden and fresh milk from the cows Stan would tend to, and fresh eggs from the hens she would be caring for. Uncle

Ted, now called Grandpa, by the children, again had someone to cook and keep house for him. The family helped greatly to fill his lonely days and nights.

In spite of all that had happened in the last several days the Neuens agreed they had much to be thankful for, this past Thanksgiving. They were already making plans for Christmas and knew it would be the best Christmas they have ever had. They thought, "Hasn't God been wonderful in the way He supplied their needs? His plan for their lives, that they did not see just a few weeks ago, was far better than they could ever have hoped for."

Several mornings later, after moving onto Uncle Ted's farm, Stan and Jonathan again went out together to do the chores. As they looked up in the heavens, the morning star shining ever so brightly, seemed to say, "Welcome home, dear ones, Welcome home." It was almost as though the verse in the thirty-eighth chapter of Job came to life. It says, "The morning stars sang together, and all the sons of God shouted for joy." Stan and Jonathan felt like they, too, could shout for joy, as Uncle Ted and the farm welcomed them home.

* * * * *